SHOT GLASS
Diva

SHOT GLASS
Diva

by

Jacki Simmons

This is a work of fiction. All of the characters, organizations, and events portrayed in this novel are either products of the author's imagination or are used fictitiously.

www.melodramapublishing.com

Library of Congress Control Number: 2007943737
ISBN-13: 978-1934157145
ISBN-10: 1934157147
First Edition: September 2008
10 9 8 7 6 5 4 3 2 1

DEDICATION

Dedicated to the last of the real people in the world. Don't let anyone or anything hold you back or hold you down.

Prologue

"Honey Davis?" a stern voice asked.

"Yes?" I was startled to find a balding, dour-faced man standing an arm's length away from me. His tall yet stocky body was encased in an ill-fitting navy blue suit, and his blue-and-gray striped tie threatened to choke him. Another man silently approached and stood sentinel on the other side; he was shorter, younger, and dressed in a similar manner, except he had a thatch of thick, brown hair that complemented the shades of brown in his tie and his tan-colored suit. I had been so preoccupied with my upcoming trip that I hadn't heard them approach. I wanted to step back and reclaim my personal space, but I couldn't. There was simply nowhere to go.

"What's going on?" I didn't recognize these men, but their sudden presence gave me a bad feeling.

They studied me intently as they flashed their badges. "I'm Detective First Grade George Mayer, Homicide, 34th Precinct," the balding man said. "This is my partner, Detective Second Grade Joshua Bingham."

My body felt frozen. Detectives? Homicide? "What … what can I do for you, detectives?" I stammered. Homicide meant someone was dead, and apparently it was someone I knew, or knew of. This was not good. This was not good at all.

"We're investigating the murder of Lola Lee."

Oh shit, I thought. "Murder!" I exclaimed. "I don't know anyone by that name. Who's Lola Lee?"

"We were told that you were pretty good friends with her husband, Sammie. Is that correct?"

My eyebrows rose as my mouth fell open in horror. Lola Lee . . . they were talking about *that* Lola, as in Sammie's wife. Blood drained from my face as the frozen feeling extended all the way down to my toes. *Lola's dead?*

"Well, I . . . ya . . . yes," I stuttered. I couldn't think; my usual fast talk had gone missing in action. I was shook! Lola Lee was dead, and two homicide detectives were asking me questions. *Do they know about me and Sammie?* I wondered.

"Do you mind if we ask you a few questions?" Mayer was obviously the alpha dog in this duo; Detective Bingham remained silent, though his sharp green eyes remained in motion. The phrase "still waters run deep" sprang to mind.

"Um, well . . . is it going to take long? I have to catch a flight; it's a family emergency."

"We won't take long, Ms. Davis." Mayer's tone implied that I didn't have much of a choice. "Let's go to your apartment, shall we? Or, if you'd like, we can go down to the precinct."

Go down to the precinct? Oh hell no! That was not an option, so what else could I say? If I didn't agree, it would make me look bad. Kyashira's newborn face flashed in my mind, but I had to push it away. I had to answer these questions so that I could focus on her with no distractions. Nausea surged in my stomach; I forced myself to swallow as I led the way, praying I wouldn't throw up, reluctance evident in every step I made.

I knew that I had to choose my words carefully. As Sammie's mistress, no one had to tell me that things could get real ugly for me, real fast. The detectives' eyes roamed around my small, one-bedroom apartment, taking in every little detail, including all of the expensive gifts that I'd thrown around in a hurry. I followed Bingham's gaze to a stack of big bills on an end table. *Damn!*

Mayer continued the questioning. He perched himself on the edge of my cream suede loveseat and removed a small notebook and ink pen from the inside pocket of his suit jacket. "How did you meet Lola Lee?"

I sighed in resignation. Lying would be futile. "I am Sammie's mistress." I took a deep breath, exhaled. "I only met her once. Apparently, Sammie Lee told her about us; she came to confront me about it at the condo where I usually stayed with him, and we exchanged words about it." I refused to mention what happened after that.

"You only met her once?"

"Yes. Most mistresses don't make a habit of socializing with the wives of their lovers," I retorted.

Mayer shot me a disapproving look. I had to remember to hold my sharp tongue if I wanted to get to Kyashira.

"And you met her at Mr. Lee's condo?"

I raised an eyebrow. "I didn't *meet* her. We didn't have an appointment. She just showed up, unannounced."

"And when was the last time you saw Mr. Lee?"

"Earlier today. We just returned from a week in Hawaii, and he dropped me off."

"What was the purpose of the trip?"

I gave Mayer a "come on, now" look. "What do you think?"

Mayer continued to grill me: my whereabouts before and after Lola's visit, who I saw, who I spoke to. I thought I was home free when Mayer tucked his notebook back into his pocket. Then he blindsided me.

"Ms. Davis, we understand that you had an altercation with Mrs. Lee, shortly before her death."

Great. Of course they knew about the fight, and I had been really hoping to avoid that topic. I may have been a high-school dropout, but I watched enough TV to know that a mistress was usually a prime suspect in the death of her lover's wife, and a fight prior to the wife's death was not a good look. "Well, yes. I mean, like I said, she confronted me about my affair with her husband, Sammie. We exchanged words, and then things got a little *heated.* But right after that I left for Hawaii. All this is verifiable."

A little heated. That was like saying someone was a little pregnant.

"How bad was that altercation, Ms. Davis?"

Uh-oh. *Careful, Honey,* I told myself. "Uh, well, we got into it a little bit. Some slapping, rumbling on the floor. You know, a girl fight."

"Were either of you injured?"

"A few scratches. And my pride, I guess." I lowered my eyes as I remembered the humiliation of being tossed out on the street—with nothing but the clothes on my back—and there being nothing I could do about it. Not right then, anyway.

Bingham examined my face and spoke for the first time. "You seem to have healed pretty well."

"Well, a week in Hawaii does wonders for the healing process," I said nervously. My smile was falsely bright and had no effect on the jaded demeanors of the detectives.

Mayer and Bingham looked at each other in an unspoken signal, and then rose to leave. "Thank you for your time, Ms. Davis. We'll be in touch. Please call us if you think of anything else." They each removed a business card from their respective wallets and handed them to me. I took them, ashamed to see that my hands shook slightly. As they walked out the door, Mayer turned and said, "Oh yeah. If you don't mind, we'd like for you to stay within the state of New York for the time being."

Hmm. It seemed like they didn't buy my story of a family emergency, or didn't care. Either way, I watched them walk away as fear gnawed a hole in my belly. Fuck what they minded; I had to get to Georgia. I had to get to Kyashira.

As I sped down the highway toward LaGuardia Airport, I knew that I would probably miss my scheduled flight to Georgia and would have to beg my way onto the next one; a family emergency just might bump me to the top of the standby list. I wondered if the detectives tailed me to the airport. I looked in my rearview mirror but couldn't see anything suspicious. The movies always showed a tail following three car lengths behind, but traffic was heavy and the only thing I noticed that distance behind me was a burgundy Ford Focus. If there was a tail, my amateur eyes couldn't spot it.

Would my flight plans be misconstrued? Would I look as if I were running because I was guilty? All I could do was hope that Detectives Mayer and Bingham did not follow me to the airport, and that I would be able to do what I had to do. All of a sudden, everything seemed to fall apart. I couldn't even say that I didn't deserve it. When I started my journey as a bad ass, I wanted excitement—and that's exactly what I got.

PART ONE
BAD ASS

Chapter One

PRETTY LITTLE MESS

My name is Honorina Estelle Davis, but you can just call me Honey. With a name like Honorina Estelle, can you blame me? It wasn't my fault that I was named for my maternal and paternal great-grandmothers. My parents thought that by doing so, they paid proper homage to my ancestors; and maybe they hoped that the genteel manners of those two "colored society ladies" (that's what they were called back then) would rub off on me and I'd become one as well. Somehow I doubted it, especially since my nickname was more appropriate for a strip club than a cotillion. But I digress.

I grew up privileged. My parents, Jerome and Valerie Davis, were doctors, and we lived in a four-bedroom townhouse in New Rochelle. My mother had her own private family practice and had been born into one of the most prominent black families in New York; they were free blacks credited as founders of churches and schools. They had roots as abolitionists and ultimately gained political power, among other things. My father's family, which had roots in Washington, DC, got their start as black business owners, right after slavery. I always heard that they had ties to the first black-owned bank, and some black-owned insurance company. My father was the third in the family to become a doctor, and the first to become a surgeon—a cardiac surgeon, to be precise. Both of my parents' families had descendants who'd attended the best schools, white and black: Howard (where my parents met in medical school), Georgetown, Fisk, Oberlin, Tuskegee, Harvard, Spelman, Morehouse. My parents belonged to the right organizations, donated to the right charities, and vacationed in the right places. In fact, my father inherited our summer cottage in Oak Bluffs, where we went every Memorial Day weekend.

My parents had head starts in many respects. Property and money were handed down—no student loans for them—and they continued the tradition of becoming educated leaders; the Talented Tenth, as W.E.B. DuBois once called them, destined to uplift the black race. My parents never told me they were millionaires, but I always knew it. I saw, heard, and experienced a lot more than most, because of my heritage. Trips to museums. Vacations in Europe. Broadway plays. My mother was looking forward to my Sweet Sixteen debut next year, in her sorority's cotillion. Yeah, like I was going to let that happen.

Unlike my predecessors, I'd always been spoiled and had a real lazy streak. I never thought I'd have to work hard for anything, or make my own way. Things like school came easy to me, I was pretty, and my trust fund guaranteed that my adult life would be just as effortless. I was a Davis, and starting from scratch just wasn't the Davis way.

Looking back, I was one pretty little spoiled mess. I never knew what it was to do chores, and I always had the best of everything that money could buy—and the worst of everything that it couldn't. I mean, everyone had issues, including my parents—or rather, because of my parents. Both of them were pieces of work, but the bane of my existence was my mother. Don't our problems always start with our mothers? I mean, they push us out and push their issues, personal opinions, and biases on us, ensuring years of expensive therapy as adults as we try to figure out how fucked up we really are. We love them, we hate them, but most of all, we can't live without them.

Valerie took the term "ice queen" to a whole different level. Her public face showed a warm yet formidable woman who gave generously of her time, talents, and money. Her energies were focused on her patients, philanthropic efforts, and luncheons with members of the various organizations to which she belonged. Behind closed doors, she did a 180. Valerie wasn't a hugger; she was more likely to pinch you mercilessly (where the bruising wouldn't show, of course), when cutting you to shreds with her sharp tongue didn't work. Ego stroking or morale boosting were not part of her program, unless there was a six-figure donation attached. No hair in my mother's chin-length, dark brown, bronze-highlighted bob was ever out of place—when I didn't make them stand on end. Her clothing was always immaculate, her jewelry tasteful yet quiet. I never even spotted her with a single run in her stockings. If she ever laughed when it wasn't required, if she ever let her hair down (literally), I never saw it.

My father, on the other hand, was her polar opposite. Dad was the good cop to Mom's bad cop, and I was totally a Daddy's Girl. Sometimes, when Valerie had been particularly hard on me—and on his rare days off—he would take me out to a local pizza place, where we would gorge ourselves on greasy slices of pizza (sausage and mushroom for me, pepperoni for him) and play Tic Tac Toe on the paper placemats. We listened to jazz—with occasional forays into Hot 97—on the radio in his black Mercedes CLK. Mom pretended not to notice the grease stains on my clothes, or that they smelled of garlic, or that I had all of Jay-Z's CDs—plus some Charlie Parker—hidden in a flowered box underneath my bed.

Any other time, though, and Valerie would be in my ass, 24/7. She never adjusted to the fact that I liked to run, skip, jump, race, and chase until my beribboned plaits came loose. If looks could kill, I would have been fertilizer for my mother's prized hybrid pink tea roses. As soon as my mother captured me, I was forced to bathe, fix my hair, and transform myself into a princess worthy of the Davis name.

"Honey, no running outside, you may scar your knees" or "How are you going to participate in pageants, with marks all over your knees?" When she got really mad, she called me by my full name. This usually happened after some major infraction, like the time I put Alka-Seltzer in the font of holy water located outside the sanctuary of our Catholic church. "Honorina Estelle Davis, you are grounded for the next month! I have never been so embarrassed, and Father Mulhaney was livid!" It took about a month for the large bruise on my upper left arm to fade; Valerie was a champion pincher. Father Mulhaney transferred to another congregation a month later, and we got the younger and hipper Father Sean Ryan, who rode a motorcycle and didn't mind sharing the leftover communion wine with a sister, under the guise of my Confessional. In the name of the Father, the Son, and the Holy Ghost— hallelujah, holla back.

As befitted a girl child of my pedigree, I was forced to sit through endless piano and ballet lessons, when I longed to play the saxophone and take modern dance (I once harbored secret dreams of dancing with the Alvin Ailey troupe; my mother would have preferred that I join the Dance Theatre of Harlem, especially since she sat on the Board of Directors). Slouching from boredom never worked; Valerie would promptly pile books atop my head and watch me walk until the books balanced perfectly—a testament to good posture. She prided herself on doing whatever it took to correct the error of my adolescent ways, to act the part of a member of the black upper class. But what kind of childhood was that? When would it be my turn to get loose, to be myself, to just be?

I recalled the time I attended my first cotillion. My mother beamed at being a part of the pomp and circumstance, watching as each girl walked out to be presented to the crowd, unaware of how disinterested I was in watching people show how well they waltzed. I ended up nodding off so deeply that my face demolished the carefully constructed tower of chilled butter pats and pinched bread balls that I'd created on my dessert plate, out of boredom. Valerie didn't speak to me for two whole weeks. It could've been worse; at least I didn't snore.

Like most people raised in a privileged environment, I had little exposure to the darkness of the world. Thieves, pimps, and murderers were characters in movies, books, and plays. The homeless were endured under carefully controlled conditions—like Thanksgiving Day dinners at the local homeless shelter—and only for short periods of time. Con artists preyed on people without education or sufficient financial resources, and poverty was reserved for the lazy and undeserving. I grew up in a home that would leave most people's living quarters looking like shacks. How was I supposed to know what the real world was like? As a result, my perception of reality was somewhat skewed, and I longed to see how the rest of the world lived.

Having too much can be just as traumatic as having too little, when the trade-off is a freedom that most would regard as a normal part of growing up. I was lonely in that big house, and I began to feel confined by my mother's precise scheduling of every available minute of my free time. My rebellions grew as I did; Alka-Seltzer in the holy water at age eleven gave way to joyrides in my mother's shiny red S500 Mercedes. Sips of communion wine with the new priest at the tender age of twelve, led to sneaking bottles from my father's bar and getting drunk with the other members of my Jack and Jill group after meetings when I was thirteen. I once skipped ballet lessons for two whole weeks, preferring to spend time in Washington Square Park, where I learned to play chess and differentiate between different drug transactions. The final straw was when I was kicked out of my Girl Scout troop at the age of fourteen for slipping chocolate-flavored laxatives into the brownies we made for a fundraiser for new tents for our camping activities. Jerome and Valerie finally put their feet down.

At first, the strict parenting worked. I had a nine o'clock nightly curfew. I had a cell phone, and I had five minutes to return any of my parents' phone calls. I had to check in once I arrived at my lessons, and my ballet instructor, Madame Gorvona, had to speak to my parents and assure them that I was actually in class. I had to sit away from my fellow Jack and Jill drinking buddies at group functions, and the chaperones kept eagle eyes on all of us. The only grass I was allowed near was the stuff that grew in our front and back yards. Soon, after a year of toeing the line, the restrictions chafed and I just wanted to stop being perfect. I wanted to stop being a Davis. I wanted to just be Honey and live a life that was free and exciting; a life with few rules, a life like any other teenager.

Be careful what you wish for, because you just might get it.

Chapter Two

I'LL FIND A WAY

It was December 1999, just before winter break. I was sixteen and in the twelfth grade. Everyone was in that crazy Y2K mode, thinking that as soon as the New Year started, everything was going to go back to the Stone Age. I didn't worry about any of that; I was more concerned with living in the present.

One day, my mother and I were on our way home, riding down the highway in her spotless Benz, listening to her favorite easy listening station. I stared out of the passenger window in silence; my mother had signed me up for her sorority's debutante cotillion in six months, which would fall right after my sixteenth birthday. In the months leading up to the event, I would have to participate in various "character-building" activities, which included waltz lessons, etiquette classes, instructions on how to wear a little black dress, and when to write thank-you notes. I slouched slightly in the heated, butter-colored leather seat as I gathered up the courage to address more immediate matters.

"Mom, a friend at school asked if I could sleep over this weekend. We want to go see a movie and meet up with some other girls. Do you think I could—?"

"The answer is no. There are way too many things that could happen."

"But you didn't even let me finish! Maybe if you hear me out, we can negotiate some ground rules."

"I can't chaperone you. I don't have time, and I don't know those children. I want you to be around people who are a little more civilized."

"How can you judge people you don't even know? And as for civilized, Judge Baron's son got arrested for shoplifting last week, and he's in Jack and Jill with me, so upbringing doesn't seem to matter." I tried to speak in a calmer tone. "You won't need to chaperone me. Mrs. Henderson will be with us. You can even call and talk to her, if you want. They're good kids, and she's a good person. Kristen and Michelle made the A Honor Roll again this quarter, Tonya is on the basketball team, and Mrs. Henderson works at the post office."

"You don't need to go, and that's my final answer!" Valerie snapped. "It's simply not an option." She snorted. "Post office, indeed."

I crossed my arms across my chest and scowled. "I just want to get out of the house! You never let me go anywhere I want to go. My friends are at the mall right now, and I had to go to some stupid fucking mother-daughter tea, where I—"

Valerie removed her hand from the gearshift and clamped down on my upper arm. Pain radiated from the spot where she pinched me. "Honorina Estelle Davis! Who do you think you are, cursing like that? See, that's why I don't want you hanging around those public school hoodlums. Look at the bad habits you're picking up."

I started to cry. "**I'm sixteen**, Mom, not sixty! I just want to do some things that other **sixteen**-year-olds do!"

"Who's the parent, and who's the child? I don't let you do the things that other **sixteen**-year-olds do because those children are going nowhere in life, and you are. You are still a child, Honey, and as a parent, it is my responsibility to give you all of the equipment necessary to thrive in this world. I knew I should have never let your father talk me into sending you to public school!" She removed her hand from my throbbing arm and replaced it on the gearshift. I knew I'd have a bruise the size of Alaska soon. "Now, I suggest you straighten up right this minute, unless you'd like all of your privileges taken away. There's no sense in arguing about it. And don't you ever let me hear you curse again." She had delivered the Gospel According to St. Valerie.

My head throbbed in time with my arm, and something inside me just snapped. "Screw you, you bitch! Just leave me alone!" I exploded.

I don't know what happened next because my head ricocheted off the window. My lip gloss left a mocha comma-shaped stain. I touched my stinging left cheek in wonder as I stared at my mother in shock. She had never hit me before, and I didn't see it coming. I didn't even know she could move that fast.

"I don't know who the hell you think you are, or who you think I am," Valerie growled. "But I will not tolerate such nonsense from a spoiled brat who is lucky to be alive! I swear, sometimes I think I should have—" She suddenly clamped her lips shut, as if she were afraid of saying too much.

"What? You should have what?" Valerie remained silent and understanding suddenly dawned. "You should have had an abortion? You should have never had me?"

She pressed her lips together tightly and gripped the steering wheel. She refused to look at me.

"Fine! If you don't want me for a daughter, then I don't want you for a mother!"

The car slowed down as we approached traffic. I removed my seatbelt and flung the door open.

"Honey! What are you doing!" my mother yelled. Her eyes widened in shock as I got out of the car and began to run. I was determined to put as much distance as possible between me and my overbearing mother.

I'd underestimated Valerie, though. I hadn't gotten far when I heard the screech of tires, then the crunch of gravel right behind me. I looked over my shoulder and the Benz was on the shoulder of the highway, its diesel engine roaring as the car gained power. Cars honked and people pointed at us from their cars. The gap between us quickly diminished, but my mother showed no signs of stopping. I panicked and flung myself against the guardrail. My mother swung the Benz at an angle to block off my escape and exited the parked car in a fury. Her features were contorted into a Kabuki mask of rage. She snatched me up with the righteous anger of a mama bear, dragged me back to the car, and tossed me into the passenger seat.

"If you move, I will run your ass over," she threatened. The look in her eyes told me that she meant it. She got back in the car and signaled politely to be let into the oncoming traffic. A car stopped and let her in, and my mother raised a hand gracefully in thanks.

Valerie's knuckles were white from the kung-fu grip she had on the steering wheel. I heard a grinding sound and dared a quick peek at my mother's face: the sound came from her jaws, which moved from side to side, as if she was chewing something extremely slowly

"Let me tell you something, you spoiled, ungrateful little bitch." Her voice was the low rumble of thunder that let you know that a storm was near. "I don't give a fuck what you think, or what you want. You have a nice life, with everything your little spoiled heart desires. But please believe that I will take that life from you if you ever pull some stupid shit like that again. Do you understand me, Honorina?"

I was too scared to speak. I'd never heard that tone in my mother's voice, nor had I ever heard her curse—especially at me.

"I said, do you understand me, Honorina?"

"Yes, ma'am," I said meekly.

"Then I suggest you reevaluate your actions and apologize to me."

"I . . . I'm sorry, Mom."

"Good. And don't go running to your father; he can't save you this time."

She turned the volume up on the radio. A flute-filled melody filled the car as she ended the discussion and continued the drive home.

Needless to say, the relationship with my mother was never the same again.

❦

My father was appalled by my behavior and actually sided with my mother for the second time that year. Nearly all of my privileges were taken away, but it didn't matter to me. I still had food, shelter, water, and nice clothes, and now even more time to devote to the life I lived when I went to school.

My parents thought that my low interaction with God played a part in how I disrespected my mother, which was why I was shuttled into regular ten-thirty service at my father's African Methodist Episcopal church on Sunday morning, after we'd attended an early Mass at my mother's Catholic Church.

"It's so nice to see you this morning, Dr. Davis," Reverend Darlene Daniels beamed.

"You too, Reverend Daniels," my dad replied. He puffed his chest out just a bit.

Reverend Daniels had short, natural hair that always looked dry. It looked like it would cut your hand if you even thought about touching it. Her smooth, even, dark complexion made her tiny gold earrings stand out. I never saw her without those little balls sitting in her ears. Reverend Daniels wasn't ugly or cute; she was just average, I supposed. What did stand out was the way she held my father's hand a little too long when she greeted him in church. I typically resented her poor attempt to flirt without me or my mother noticing, but this time, I was glad she'd done it. If I couldn't get revenge on my mother, Reverend Daniels could do it for me. She greeted my mother and me quickly and flashed a much cooler smile at us than the one she gave my father. You could tell she really didn't care for us.

"Valerie and Honey, it's a pleasure to see you both in the house of the Lord." Reverend Daniels looked my mother up and down, her eyes resting briefly on my mother's five-carat diamond-and-platinum wedding ring set, which had been handed down to my father from his mother.

"Thank you, Reverend Daniels. We enjoy your services," my mother replied with a fake smile of her own. Sometimes I wondered if Valerie knew what Reverend Daniels was up to.

We took our seats in the first pew and listened to Reverend Daniels preach, ironically, about David and Bathsheba.

My father was a faithful donor to Mount Calvary AME, which had been his home church for quite a number of years. Even though my mother a devout Catholic, I had a feeling that she'd passed on attending Mass more than usual because she wanted to keep an eye on Reverend Daniels.

Several hours later, church was over. My parents chatted with a few people, exchanging social pleasantries that were faint masks for the social warfare that ruled our world.

"Isn't Honey graduating this year?" Mrs. Callahan asked.

"Yes, she is," my father answered proudly. "Graduating high school at the age of sixteen is quite an accomplishment."

Mrs. Callahan's eyes narrowed as she kept her smile plastered on her face. One of her sons was in danger of repeating the seventh grade, and Mrs. Callahan and her husband spent a lot of money on not only a private tutor for him, but also on a donation to the school headmaster's favorite charity. "Where will she be attending college? We're so proud of Melissa. Harvard was her only choice, and she was accepted."

Of course she was accepted. Mrs. Callahan attended Radcliffe College where she met Mr. Callahan, who was a Harvard man himself. Melissa was too dumb to get into another college on her own; her brother's school problems were hereditary.

"Wonderful," my mother answered dryly. "Honey will be attending Howard. We've discussed Yale and Harvard, but she decided she wanted to continue the family tradition. She'll be a biology major with a pre-medical focus."

That was news to me! Even though I had been accepted to Howard (big surprise), I hadn't decided on a major since I was being forced to attend college. I wanted to take a year off and maybe backpack through Europe but nooooo . . . Jerome and Valerie weren't having it. My mother filled out all of my applications and just used the same personal statement for each one.

"Congratulations, Honey. I do hope to see you before you leave," Ms. Callahan said, as she gave me a brief hug.

"Thank you, ma'am. You will," I answered with yet another fake smile.

Between Reverend Daniels and Mrs. Callahan, Valerie was not in a good mood by the time we arrived at my father's car. As soon as the doors shut, she went off on my dad.

"I don't like that woman!"

My dad chuckled. "Naomi Callahan is in your alumni fundraising group. Why don't you like her?"

"I'm not talking about her," Valerie snapped. "I'm talking about *Reverend* Daniels. I don't know why you insist on coming to this church. I wish you would convert to Catholicism, like we'd discussed before we got married."

"We've talked about this many times," my father hissed back. "This is my church, and I like it. Reverend Daniels has done a good job since

Reverend Michaels retired a few years ago. Respect the house of the Lord and remember why you're here, Valerie."

My mother sucked her teeth. "Why does she have to be your spiritual advisor? I don't trust her. What makes her an authority on anything?"

"I'm not going to entertain any more of this conversation," my father said in a stern tone.

I laughed silently at my mother.

❧※❧

At home, my friends were picked for me. At school, I made it a point to find my niche and got to know everyone who was good to know socially, although I did make it a point to keep my grades up to avoid further scrutiny from my parents. Eventually, I managed to gain status as the most popular girl in school. My confidence, fly clothes, and cocky attitude helped me to become the "It" girl. It didn't hurt that I had been blessed with the body and face of an eighteen-year-old, and was invited to the hot parties that were usually by and for seventeen and eighteen-year-olds. When I got the invites, I often acted as if I had bigger, better plans happening and couldn't attend. My "unavailability" was quite far from the truth: Outside of school, I wasn't allowed to mix and mingle with those outside of my carefully chosen social circle. The funny thing was that I put a lot of time and effort into landing those invitations. Not showing up to their parties made more invitations pour in; it was the law of supply and demand, just like I learned in school.

Although I was considered popular, I tried not to let it get to my head too much. Hangovers, however, were a different matter. I'd gone from sneaking drinks with my social group buddies to more solo exploits. Drinking, I discovered, helped me deal with my dissatisfaction with my life—or rather, with my parents' life for me—or, more specifically, my mother's life for her privileged upper-class daughter, since she was the one primarily responsible for arranging my life to her heart's content. I helped myself to my parents' well-stocked bar in the basement while they were out. Sometimes I even drank while they were in another part of the house.

My parents' wet bar—and the adjoining wine cooler—were littered with bottles of liqueurs and wines that I couldn't pronounce: Stolichnaya, Jägermeister, schnapps, Jose Cuervo, vermouth, Pouilly-Fumé, ouzo. There were also the ones whose names just rolled off my tongue: Bacardi, Maker's Mark, Bombay Sapphire. I quickly took advantage of Jerome and Valerie's naïveté with regard to my alcoholic self-education and experimented with everything, including designer beers, lagers, and ales. After I vomited a time or two (especially after a bottle of Guinness), I developed such a tolerance to alcohol that a shot or two no longer gave me even the slightest buzz. I needed at least half a bottle, and often could polish off an entire bottle by myself.

I remembered my first drink: it was after my parents' Christmas party, when I was fourteen, and they left some brand of high-end champagne on the bar. The bulk of the adults were outside in a heated tent with catered food and a makeshift dance floor. Inside, it was only me and Camille Jordan, a girl I'd known since we were in diapers. Camille's father owned a chain of sporting goods stores, and her mother was a successful real estate agent; in fact, she'd sold my mother the office of her private practice.

"How's school, Honey?" Camille asked. She still attended the private school that I couldn't wait to leave.

"It's all right, I guess." I studied the bar from my vantage point on the loveseat, searching for any new additions for the party.

She pushed her glasses up on her nose. "Well, I have a project due the day our break ends."

"What subject?" I asked absentmindedly. There were some pretty bottles grouped toward the end, plus some blue bottles of that Bombay stuff. On the other end was a crate filled with champagne flutes. Hmm . . . I'd never tried champagne before.

"History. I have to go a scavenger hunt. I have to find ten historical hot spots in downtown New York." She looked excited at the prospect.

I nodded. I wondered if there was any more of that schnapps stuff; it was probably sweet. "I guess that sounds like fun. We don't do things like that in public school," I replied.

"You don't?" Camille looked confused; she couldn't imagine such a thing. "Why did you leave private school last year? I miss not having you around."

"I begged my parents to let me go to public school this year."

"But why? Our school is one of the best schools in New York."

I wasn't in the mood to debate the merits of private vs. public education. "I wonder what that tastes like?" I nodded at the bottles on the bar.

"What?" She sipped her (virgin) eggnog and looked around the room.

"That." I got up and walked to the bar for a closer examination of those bottles. They were dark green with white flowers and green vines painted on it. The label read Perrier-Jouët. I tried to sound out the name using my high school French, but couldn't quite get it right.

Camille frowned. "Honey, I know you're not thinking of —"

"You know I'm not thinking of what?" I retrieved a flute. "Our parents are outside, and the liquor is in here." I gave Camille a winning smile. "Come on, Camille! Let's try a little. No one has to know. It'll be fun!"

Camille's worried frown turned into a disapproving scowl. "Maybe you need to reevaluate your idea of fun. You shouldn't be drinking.

We're underage, and it's against the law!"

"Fuck being underage! We're in a safe environment; if we're going to try this, this is the best time to do it. What are you afraid of?" I peeled the foil from the neck of a bottle and examined the wire contraption that fitted snug against the stopper.

Camille simply stared at me in shock. "What has happened to you, Honey? You've changed so much!"

I didn't know why Camille acted so surprised. Public schools were known to be much more lax than private ones, and they had all types of kids in them. I got back to the matter at hand. "Hey, do you know how to open this?"

Camille shook her head. "I don't know."

I tried to pull the wire part off, but it wouldn't budge.

"You have to twist the wire part off, silly," Camille said in exasperation. "Give it to me." She twisted the contraption off and tossed it aside. She tried to pull the stopper out but it was too hard for her. We both stared at the bottle in frustration, then Camille had an idea. "How about you hold the bottle, and I'll pull the stopper out? You pull from your direction, and I'll pull from mine."

"Okay." I was game for anything that would enable me to taste the contents of that pretty bottle. Anything in something so attractive had to taste good. I got a good grip on the neck of the bottle while Camille grabbed the stopper. She pulled, I pulled, and eventually the stopper slid out of the bottle with a sudden and loud *POP!* Champagne fizzed from the bottle and onto the floor.

"Oh, my God!" Camille exclaimed. She went back behind the bar and grabbed some towels, handing one to me. We both got on our hands and knees and wiped up the pale golden liquid. When we were done, we rose and looked at the open bottle, then at each other.

"Well?" I challenged Camille. "The bottle is open, now. We can't let it go to waste."

Camille thought about this, then reluctantly nodded. I got another flute and poured each of us a glass full of champagne. I handed Camille hers and raised mine in a toast. "To breaking out of our cages," I proclaimed as I clinked my glass against Camille's. I took a sip and bubbles floated up my nose. I sneezed and choked at the same time.

Camille slapped me on the back in alarm. "Honey! Are you okay?"

"I-I'm okay," I sputtered. I let my throat calm down then took a more careful sip. The slightly bitter liquid eased down my irritated throat. I smacked my lips and decided that I liked it.

"That's what's up," I said. "How is yours?"

Camille took a sip and wrinkled her nose. "Ewww!" She put her flute down. "I don't like it. It's nasty." She walked back over to the sofa and picked up her cup of eggnog.

Oh, well. More for me. I downed the rest of my champagne and enjoyed the warm, tingly sensation that flowed through me. I quickly poured another flute and took a huge gulp. Camille looked at me disapprovingly as I twirled around with the flute in my hand, dancing to a tune in my head. I had this crazy feeling inside, and I loved it.

"What has gotten into you, Honey?" Camille snapped. "After all your parents do for you, this is how you repay them? Continue this madness if you want to; you're going to end up nothing but a high-class drunk from Harlem!"

I bowed deeply to Camille. "That would be a shot-glass diva from Sugar Hill, thank you very much." I swept my hand—the one with the glass in it—in a dramatic gesture, spilling champagne on Camille in the process.

"You're pathetic," she sputtered as she rushed to find napkins to dry herself off. I laughed and took a swig of champagne straight from the bottle.

Camille was right; I was headed down a sketchy path. It didn't matter, though. I kept coming back for more.

Chapter Three

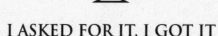

I ASKED FOR IT, I GOT IT

My parents were going to a New Year's Eve get-together at the home of one of my father's colleagues, and the twenty-year-old Catherine Alexander was appointed my babysitter for the evening. Catherine was one of the preferred sitters in our circle of the young and privileged. Her father, George Alexander, was an attorney and her mother, Christine Tyler Alexander, was a dentist. Catherine was a straight-A student on winter break from Yale, and took babysitting gigs to make side money (she was at Yale on a full scholarship). Most of her pocket money went toward books, particularly romance novels. I'd given her three of them as a Christmas gift, part of my plan to escape for the evening. I handed Catherine the gift and she ripped it open, curious and tickled.

"Oh, Honey! You got these for me?" she asked with widened eyes as she stared at the couples entwined in heated embraces on the covers of the books.

"Yeah. Just a little something for Christmas, even though Christmas is over."

"This is so sweet. Thank you!"

Catherine gave me a big hug and immediately curled up on the sofa with one of the novels. When she got about twenty pages deep into the storyline, I knew it was time to place a call.

My first date was with one of the flyest catches in my school. Mikaylo Jones was half black, half Puerto Rican, eighteen years old, and 100% fine. He spoke fluent Spanish when he felt like it, thanks to his mother, and fluent Ebonics when he wanted to keep it hood, thanks to his father. He grew up on the East Side, in what is known as Spanish Harlem, on 116th street. His parents split up when he was young, but his father only moved a hop, skip, and jump to Taft Projects, on 112th street. We met when I got sent to the office because I broke the school's dress code (thanks to the stash of clothes I kept in my locker), and Mikaylo was waiting to talk to the principal about something screwed up he'd done.

He had a little thug in him, but managed to be smooth. He was a pretty boy—trouble waiting to happen—but I thought I could handle it. Since I was a bit developed, Mikaylo thought I was his age and hounded me for my phone number until he found out the real deal. It was too late by then; he was hooked. When I still refused to give him my number (best believe I didn't want Valerie catching wind of a boy calling me!), Mikaylo's best friend, Steve, shuttled our love notes back and forth, since we took different classes in different parts of the building. I was too shy to admit that I liked him, and maybe Mikaylo was too ashamed that he liked a sixteen-year old, but after about one week of passing those notes back and forth, I finally broke down and gave him my number. About a month later, he asked me to go to a New Year's Eve party with him. I figured this was a test, and I was determined to pass it. I slipped out the back door in my brand-new jeans, fitted cashmere mock turtleneck, and fly black boots, and met Mikaylo at the end of the street, near a stop sign.

For the party, those of us who were underage (which was most of us) had all gotten some decent fake IDs. The ringleader, who just so happened to be Steve the note-passer, used his new ID to rent a suite at this nice hotel where his cousin Bernard worked part-time. Bernard said he'd watch out for us on his shift at the desk, so long as he didn't have to take responsibility for the room; he wasn't trying to take the heat for a bunch of rowdy adolescents. Thankfully, the party wasn't a word of mouth thing. You had to be on the top dog list to get an official invitation, along with last-minute details of the time and location. We tried to keep the riffraff out, and for the most part, we did.

When I walked into the party, I felt like a superstar; I even wore designer shades with my outfit. Music was already playing, but not too loud. I greeted the folks I knew, laughing and chatting them up like this was the best thing in the world. It was all an act because I was scared as fuck; most of the people there were popular juniors and seniors, and even a few college students. I forced myself to breathe easy as I removed my shades and literally showed my face.

"What's up, Honey?" Demetrius Williams said. He was in my history class. In fact, we didn't hold long conversations much, so I was surprised he even stopped me. His eyes were all over my C cups and curvaceous hips.

"Hey. What's going on?" I answered with a smile.

Mikaylo wedged himself between us and gave Demetrius a pound. Then he whispered in my ear, "So you've got a boyfriend, huh?"

"Oh, you got jokes. He's a boy that's a friend." I danced around the question. The sudden thrill in my stomach that Mikaylo might actually be jealous made me want to drag the moment out a bit longer. "A *good* friend." I tilted my head and smiled at Mikaylo.

Mikaylo frowned. "A good friend, huh? Well, maybe your good friend can give you a ride home tonight."

Okay, maybe I wasn't as good at this flirting thing as I'd thought. "It's not like that, Kaylo," I explained hastily. "I like him, but I don't like him like that."

"Good. Don't be liking that meathead just because he's on the football team."

One of my best friends, Yolanda McCoy, ran to me. "Girl, you made it," she said with a hundred-watt grin that matched the sparkly gold sweater she wore with dark brown jeans and brown ankle boots. Her freshly permed black hair was parted on one side—like the late singer Aaliyah—and hung in a straight curtain past her shoulders. Small gold hoops adorned her ears. We exchanged hugs.

"You know that's right. Honey's in the hooouse!" I twirled around.

"You look good," Janeisha "Pookie" Parker added. "You always have the coolest gear." Her eyes ran over my outfit hungrily.

"You look nice too, Pookie," I replied. She wore a pair of fitted Lee jeans, black knee-length boots, and a black sweater with little black beads sprinkled across it. Her hair had been pulled back from her face and hidden beneath a large, burgundy-highlighted fake ponytail. Gold door-knocker earrings with "Pookie" scripted in the hoops hung from her ears.

Her eyes paused on the Gucci logo on my boots. "I got the knock-offs. You got the authentic. Big difference." Her mouth turned downward in disappointment.

"It's all good. You still know how to put it all together," I assured Pookie. "You got some shit you can use to your advantage, and won't." I pointed at her ass. "You could make a fucking killing!" Pookie had one of the biggest asses in our school, which made her the object of a lot of attention, not all of it good. We shared a laugh and exchanged high fives.

Almost everyone was drinking, and some were puffing on blunts, too. I needed some liquid courage flowing through my bloodstream, so I got some beer. After downing four of them, I was dancing like someone in a Lil Jon video. I shook the stress away and got low, bending over and backing it up on whatever guy was nearest. Mikaylo tore himself away from his boys to break it up.

I giggled as Mikaylo gave my dance partner the screw face. I draped my arms around his neck and asked, "Does anyone have some real alcohol around here? Fuck the beer, let me have a shot."

"Be right back." Mikaylo left, then came back with an unopened bottle of liquor. I looked at the label: Hennessy.

"Give me a pimp cup," I joked. I poured some into a cup, started drinking, and didn't stop. Soon, I slurred, "Look it there. Look, look! I drained this bottle." I held the bottle up to the light; only a corner of the cognac was left. "Mikaylo, why'd you let me drink that whole bottle of Henny by myself?" I was beyond tipsy and wrapped my arms around him. I felt so good, so loose and free . . . and horny.

Mikaylo took advantage of the situation and pressed his body closer to mine. "This may come as some surprise, but I'm feeling you," Mikaylo murmured in my ear before he nibbled on my earlobe.

Damn, that felt good! I laughed and snuggled closer to him.

"Who put on Three 6 Mafia? This song is whack!" Yolanda yelled. Her face was flushed and her hair was a bit disheveled as she continued to grind against Demetrius.

"You're crazy as hell. You don't like this? I loooove this song," I slowly swayed my hips, grounding them against Mikaylo's crotch. "It's a fun track that you can just groove to."

"Then let's dance. That's the only way we'll really know if you love this song." Mikaylo ground his erection into my ass. I got caught up in the sparkle in his eyes, the music, the liquor, and his touch.

"You know what, Honey? Can I tell you something?"

"What's that?"

"You're sexy."

"That's old news," I teased.

"We belong together. That's new news. I never messed with anyone younger than me. For you, I'm willing to make that exception, if you act right." He held me tight. "Cutie, you turn me on. Stay with me. Don't go home. Let's make this a real special night."

Oh wow. He wanted me to spend the night with him! "I can't. I would, but I can't stay long. I—"

Mikaylo pulled back with a disgusted look on his face. "Shit, Honey! I thought I had a new lady in my life."

I was torn. What to do, what to do? "Are you asking me to be your girlfriend?"

"Let me tell you again: I thought I had a new lady in my life, not some scared little girl. And if you're all mine now, we should make this night memorable." He pulled me close again and tongued my ear. "Come on, baby. Do this for me," he urged.

I felt my nipples harden at the sensation of his tongue in my ear. I opened my eyes slightly and saw one of his homeboys walking toward a room, wearing only his boxer shorts. I opened my eyes completely and saw a couple feeling each other up like they were in a porn movie. Further inspection revealed a lot going on around the room: threesomes, blow jobs, sex games. I got even more turned on.

Still, the prospect of having sex for the first time—and with someone as mature as Mikaylo—was scary. I tried to stall for time. "Do you have any condoms?" No way was I about to have any kind of sex without protection. Valerie would literally kill me if I got pregnant.

Mikaylo pulled away again. "Why are you fucking with me, Honey?"

"That means you don't." I figured I could call Mikaylo's bluff and get out of this with my virginity intact, so I staggered over to an empty couch and plopped down. Mikaylo sat next to me and took my hand.

"I don't have any reason to gas you up," he started. "I tell it like I see it, and see it like I tell it. No matter what, I want to always be around." The look in his eyes seemed sincere.

"I'm not fucking with you, Mikaylo. I'm going to sleep." I was drunk and exhausted. My eyes closed and my head fell on the overstuffed arm.

"I know you didn't tell me to pick you up and come all the way down here, if you were going to sleep," Mikaylo snapped.

"Uuumm . . . umm." I couldn't concentrate enough to put my fear into words.

He nudged me awake, and he wasn't gentle. "If you aint gonna give me none, you're not who I thought you were."

Mikaylo placed my hand on the crotch of his jeans; the feel of his rock-hard dick had my hormones jumping and lust shot through my drunken haze. I couldn't tell him he was my first; I was drunk, but still mindful of my image. I just played it off by laughing.

"Oh, you think that's funny?" Mikaylo pressed my hand harder into his crotch. "You're lunching. I got something for that laugh." He rubbed my hand over his crotch.

"Wait a minute. How do I get out of here? Which way do I go?" I slurred.

I was so twisted that I was no longer making any sense at all. My crew was nowhere around, gone off to do their own thing. The next thing I knew, my feet were moving and the room moved through half-closed eyes. I didn't have energy to open them too wide.

My body hit a mattress. Then a body cuddled up next to me. Hands peeled off my clothes as my limp body offered no resistance. Then I was moaning, felt out of my mind, and Mikyalo was pumping away on top of me, saying, "Yeah, baby," over and over. Then he said, "You a'ight with me, and I love your titties. I'm going to bust this nut." Then I passed out.

When I finally woke up, I looked at my watch. It was seven-thirty in the morning—the *next* morning. *Oh shit.* I'd stayed out all night! I only meant to stay at that party for three or four hours, but the liquor led me astray. I wondered exactly how much I'd drunk at the party.

I looked over at Mikyalo, who was in a deep sleep, snoring and drooling like some old head who'd worked all night to feed his crumb snatchers.

I shook him vigorously. "Get up, boy! I need to get home." He didn't budge. I shook him again, feeling panicked. "Mikaylo!"

He grunted. "Huh?"

"I gotta get home! You gotta get me home. My parents are gonna kill me!"

Mikaylo grunted again and turned over, pulling the covers over his head. We went through this for another ten minutes until he finally woke up—with an attitude—and got ready to take me home.

I held my pounding head and looked at my clothes on the floor, wondering what had happened the night before. I stepped over sleeping bodies in various stages of undress, beer cans, bottles, and pizza boxes. When I made it to the bathroom, I peered into the mirror, gazing at my bloodshot eyes. Before I could even use the bathroom, a sticky liquid trickled down my thighs. I looked down, wiped some of it off with my finger, and examined at it. That's when I realized what I'd done. *Shit.* I was no longer a virgin.

Chapter Four

A HARD HEAD MAKES A SOFT ASS

It goes without saying that my parents lit into my ass when I got home. They were waiting for me in the sitting room right off the foyer, their identical expressions of disgust, anger, and anxiety speaking volumes as to my fate. I was caught off guard, and never expected both of them to be positioned just on the other side of the door. Telling a lie wasn't possible; the truth spoke for itself, since it was nine o'clock the next morning. I deserved whatever I had coming; I couldn't deny it for one second. No matter how I sliced it, I'd pushed my quest for freedom much too far.

"You know, Honey, I'm starting to think that you can't hear me when I talk. The funny thing is that everyone else can." My mother slid her glass around the top of an antique end table. She had a flat, half-filled bottle of Bacardi in front of her. I remembered that bottle; I'd had a few drinks before I snuck out to meet Mikaylo, and then hid the bottle in the little niche between my bed and my nightstand, and tried to cover it up with a teddy bear I'd had since I was six. Yes, I was in deep trouble. My father just cut his eyes at me. It hurt me to know I'd disappointed him so much. He only gave me that look when I really left him unable to defend his darling, sweet daughter.

"There was a reason that we hired Catherine to watch you; it was so you would stay your sixteen-year-old ass at home. That's usually the purpose of a babysitter." She continued to make circles with her glass on the table. Her refusal to make eye contact with me was almost as frightening as the evenhanded tone in her voice. "It's also funny that my liquor is running low. That's a rather strange coincidence, don't you think?" Valerie raised the bottle of rum. "I found this in your room. The last time I saw it, it was behind the bar downstairs. I doubt that Consuelo put it there, so perhaps you can tell me how it got in your room—and in such an odd place." Consuelo was our maid, and she'd been around since before I was born. She was a devout Catholic who would no more take a sip of rum than she would dance naked on the roof in broad daylight. Her husband had died of alcoholism and Consuelo was definitely anti-drinking. She was also fiercely devoted to my parents, particularly my mother. Valerie poured herself a glass of rum and raised it to me in a mock toast. I gulped as I waited for her next round of words.

"I specifically told you not to cause any trouble. Instead of getting better, you're getting worse." Her hands shook as she downed the liquid without missing a beat. Her usually immaculate hair was a mess; she didn't even have on the silk scarf in which she normally slept. Her eyes had bags under them, and her unmade face was ashen and filled with wrinkles. I'd never seen her act or look like that. It scared me.

My mother got up and walked toward me. My father just stood there with his hands buried in his pockets.

"You obviously don't care how hard we work to give you a nice life! You don't seem to appreciate the opportunities you have. I'm tired of fighting with such an ungrateful child." She poked me in the chest with her index finger. "You want to run with trash in the slums? Well, I hope you had a good time last night. Congratulations, young lady; your trust fund has just been cancelled!"

My jaw dropped. "But, Mom, I—"

"But Mom, nothing! Get the hell out of my face, Honey." She picked up the bottle and her glass and turned to leave the room. She turned back and looked at me. "As of today, I no longer have a daughter. I regret ever having you. I will only do what I am required to do for you under the law, and nothing more. I'm finished with this conversation, and I'm finished with you!"

I could only stare in shock as she stomped up the stairs. The thought of my cancelled trust fund made me even more nauseous than my hangover. Despite my wild ways, I always knew that my trust fund was my safety net. I wouldn't really ever have to work, because my grandparents left me money that had been carefully invested since my birth, and that I would inherit when I turned twenty-one and thirty; that way, if I blew the portion I inherited when I turned twenty-one, I'd still have some left when I turned thirty. *Maybe Mom didn't mean it*, I tried to tell myself, but in my heart of hearts I knew she was dead serious.

I followed my mother upstairs and went to my room to digest this latest turn of events. I wished I still had that bottle of rum; I needed something to calm my nerves. I didn't even get the door to my bedroom closed before my mother flew into my bedroom with a leather belt in hand and fury in her eyes.

"Valerie, don't!" my father yelled from the hallway. His face showed something that I hadn't ever seen before: fear.

"She needs to stop this! She needs it! The reason why she's become this way is because I've never beat that ass! I just can't take any more of her." She lifted the hand that held the belt and prepared to strike.

I tried to scramble across the bed, but Valerie grabbed my ankle and pulled me back. Her strength was surprising. She brought the belt down with a force and precision that reminded me of the movie *Glory*. Pain shot through my side, my back, my arms—my mother was on a mission and didn't care where the belt fell. I ended up on the floor, where I tried to curl up in a fetal position, but my mother pulled my leg again to straighten me out. Her eyes blazed as her arm moved up and down, the belt whistling through the air before landing with a resounding *THWAP!* on whatever part of my body that I was unable to protect, each stroke punctuated by a scream. I managed to cover my head and tasted salty tears as my mother literally beat me like a runaway slave.

"You (*THWAP!*) fucking (*THWAP!*) ungrateful (*THWAP!*) little (*THWAP!*) bitch! (*THWAP!*) You (*THWAP!*) drunken (*THWAP!*) bastard (*THWAP!*) whore! (*THWAP! THWAP!*)"

It was official: my mother had lost her ever-loving black mind.

My father finally grabbed her arms from behind, yelling, "Valerie, STOP!"

She allowed him to hold her back, her chest heaving from her exertions, sweat beaded on her forehead. The belt dangled from her hand, waiting to be brought into service once more.

"That's enough, Valerie," my father said.

I uncovered my head enough to peek at his face, and was surprised to see that tears rolled down his cheeks. He dragged my mother from the room, her hatred-filled eyes never leaving mine.

※

Days came and went. I didn't get any forgiveness from my parents. Knowing I was on their shit list took all of the fun out of wilding out. I never pulled a stunt like that again and tried to kiss up to my mother in a desperate attempt to change her mind about my trust fund. I attended every extracurricular activity, got up early for Sunday Mass, volunteered for committees, asked to accompany her to teas and luncheons. I even stopped drinking. I was the model daughter she'd always wanted, but I was a day late and a dollar short.

I did get a present of sorts. My period didn't come the first month. By the second month, I figured something was up. I panicked and knew I had to get checked by a doctor. I couldn't tell my parents because if I really was pregnant, Lord knew what would have happened at that point. I couldn't tell Yolanda, or even Pookie—especially Pookie, because then the whole school would know. The last thing I wanted was to have my business in the streets.

I cut class the next day and went to the free teen clinic. I waited for an hour before I was called into a back room. A lady in pink scrubs and a nametag that read, "Junie Braithwaite, RN," gave me a cup for a urine sample, which I filled nearly to the brim because I was that damned nervous. When I returned to the room, Junie handed me a gown and a thin sheet, and told me to change. I changed into the gown, climbed under the sheet, and lay back, wondering what was in store for Honey Davis.

I studied the ceiling and walls for at least twenty minutes until the doctor arrived, with Junie in tow. The doctor was a tall, extremely light-skinned black woman with sandy brown hair and hazel eyes. Freckles dotted her nose and almost matched the pattern of her tan silk blouse with small brown polka dots, which she'd paired with dark brown slacks and low-heeled brown leather shoes.

"Hello, Honorina. My name is Dr. Stevenson," she greeted. "You've already met Junie." Junie smiled at me.

Hearing my birth name brought back memories of my mother's disapproval. I swallowed my fear. "Hi, Dr. Stevenson. Most people call me Honey."

"Okay, Honey. Let's start with why you're here today. Can you tell me what's been going on?"

"I, uh, well, my period is late." I felt the heat in my face as blood rushed to it. I was sure that my face was as red as the period that was suddenly missing in action.

Dr. Stevenson nodded and asked, "How late?"

"About eight weeks."

"Okay. When was the first day of your last menstrual period? The last one you remember having?"

I tried to remember; I never wrote them down or anything. Who had time for that? "Um . . . like, around the middle of December. It was not too long before we got out for Christmas break."

"Are you usually regular? I mean, do you have a period every month?"

"Yes."

"How long does it last?"

I shrugged. "About a week, more or less."

"Do you play sports, or do any other strenuous activity?" I shook my head. "Have you been under a lot of stress lately, with school, or at home?" I nodded; she had no idea.

Dr. Stevenson nodded again as she looked down at my chart. "You're sixteen, Honey?" When I nodded, she asked, "Are you sexually active?"

I hesitated, then nodded.

She saw my hesitation. "How long have you been sexually active?"

I looked away from her kind gaze. "I . . . since New Year's Eve. It—It was my first time."

"Did you use any birth control?"

I closed my eyes in shame. How could I tell her that I'd been too drunk to remember that first night, or that Mikaylo and I didn't use any condoms?

"I see. Well, Honey, have you ever had a Pap smear, or a gynecological exam?"

I shook my head.

"Okay. What I am going to do is give you a Pap smear, which will check for any cancer in your cervix. I'm going to use a speculum, which will keep the walls of your vagina open and allow me to take a culture for the Pap smear, and also for sexually transmitted diseases. Then I will give you a pelvic exam, where I check the size and shape of your uterus and ovaries, and see if I can feel anything abnormal. I will finish with a breast exam, to check for any unusual lumps. You can do these yourself once a month. I'll give you a brochure before you leave, that tells you how."

Dr. Stevenson put on latex gloves and asked me to lie back and put my feet in the stirrups. "Try to relax," she instructed. "Scoot all the way to the bottom of the table and let your knees fall way apart. Now take a deep breath, and let it out." I heard her fiddling around and the clang of metal on metal. "Now you're going to feel some pressure, and it's going to be uncomfortable. Just try to relax. Keep taking deep breaths." I felt something cool slide into my pussy, then a click. The pressure was crazy, and I cringed. I remembered Dr. Stevenson's instructions and took deep breaths. She murmured instructions to Junie, who handed the doctor different things and took them back again. A few minutes later, the metal slid out and I felt relief.

She accepted a tube of surgical jelly from Junie. "Now we'll do your pelvic exam. This will be more uncomfortable, so try to relax and take those deep breaths, okay?" She squeezed a dollop of jelly onto the fingers of one hand and pushed it inside my pussy, while she felt my abdomen with the other hand. I squirmed from the pressure; I needed to pee again! "Try to relax," Dr. Stevenson said. She maneuvered her hands some more, then pushed against what I guessed were my ovaries. She finally removed her hand and peeled off her gloves, then donned a new pair for the breast exam. I almost leaped off the table, my breasts were so sore when she touched them. When she was done, she removed those gloves and threw them away. Junie left the room with test samples in her hand and Dr. Stevenson followed.

"I'll be back, Honey. You can get dressed now," she informed me and closed the door behind her.

After I'd gotten dressed, I sat in the chair beside the examination table. Shortly thereafter, Dr. Stevenson returned. She sat down at the other chair in the room and opened my chart.

"Well, Honey, we did the Pap smear, as I explained, and also tested you for Chlamydia, gonorrhea, herpes and HPV—the human papilloma virus, which causes genital warts and can also cause cervical cancer. You can also get tested for syphilis and HIV—the virus that causes AIDS—but that will require a blood test and Junie can do that for you, if you'd like. Your test results should be back in a couple of weeks, and we'll contact you only if they are positive." She paused. "Your pregnancy test was positive, and your cervix was that of a pregnant woman in the early stages of pregnancy. Your uterus is enlarged as well, another sign of pregnancy. By the feel of your uterus, and based on the estimated time of your last menstrual period, I'd say you were nine to ten weeks pregnant. A blood pregnancy test would narrow that time period down, along with a sonogram."

Terror coursed through my veins as I shook my head in denial. "Oh, my God! My parents are going to kill me. Oh no!" My eyes teared up and I dropped my head in shame.

Dr. Stevenson handed me a tissue. "I take it that this wasn't planned?"

I shook my head as I continued to cry. Hell no, I didn't plan to get pregnant!

Dr. Stevenson sighed. "Well, I'd like for you to consider your options. You can keep the baby, in which case I'd like for you to start your prenatal care as soon as possible; you can give the baby up for adoption, which would still require prenatal care; or you can have an abortion. New York does not require parental consent for this procedure. I can give you information on all of these options." She looked at me with concern. "You don't have to make a decision today, but I will advise you that if you choose to have an abortion, it is safer to have it done before you reach the twelve-week mark."

I continued to cry. Me, Honey Davis, pregnant. "How could I be so dumb?" I mumbled.

Dr. Stevenson patted my hand. "You're not dumb, Honey. Things happen. What's important is that we learn from our mistakes." She handed me a stack of pamphlets on STDs, abortion, adoption, prenatal care birth control methods, HIV, and self-breast exams. She gave me a piece of paper with my estimated due date and current weeks of pregnancy, then wrote a prescription before she handed me a small brown paper sack filled with little pill packets. "I'm writing you a prescription for prenatal vitamins, should you decide to keep the baby or put it up for adoption. In the meantime, I've given you some samples that will last you a couple of weeks. You will need to find an obstetrician for your prenatal care, if you need it. I can recommend someone for you, if you'd like?" I nodded; I didn't know of any doctors other than my parents' friends, and going to one of them was a definite no-no. She handed me a sheet of obstetricians that were in the area, who catered to lower-income girls. I didn't tell Dr. Stevenson that I could afford a doctor under my parents' insurance.

What was I going to do? I had to tell Mikaylo, of course, but what the hell was I going to tell everyone else? I couldn't tell my friends, and I damn sure couldn't tell my parents. Valerie would beat this baby out of me, and kill me in the process—and my dad might not be able to stop her this time. It was at that moment that I felt a connection with this baby. My baby. Our baby, mine and Mikaylo's. Yep, this was between Mikaylo and me, and it was going to stay that way.

"Honey?"

"Huh?"

"Did you hear me, sweetheart?"

"I'm sorry, Dr. Stevenson. What did you say again?" I sniffled.

She patted the top of my hand. "I know you're scared. You can't take your actions back now. All you can do is learn from this, okay?"

"Yes, ma'am."

I let Junie draw my blood for the pregnancy test, syphilis, and HIV, and went home. After I got out of the taxi, I didn't know what to do. I called Mikaylo on my cell phone as soon as I shut the door.

"Hi, baby girl," he greeted. "You wasn't in school today. You all right?"

My throat tightened. Hell no, I wasn't all right! "Can I come over? Can you come over? I mean, can we meet somewhere?" I babbled.

"Slow down. What's wrong? You sound real upset."

"I gotta tell you something. We have to talk. It's very important."

He heard the fear in my voice and didn't hesitate. "Yeah, a'ight. Matter of fact, I'll pick you up at the stop sign in half an hour. My brother should be back with the car in a few minutes," he explained. Mikaylo used his brother's car to get around. I hung up, changed my clothes, and walked down the street to meet him. It was best if he didn't pull up right in front of our house, because there were too many nosey people around and too much shit flying already. I waited twenty-five minutes for Mikaylo to arrive. When he finally pulled up, my nerves were strung tighter than a piano's. Mikaylo got out of the car.

"Where have you been?" I snapped.

He looked at me in confusion. "I got here as soon as I could." He gave me a big hug and kiss before opening my door for me. I got in and he shut my door, climbed back behind the wheel, and pulled off.

"So what's goin' on, ma? You feelin' all right?"

No matter how I was feeling, I rarely missed class, so I knew my sudden absence needed an explanation.

"Yeah, yeah. I'm all good," I lied. I didn't want to talk about it in the car. Mikaylo must have sensed this because he turned the radio to Hot 97 and took my hand. If he was good at anything, it was changing the subject. He knew me well enough to know I'd talk when I felt like it, and at the time, I just wanted to be near him.

Mikaylo bought some Chinese food from a corner store, then we went around the corner to his place. After we walked upstairs, I wiped my feet on the mat at the entrance to the apartment. Mikaylo's mother was a stickler for neatness. Mikaylo went in first, to make sure his mom wasn't home. She didn't mind me coming over, but she made it clear that she didn't like the two of us alone. She worked and was taking a night class at City College, so she mostly didn't get home until the middle of the night. We went to Mikaylo's room and shut and locked the door behind us.

He gave me a carton of food, along with a plastic fork and some soy sauce. My stomach did back flips as I watched him open his own carton, thinking that he was the father of my child. It just felt so weird to know that. There were no words to describe how I was tripping, realizing that we'd made God's creation, and our baby was living in my belly. I wasn't hungry. How could I have been?

Despite my lack of hunger, we blessed our food and Mikaylo made the sign of the cross; he, too, was Catholic.

"¿*Que paso*?" he asked, taking a big bite of his fried rice. "So what do you wanna talk to me about?"

My time had run out. "I wasn't in school because I went to the doctor today, Kaylo."

"Why? Everything where it belongs?" he teased.

"I'm pregnant."

Fried rice flew out of his mouth and a couple of grains landed on my face. The remainder landed on the floor at his feet. I think some of it went down the wrong pipe, because he started choking and coughing like an asthmatic. His face was beet red.

"Kaylo! Kaylo! Are you all right?" I asked frantically, smacking him on the back.

When he sat back up, tears streamed from his eyes.

"Oh shit," he said weakly, still coughing. He finally used one of the napkins to wipe his mouth and the sweat that ran down his face. "My bad, ma. Excuse me." He cleared his throat a final time and took a sip of soda. "Are you sure?"

"Yeah. The doctor said the test was positive, and that I'm about eight or nine weeks along. I won't know for sure how far along I am till the blood test comes back and I have a sonogram."

"Sometimes there's such a thing as a false positive. Look, why don't we check one more time? Let's go to Walgreen's and get a test." He grabbed his keys and made for the door, but I stopped him.

"Kaylo, I got checked by a doctor! You know, one who graduated from medical school! She did a pelvic exam! She felt the pregnancy, and said that my cervix looked like that of a pregnant woman. Why do I need to take another test, and from a drugstore at that?

"Well, a false positive could still happen," he insisted.

My suspicion kicked in. "How do you know that?"

"I just know, okay?"

"But how?" I pressed.

"It happened with another girl, okay?"

You could've heard a pin drop, and that's when I had to accept the situation on my hands. Mikaylo probably never used protection, and he probably couldn't keep his dick in his pants to save his life. I handed Mikaylo the paper from the doctor, which stated approximately how far along I was, along with the pamphlets for abortion, adoption, and prenatal care. He held the paper with my due date on it for a long time, staring at it as if his gaze could somehow change the outcome.

"What are we gonna do?" I finally asked.

It took a long time for him to say anything. "What do you wanna do?"

"Aren't you Catholic?"

"Yeah."

"Well, you know I am, too." The fact that I usually had to be dragged to Mass was beside the point.

"I know, but that doesn't mean you can't get rid of it."

"Don't call our baby 'it'! I have a baby inside of me," I snapped. "A human being."

"So we're keepin' it—um, the baby?" He sounded disappointed.

The more I thought about it, the surer I felt. "Yeah. I can't get rid of my first child. I just can't do that." A strange sense of peace crept over me as I spoke the words aloud, to quickly be chased away by fear. "But my parents can't find out. Ever."

"Well if you keep it, how are you going to manage them not noticing that you are?"

I sighed. "I haven't thought that far ahead yet."

Mikaylo shook his head. "You're gonna show eventually. There's no way to stop that. " He took my hand and stared into my eyes. "Honey, your parents are loaded. The baby will have everything it needs. We'll have everything *we* need. Be reasonable about this. Tell them."

"You don't know my parents, Kaylo. You have no idea how I grew up, and how I really live."

"I'm not sayin' they'll be poppin' bottles over this, but you don't know what it's like to want for anything, Honey. That much is obvious. They'll have your back."

I shook my head. "I don't think so. You don't know my circumstances. There's more to my story than I mentioned. I hid a lot from you, because I was embarrassed. You never asked me why I never invited you over. There's a reason for everything, and they will make my life miserable. They will make your life miserable. No, they will make *our* lives miserable." I stopped and took a deep breath. I had to make Mikaylo understand. "Do you know how much business my mama is gonna lose if any of her rich-ass friends find out she couldn't manage her own house? Do you know how people will laugh at my father? It'll be my fault. You gotta see where I'm comin' from. If they find out about this, I'm done for. They'll kill me!" I saw Valerie's belt lashing in the air before it came down on me with the force of a sledgehammer.

Mikaylo shook his head in frustration. "I don't understand what you want me to say or do. You say you want to keep it, but you're telling me that your parents will give you hell if you do keep it. So what is your plan?"

"My plan?" I couldn't believe my ears; he was putting this all on me! "I didn't make this baby by myself! This is our future you're talking about! I just turned sixteen. I don't have a plan!" My voice cracked. "I'm scared, okay?"

Mikaylo put his arm around me and did his best to comfort me.

"I'm sorry, ma. That came out all wrong." He kissed my forehead. "This has been a long day for you, I'm sure. Let's pick this conversation up tomorrow. Let me see what I can come up with, okay?"

I nodded, my face buried in his chest.

"I have to take you home now. Just lay low and get some rest, okay?"

I planned do to just that. But someone had other plans for me.

Chapter Five

NO ROOM FOR MISTAKES

Valerie was lying in wait for me by the time I got home. She sat in our immaculate living room, flipping through a magazine. A half-filled crystal glass of either scotch or whisky sat beside her on an end table. I mumbled a greeting and headed for my room, but she stopped me. "Where were you this afternoon, Honorina?" she asked.

Oh shit. She called me Honorina, which meant I had committed yet another major infraction. I racked my brain, trying to figure out what I'd done this time, as I lied, "Nowhere special. I went by the library for a school project."

"I see. Did the library relocate to the free teen clinic on the other side of town?"

I stood there like a deer in headlights, trying to figure out how my mother found out about my clinic visit. As if reading my thoughts, Valerie said, " I'm on the Teen Pregnancy Prevention Campaign, and we work closely with that clinic. In fact, Dr. Stevenson is one of my sorority sisters and she is very active in the campaign." She closed the magazine and put it aside before standing. "Now tell me, Honorina, why I had to find out from her that my own daughter is sixteen years old and hot in the ass?"

Oh, God.

"Dr. Stevenson called me because you are underage, Honey," Valerie continued. "By law, she had to notify me of any medical examination or procedures that you underwent." She stalked toward me with her hands clenched in fists. "She also told me the news. Happy Mother's Day." Her tone was laced with sarcasm. She walked up to me and I braced myself for one of her famous pinches, but she kept her fists balled up at her sides. She looked me up and down and turned to walk away. Before she left the room she tossed over her shoulder, "There will be no school for you tomorrow. You have an appointment for an abortion."

A chill swept through my body. An abortion? Kill my baby? "But Mom, I want to keep my baby, and I know I messed up. Please don't make me have an abortion! Please!" I pleaded with my mother, hoping to reach that maternal part of her.

"Oh, so I'm 'Mom' now?" Valerie snorted. "Be serious. How are you going to take care of a child when you can't even take care of yourself?

I fell to my knees in despair. "I'm sorry I've given you so much trouble lately. I put you through hell, but I learned my lesson, I swear. Please, don't—" I begged.

"Honorina, you have no money of your own, you have no job, and you will be starting Howard in the fall. We are going to get this taken care of before anyone else finds out."

"But I can get a job," I said in desperation. "I can postpone school a year, I can—"

Valerie shook her head. "No. I don't like who you've become, Honorina. You wanted to make a hard bed, now lie in it. However, I will not allow you to ruin our family name in the meantime. Tomorrow you will have an abortion. End of discussion."

Even as my heart sank at the finality of my mother's tone, another thought made me panic. "Does Dad know, Mom? Does Dad know?"

Valerie cocked her head and looked at me. A small smile played around her lips. "Why don't you ask him yourself, when he gets home? I'm sure this is exactly the sort of thing he'd like to come home to, after a hard day of surgery. He's trying to save someone's life right now. How you would feel with that sort of pressure, coming home to some bullshit like this?" She shook her head again. "You have a mouth, so face your father for a change."

The thought of having to tell my father that I was pregnant made me even more stressed. I rose from my knees and threw my arms around my mother. "Mom! Mom! I need you. I'm scared."

Valerie stepped out of my embrace. "That's not the way it sounded a few months ago, when you called me a bitch and disrespected me." She retrieved her magazine and drink and marched up the sweeping staircase toward her bedroom. A minute later, I heard her door slam.

I sat at the bottom of the steps, shaking and numb. I'd gotten myself into a huge mess for sure, and I didn't know how to get out of it.

⚛

"It's real rough at home, and I can't take it anymore. My mother knows that I'm pregnant." I was on the kitchen phone, venting to Mikaylo. I had to make it quick because if my mother caught me on the phone with him, there was no telling what she might do. The fact that she didn't beat me to a pulp when she confronted me about my pregnancy had me scared. That wasn't like Valerie to keep her cool in the face of something so huge, especially when it came to me.

"Damn! She does? How did that happen?"

"No time to explain right now. Did you get a chance to think of anything?"

"It's funny you should ask. I do have a plan."

"Please, hurry up and tell me! My mother is really tripping, and she's going to force to get rid of the baby if I don't do something before morning. Please tell me we're going to make this work somehow!"

Mikaylo's voice was soothing. "We will, baby. If you're serious, pack a small bag."

"I'm very serious. I'm keeping this baby, Kaylo."

I managed to get the most essential details about meeting Mikaylo before hanging up. We agreed that he'd pick me up around three AM, which was a few hours from now. We had to be at the Greyhound Station at four. I took my small, packed bag and snuck out of the house to our usual meeting place. Mikaylo arrived in a taxi and it pulled off as soon as I got in the car.

"I found a place for us to stay with friends," he explained as the taxi sped toward Port Authority.

Friends? Well, that was good, wasn't it? "How did you get them to take us in? What's the catch?"

"They were looking to rent out their basement apartment. The only catch is they are in Georgia."

Georgia. I didn't know much about that state except for it seemed to be associated with peaches. We visited Atlanta once when my dad went there for a medical convention. I remember it as being hot and humid and everyone talked slowly, and with a twang. The prospect of going so far kind of appealed to me because I wanted to be as far away from my parents as possible when I had the baby.

"So who are these friends, Kaylo? How do you know them?"

Mikaylo squirmed. "Let's just say they're good people." His tone discouraged further inquiry or discussion. I decided to just let it rest; I'd get the entire scoop later.

We had been in the bus station for twenty minutes, and I had thrown up twice already. I hurled everything I'd eaten earlier. I couldn't even focus on what Mikaylo was saying. Between the physical and emotional turmoil, and morning sickness, I just wasn't in the position to press the issue about his friends.

"I don't know why they call it morning sickness. They need to call that shit 'all-muthafuckin'day sickness,' 'cause it's too damn early to be throwing up," Mikaylo commented. He rubbed my back in attempt to make me feel better.

"Shut up! You did this to me," I snapped. I was irritated that I had to stand in line. Mikaylo held our places for a while, but after an argument over cutting in another line jumped off, a bus station employee came by and told everyone they had better stand in line for themselves. Under the circumstances, it just wasn't worth arguing over.

Mikaylo stopped rubbing and shot me an annoyed look. "Give me some credit here! I'm trying, okay? And by the way, you did this too."

I didn't feel like arguing. I just want to get started with our new life.

Finally, our bus pulled into the station. I looked forward to sitting down, at the very least. The ride from New York to Georgia was twenty hours, though, and I was hardly thrilled about that. We boarded, found seats near the bathroom, and settled into uneasy sleep.

❦

Georgia was nothing like New York. We ended up in a small town called Barnesville, forty-five minutes from Atlanta. I guess that all made sense, since it would be harder for anyone to find us if they came looking. At least I was sixteen, and Mikaylo would soon be eighteen. I'd declare myself an emancipated minor, if my parents wanted to make things even uglier than they already were.

Neither one of us knew where to go when we got off the bus. The air didn't even smell the same down there. Everyone smiled politely when I looked at them. A couple of people even waved.

My hair started getting frizzy and stuck to my neck as soon as I got off the bus. Mikaylo looked around and then smiled as he took my hand and pulled me toward two older women, standing closely together. When we reached them, Mikaylo gave each of them a big hug. "Honey, this is Jessica, and Paula," he introduced us.

"You can call me Jessie," Jessica said as she gave me a hug. "I'm so glad to meet you." Paula simply smiled her greeting. "You two must be so tired! I'll go and get the car." Jessie left to start her air-conditioned SUV, so it was worth the five minutes it took to locate our bags and reach the car. After that long-ass bus ride, all I was trying do for the next couple of days was sleep. I was glad that Jessie and Paula were there. If they hadn't been at the station to pick us up, we would've been lost.

As we rode in silence, Paula turned to us in the backseat and said, "I know you guys must be exhausted from your trip. Jessie and I will make you some lunch, and then we'll show you to your apartment."

I looked over at Mikaylo, who had a serene look on his face. He seemed to have figured everything out. I relaxed into the leather seats and nodded off until we reached Jessie and Paula's house.

Mikaylo and I sat in the living room, which gave a direct view of the kitchen. Jessie and Paula moved around the small kitchen with familiar maneuvers, complete with occasional brushes of thighs, hips, arms, and hands against each other. They were polar opposites: Paula was tall and solid, like a basketball player, with a playful personality and a high voice. Jessie was shorter, slimmer, and spoke with her hands and eyes. She liked to talk and her no-nonsense voice provided the background melody to their kitchen dance. It took me a minute to realize that they were a lesbian couple. It really didn't bother me, though.

After eating fried chicken and collard greens, Jessie helped Mikaylo take our bags downstairs. Our basement apartment was small, but it was adequate for the two of us. I turned on the shower while Mikaylo made the bed. Since I was used to riding in style, and not on public transportation, I felt the need to promptly wash the bus grime off me. After fifteen minutes of vigorously scrubbing my skin, I stood still and let the hot water pelt my body and ease all my tension. Just as I was wrapping the towel around my body, I felt a rumble in my gut. All of that scrumptious Southern food was on its way back up.

Mikaylo knocked on the door before opening it. When I didn't answer, he opened the door and found me leaning over the toilet, throwing up like crazy. I felt his arm around me. He brushed my hair back, comforting me while I let nature take its course. He could tell that I was pretty weak and depleted, so he picked me up and carried me to the bed. He laid me down, snuggled up next to me, and held me until I drifted off to sleep. I felt so safe and secure that even the troubles with my home life began to fade away.

The next day Mikaylo found a job, which was a good sign. He was working at The Waffle House as a bus boy, which was the best he could do for his age. I was proud of him for doing what he had to do. I missed my crew at school, and even wondered about my parents, but Mikaylo was on point and Jessie and Paula were supportive.

The two women were like a personal gift sent to me from the heavens. I had no idea that Jessie was a retired college professor. When Mikaylo went to work, she would come downstairs to check on me, or bring me upstairs and tutor me on twelfth-grade subjects. And yes, she gave me homework, and graded the shit, too. She became a mother figure to me and, in some odd way, we bonded far more than I ever thought we would. Hell, we had more heart-to-heart talks than I ever had with my own mother. Jessie was tough on me, but she didn't put me down or make me feel like I was a hard-headed girl, going nowhere fast.

The two women were also available when it came to my prenatal appointments. As embarrassing as it was, I had to seek government aid, since I didn't want to use my parents' medical insurance.

Either Jessie or Paula got me up, dressed and fed me, took me to my appointments, and picked me up as well. In fact, Paula found the magic remedy to make me feel better when I couldn't eat: weed. She literally made me swear on a Bible that I wouldn't say anything to Mikaylo or Jessie. Since I didn't want the "What the fuck do you mean, you smoked a blunt?" speech from Mikaylo, I didn't tell anyone about our afternoon ciphers. We talked about everything under the sun during those afternoons on the back porch. I knew it wasn't the smartest decision to puff and pass, but it kept me mellow and it kept my mind off drinking. I did sneak a few watered-down beers, but my newfound remedy helped more than I care to admit. And when I got mellow, so did Paula. During one of our smoking sessions, she revealed to me why Jessie paid me so much attention, and why she had been so open to Mikaylo and I laying low on their turf.

"She's sterile," Paula said while holding a lungful of smoke. She blew the smoke out and continued. "We found out that she couldn't have kids on her thirty-fifth birthday. It's not like she wants to be with a man or anything, but it still messes with her. She really wanted to be a mother. So I guess she's kinda thinking of your baby as her closest chance at having one." She passed me the blunt.

I took a toke while I thought about what Paula just said. "What about artificial insemination? Or adoption?"

"We looked into both of them. Artificial insemination is extremely expensive, and we can't afford it. And as for adoption, well," Paula snorted as she took the blunt from my outstretched hand. "Adoption agencies don't want to let gay couples adopt, and Jessie is retired; she doesn't make enough money on her own to suit the agencies, so she can't adopt as a single parent." She sat and stared into the distance for a moment, then shook her head and passed the blunt back to me.

As I smoked, I was more aware than ever of how sheltered I was, and of how unfair the world could be. Jessie and Paula were better parents to me than my own parents, but because of their sexual preference, they weren't allowed to be parents while my parents had the financial means and the right preference, but weren't that great at raising kids. What kind of sense did that make?

❧❦

As the months passed, Mikaylo got tired of collecting dirty dishes and getting wet from head to toe with dishwater at that Waffle House.. My belly started to poke out and I noticed a drastic change in him. I was only seven-and-a-half months pregnant, but he was already acting like I'd pushed the baby out and we were some unhappy married couple. He became distant, short-tempered, and, on occasion, downright cold. He ignored me when he was at the apartment, he ignored my calls when he was out, but he pretended that we were a happy couple when we were out and about, and especially around Jessie and Paula. Whenever he saw someone who looked familiar, the two of us were lovey-dovey, holding hands, kissing, giggling, whispering, "I love you," to each other, and just plain appearing like it was all gravy. But when our front door closed, we were suddenly no more than just two people who lived together. His behavior truly was a contradiction that I didn't understand. There was a person growing inside me, yet I had never felt so alone. Every now and then, I rubbed my belly and just cried. I waddled everywhere, my feet were swollen, and Mikaylo even stopped holding me in bed like he used to.

The turning point came one night when he stomped past me after coming home from work. He looked tired, his uniform was dirty as hell, and he didn't utter one word to me.

"You can't speak, Kaylo?" I asked.

"What?" he shouted. Mikaylo rarely shouted at me; he had to be heated to even raise his voice. I heard him moving around and opening drawers.

I tried to remain calm. "I asked you if you had a problem speaking or something."

He walked out of the room in a pair of jeans and a hooded sweatshirt. The look on his face was borderline demonic. "What in the hell is your problem? I bust my ass in that damn Waffle House, while you sit around eating and watching TV all day. You need to check yourself."

Oh, no he didn't! "I don't know where this bad attitude is coming from, but no, you need to check *your*self, Kaylo. I'm not having fun. Being pregnant is a bitch!"

"Speaking of a bitch, all you do is complain. I'm going out to get some air." He turned and stomped toward the front door.

"I don't give a fuck where you go to get it. Take all night if you need it, just don't bring that stank attitude back up in here!" I shot back.

The door slammed behind him. The phone rang soon after.

"Kaylo, it's me. I wanna know why you ackin' like yo' fingas is broke, nigga. Call if you ain't coming," a ghetto voice said.

"Who in the hell is this?" I asked. I felt a flutter in my belly, but it wasn't the baby. I knew something wasn't right.

The line went dead. I dialed *69 and called back.

"Hello? Who called me from this number?"

"Bitch, ain't nobody call you. Get your facts straight."

"You think I'm stupid? I used*69 to call this number back."

"I already told you, we ain't got nothin' to talk about. I called to talk to Kaylo, not you."

Called to talk to Kaylo? What was going on? "Apparently, we've got a whole lot to talk about, because Kaylo is my—"

The girl on the other end giggled, cutting me off. "You're nothing!" The line went dead again.

All of a sudden, a sharp pain raced through my stomach. "Ooooh shit!" I exclaimed aloud, dropping the phone. The shooting pains had been happening lately, ever since Mikaylo started coming home when he felt like it. I was hot, to say the least. How could Mikaylo cheat on me at a time like this? I knew I was missing some information, but a woman's intuition never lied. I flew into a sudden rage; I went to work and went around the apartment, grabbing everything that belonged to him. I picked up hoodies, jeans, boots, sneakers, pictures, even his bath towel. Like a madwoman, I stuffed it all in a big, black garbage bag and dragged it out to the trashcan in front of the house. I was wondering how I could've been so stupid to get knocked up by an asshole like Mikaylo, when the sharp pain stabbed me again as I walked back to the house. I tried to lie down but it got stronger and when I stood, it only got worse. There was no relief, no matter what I did. When I was crying in a ball on the bathroom floor, I knew it was time to go to the hospital. I crawled to the bedroom and called Jessie.

Paula answered. "Hello?"

"Paula, it's Honey. I-I gotta go to the hospital."

"What happened? What's the matter?"

"Kaylo's not here. Just please come and help me, and fast!" Another spasm rocked my body from head to toe. "Please, Paula," I sobbed.

"We'll be right down."

I could hear both of them scurrying above my head, frantically running back and forth, trying to get themselves together. I let out a bloodcurdling scream as I forced myself to walk to the door and unlock it.

Paula got to me first. "Come on! Come on . . . it's going to be okay. Breathe the way you've been practicing." They were both holding me by the elbows. I struggled to inhale deeply then exhale slowly, to keep myself as calm as possible.

"It hurts so bad. Oh my God, it hurts so bad! Please get me out of here!" I whined as they led me toward the SUV. "Ooooh! I can't make it!" I sagged in their arms; my legs were no longer strong enough to hold me.

Jessie tossed Paula the keys and her purse. "Pull the car up!" Paula dashed off.

"Clothes. I need my bag," I panted as I struggled to do my breathing exercises.

"Forget the clothes," Jessie snapped. She wrenched open the back door of the truck and Paula ran around to try and help me into it.

"Please, get my clothes! I really need my things," I insisted.

I fussed so much that Jessie did get my bag, and she and Paula finally got me into the truck. I lay in the back seat, writhing in what I could only describe as the most intense pain I had ever felt in my natural life. It was like someone was trying to tear the bottom half of my body away from the top half. When we made it to the hospital, an emergency room nurse had just gotten me into a wheelchair when I felt a pop between my legs. Warm fluid ran down my thighs and calves and onto the floor.

"Oh, holy shit!" Paula exclaimed. "Doctor! Nurse! Her water just broke!" She looked around frantically for medical help.

The nurse looked down and yelled to another nurse behind a desk, "Call L&D and tell them we have one coming up whose water just broke!" To me she said, "Hang in there, sweetheart. We're going to take good care of you." She pushed the wheelchair toward the elevator. Paula went with me while Jessie stayed behind to answer questions about my medical history and insurance coverage.

I started to feel a little dizzy and I felt like I was going to pass out. I was wheeled into a white room and several attendants lifted me onto a bed. A male doctor with a green mask stood over me.

"Can you hear me, sweetheart? What's your name?"

"Honey," I whispered in a raspy voice. "Honey Davis."

"Okay, Honey. I'm Doctor Vasquez."

I don't remember being sedated, pushing the baby out, or any of the subsequent events. About an hour after I came through the hospital doors, I was staring down at a tiny person with her eyes closed, wrapped in pink blankets. The doctor told me I was suffering from extreme stress and dehydration, so a nurse administered an intravenous saline drip for the rest of the night. Jessie and Paula came in to see me after a while, both of them grinning from ear to ear, like schoolgirls. "You did it," Jessie crowed.

"You sure did," Paula agreed. "You handled it like a real trooper."

"We went by the nursery to see her," Jessie added. "She's beautiful."

"What are you going to name her?" Paula asked.

I named the baby Kyashira Star Davis. My bundle of joy weighed five-and-a-half pounds, which the doctor said was not bad for a baby born a month-and-a-half ahead of schedule. Thankfully, she was healthy and didn't need any specialized medical care. She was beautiful and looked just like her father who, after two whole days, was nowhere around. I knew I had a big decision to make. A tear streamed down my cheek as I thought of doing the unthinkable.

Chapter Six

THANKS FOR NOTHING!

Two days after I had the baby, Jessie and Paula came to get me from the hospital. I was depressed, knowing that Mikaylo didn't care about the baby enough to check on us despite whatever was going through his head about me. It was clear that Mikaylo and I were finished, done, however you want to put it. There was nothing left for me in Georgia. I had no way to pay rent without a job, and I wasn't about to ask for a handout.

I had made my decision and I knew how desperately Jessie wanted a child. I also knew that my baby would never want for anything. The biggest problem was that every time I looked into Kyashira's eyes, I saw her father staring back.

I felt that it was better if the two of them, Paula and Jessie, raised my child. I just hoped and prayed that the women would see things my way and agree.

When we made it back to the apartment, I began to unpack my hospital bag.

"There's plenty of time to do that. You need your rest," Jessie said as she took the bag out of my hands and pushed me toward the bedroom.

She and Paula followed.

I walked in the bedroom where Mikaylo and I once slept together, only to find a crib and several gifts adorned in pink bows. A rocking chair sat next to the crib.

"You all did this?" I asked, smiling.

"Did you think we were just going to leave you hanging like that? It's just a few things to get you started with the baby," Jessie explained. She seemed happy that I was happy. Paula just smiled at me.

My eyes teared up. The couple had already done so much for me; I never expected more of their generosity. I lay the baby down in the crib.

"Thank you both," I said, hugging each of them. "You'll never know how much this means to me."

"Don't mention it," Paula said.

"She's got your smile and his eyes," Jessie commented.

Paula plopped down in the rocking chair. It was quite obvious that she was really smitten by Kyashira. She hadn't taken her eyes off the baby since we arrived home from the hospital.

"How would you feel about being her mother?" I blurted out.

"What do you mean, Honey?" Paula tore her attention from the baby and stared at me in shock. Jessie's expression was practically identical.

"I've thought about you and Jessie being her parents for a long time now. Would you consider raising Kyashira? I have no idea where Kaylo disappeared to, and she deserves a lot more than I'm prepared to give her. I would rather her be in a loving home, with parents who can love and support her. Enough has happened already and I'm not up for applying for welfare or chasing Kaylo for child support. Right now, I can't even afford to take care of myself, let alone a child." I broke down and cried, feeling overwhelmed. "Why did he leave me? Why did he do something like this? I thought he wanted me as much as I wanted him."

I lost it. I just flat out lost it, although I'd managed to play tough for the past few days. The pair just looked at each other and I could tell they felt sorry for me. Still, they remained strangely silent.

"Why won't either of you answer? You're not telling me something." I wiped my eyes on my shirtsleeve and looked at them. They looked at each other and Jessie shook her head. Paula sighed and turned her attention back to Kyashira.

"Tell me what it is . . . *please*," I begged.

"It's about Kaylo," Paula said finally.

"What about him?" I asked.

Jessie's entire demeanor changed. She went from proud to defensive. "Don't! No, Paula." There was a plea in her voice that was unlike anything I'd ever heard from Jessie.

"She needs to know, Jessie. We've kept this long enough." To me, Paula said, "We're not Mikaylo's friends; he's my nephew. His father is my brother. That's the real reason we allowed him to come here. He was stuck, and we didn't want to tell you." She sighed deeply, as if the weight of the world was on her shoulders. "We weren't ever supposed to tell you. Mikaylo was supposed to bring you here, and we were supposed to try to talk you into having an abortion, or giving the child up for adoption." She shook her head. "I guess he got scared and ran off when he saw you weren't going to do that. I'm sorry."

I was stunned. I shook my head in disbelief. "I don't believe it. I trusted you both. How could you!" I yelled. I don't know if I was more hurt than mad, or more mad than hurt. My parents lied, Mikaylo lied, and now Jessie and Paula lied too. I buried my head in my hands and began to sniffle. The baby began to stir. I guess she was scared and picked up on the somber mood in the room.

Jessie walked over to the crib to soothe Kyashira. Paula got up and left the room. There was nothing but silence, and I suddenly questioned what kind of people they really were.

Paula returned with an envelope.

"It's not what you think," she said hastily as I looked at both her and the envelope with distrust. We've been thinking of you the whole time. We've grown to really like you, no bullshit. That's why Jessie was trying to tell you to go back to high school, or at least get your GED. " She ran a hand over her hair, which had been brushed back into a ponytail, in frustration. "Please forgive us and read this." She pushed the envelope into my hand.

I closed my eyes and sighed. Curiosity got the best of me, so I opened my eyes and read the letter.

You had no right to intervene with my son, bitch! That ain't my daughter, so I don't give a fuck what happens to that girl. Her parents could've afforded to clean up her spilled milk. This would've taken care of itself, but you had to go drag Kaylo into this. She probably lying, anyway. I bet that baby ain't even his. He ain't start none of this foolishness 'til he met her little ho ass anyway. I never did like her. If he doesn't graduate this year, it'll be your fault for telling him he could run to Georgia to stay with you and your lesbian love to play family. If you're such a positive, motivating force, then what kind of shit is that? And if you know it all about telling kids what to do, why the fuck you don't have a child of your own? You need to handle your own before you start trying to call me on mine. I'm in New York, busting my ass to be a good mother to my children, while your brother don't do shit! As a matter of fact, all he was good for was a wet ass and a headache. I'm tired of you poking your nose in my children's business. You are out of line, and I don't appreciate it. Fall back, or I'll personally come to Georgia to put your ass in check, okay?

I threw the letter to the floor in disgust and hurt. The letter was longer and more detailed, but I couldn't read anymore. "Kaylo's mother pretended like she liked me," I said in confusion. I began to tremble all over and my head began to ache. I rubbed my temples.

"Kaylo ran away when you needed him the most. Just because I'm his aunt doesn't mean I condone his behavior," Paula explained. "I was wrong for even entertaining his scheme, but sometimes we do crazy things for the people we love. Just keep telling yourself that you're better off without him, because you are. You can't expect a boy to be a man. You have your whole life ahead of you, so find comfort in your future." Paula sat next to me and put her arm around my shoulders. "We will make sure the baby is well cared for in every way. We've tried to have a baby for so long, and it just didn't happen. Maybe this is a blessing in disguise."

"Please don't hate us, Honey," Jessie added as she knelt in front of me and took one of my hands in hers. "We're good people."

I didn't say anything. Too much information was coming at me, and I felt like a cross between a zombie and a complete idiot who took one for the team. I just climbed into bed and curled up in a fetal position, watching a lone stream of light piercing through the curtains, bathing a corner of the room bright yellow. I hugged Mikaylo's pillow tight to my body. If I couldn't have him, at least I could have his scent right after having his child. I was experiencing a loss of love and trust. I suddenly felt like a little girl caught up in a grown woman's dilemma, and I was having a serious reality check. I rubbed my eyes and looked at the other side of the bed. Empty. Very slowly, I felt my heart begin to sink. I didn't know how to feel or what to say, or what to do, so I just closed my eyes and curled up tighter. I suddenly missed my mother's dumb mother-daughter teas and my father's secret trips to help me sneak a piece of greasy pizza. As slumber took over my body, I could feel Jessie and Paula's presence in the room. Through it all, they sat and watched the baby. I didn't say so, but it did give me comfort.

As I drifted off to sleep, I set a few personal goals for myself. After Mikaylo's untimely departure, I knew there were a few things I would no longer stand for. Never again would another man fuck me unless I was prepared to accept the possible consequences —after using protection of course. I decided that it wasn't worth it to love someone, in the end. From that point on, whatever I wanted, I was going to get on my own. Men were liars, deceivers, and cheaters, and deserved to be treated as such.

※

It was time to say goodbye to Georgia even sooner than I thought. I can't remember everything leading up to the day of my departure, but I do recall finding my cell phone, which had been lost since Mikaylo and I had run away. I charged it and was grateful that my parents hadn't canceled the service on it. I figured my dad was trying to leave the door open for me to at least communicate. My voice mailbox was full and I was curious to know if Mikaylo left any messages, but he hadn't. My whole crew back at school left most of them. I was too embarrassed to call anyone back, including Yolanda or Pookie. I checked my text messages and saw a unexpected and strange text from my dad, dated a week ago.

HONEY, YOUR MOTHER IS ILL. PLEASE CALL ME PROMPTLY IF YOU GET THIS. LOVE DAD.

My hands were shaking so badly, I almost dropped the phone. My throat felt like it had a lump in it and I could barely hit the speed dial button.

"Dad, what's going on?"

"Honey?" he said. My father sounded afraid and alone. I had never heard him sound like so sad. Although I hadn't spoken to him in almost a year, I knew something was wrong, just from the tone of his voice. "Oh baby, thank God you called! It's your mother."

The lump in my throat grew larger. "What about her, Dad?"

"Look, I don't care where you are, or where you've been. I need you to come here as soon as you can."

"I'm not sure if you're aware of the reason I ran away. I was pregnant, and Mom tried to force me to get an abortion. I just gave birth, but my baby could've been dead right now."

"Your mother is in the hospital, and it's bad. Let bygones be bygones. We'll sort things out between us later. Please, Honey," he pleaded. "It's serious, and she's in intensive care. She isn't expected to pull through, but I'm trying to stay strong. I've been trying, and I need your support. If you don't come for her, at least come for me."

My father began to cry. My heart sank even as I tried to process his words.

"Intensive care? What happened to her?" I asked as I began to cry too. The circumstances made me forget that Valerie and I were opponents in a brutal mother-daughter war.

As my father explained, my mind began to drift some other place. I closed my eyes and looked upward. *Why, God? Why today, of all days, do you want to test me like this?* I tried to remain calm because I didn't want to upset my father further. "Where are you?"

"I'm at the hospital. Are you coming?"

"I'm on my way right now, but I'm in Georgia. Stay by your phone, Dad. I love you."

He seemed shocked to hear those words come out of my mouth. "I love you too, sweetie," he replied. Even though things at home weren't cool and I'd made a mess of my life, I suddenly felt something for my mother. I tripped over things, cursing and swearing as I tried to quickly gather my most important possessions. I was dressed and outside before I even remembered moving. I banged on Paula and Jessie's door, hoping someone would answer. I pounded nonstop, wondering what was taking one of them so long to answer. I was so desperate to get in that I turned and twisted the doorknob. I wanted the pain to stop, and I just wanted to get to my father as quickly as possible. I needed them to help me.

"It's Honey! Open the door!"

Paula came to the door with her hair wrapped up in a scarf. Obviously, she'd already taken her nightly bath and gone to sleep. After I explained what happened, it became clear that it really did make sense to leave my baby with her and Jessie. I called my father back to ask him to charge a plane ticket for me to his credit card. I inhaled deeply, feeling sick to my stomach. Paula drove me to the airport, telling me over and over again that she and Jessie would treat Kyashira as their own. When we arrived at the airport, I wiped away tears with both hands. I was on my way to confront memories that I hadn't buried all that long ago.

Chapter Seven

TROUBLED WATERS

I stood in the doorway of my mother's hospital room for a while, taking in what I saw. My father sat vigil by her bedside. As I walked in, a nurse with a chart was walking out. My mother's face was covered by an oxygen mask and tubes were everywhere. She looked fragile and weak, when I was used to seeing her so vibrant and strong. I felt apologetic by virtue of the shape she was in alone. I felt the tears build as my mouth went dry. All I could do was bend and kiss her on her cheek.

I saw her fingers move a little bit, although her eyes were closed. I kissed her again, on the forehead, then walked away. My father and I stepped out of the room and went to the lobby. I spotted a few of my mother's friends sitting around, talking. Others were scrolling through email messages on their Blackberrys. Mrs. Taylor, one of her fellow Links members, came over to me and chewed me out.

"Where have you been, *Hollywood*?" she snarled, eying my belly. It had really gone down rather quickly after the birth of Kyashira, though I could tell that she knew I'd had a baby. "She put every ounce of trust in you. You have no respect, Honey! That's your problem. There's just something in your head that makes you just not care about anyone but yourself. Do you know what your parents went through, wondering where you were? You did this to her, and you'll just have to live with that for the rest of your life."

I was rendered speechless as she continued to rip me a new asshole. I didn't even have words for a rebuttal. All I could do was watch her give me one last hostile look, move away toward the elevator and get inside. A cold sweat broke out on the back of my neck. *God damn it!* My mother's friend sure knew how to hold a grudge and make me feel like shit, all in the same moment.

My chest heaved; I felt overwhelmed and was about to burst into tears. I wasn't going to let the rest of Valerie's cronies see me cry, but they didn't know that I was long overdue for a nervous breakdown, which was the last thing I needed right then. No one knew what had happened to me with Mikaylo during my extended hiatus. I was drained, and may have even been battling post-partum depression. Honestly, I was probably also long overdue for therapy, but I had to focus my energy on the new problem: my sick mother.

My father watched the exchange from afar. He looked at me briefly before speaking.

"Honey, could I talk to you?" Without looking at him, I stood and led the way toward the elevator. Too many ears and haters were around. I guess my father was trying to spare me from any more random attacks, so we ended up in the chapel of the hospital. I sat down in a pew and folded my hands in my lap. He sat down beside me but before he could speak, I did. I just couldn't take it.

"I understand that you gotta be pissed at me."

"I don't know if pissed is gonna cover it, baby doll."

I hung my head. "I know I messed up. Sorry about Howard, Dad."

"All we wanted was for you to be a responsible woman we could be proud of."

That shut me up.

"What about the baby?" he asked.

"She's with some good people."

"A girl, huh?" He smiled a bit.

"Yes, I had a girl. Her name is Kyashira Star Davis." I managed to force a smile.

"Kyashira Star. That's a pretty name." He was silent for a moment. "Baby doll, I will always love you, no matter what. I didn't call you here to beat you up. Like I said, maybe we can sort out your issues a bit later." He took off his glasses as he peered at the cross in the front of the chapel. "Your mother is dying. In fact, she's been sick for a while. She could go at any time now."

We both wiped our eyes. I hugged my father.

"What's wrong with her, Dad? If she'd been sick for a while, how come I never knew about it?"

He sighed deeply. "Well, Honey, your mother has been hiding things for a very long time. It's not my place to get into them. She actually asked me to call you. I think she'd prefer to tell you herself. No matter which way this whole thing pans out, just know that we loved you, and still do." He put his hand on mine. "I think we'd better get back up to the room now. We'll see if your mother is up to seeing you now, okay?"

"Okay."

We both rose to our feet. My father put his hand in mine. We walked out of that chapel with heavy hearts. I had no idea what my mother needed and wanted to tell me, but I figured that at least the door was open for conversation, even if she was on her deathbed. I never imagined something like this could happen, not even in a million years.

"Valerie, Honey's here," my father explained, when we arrived in my mother's room. By that time, all of her friends were gone. Visiting hours were up. I knew my parents' status in the medical community had something to do with us being able to stay beyond the regular visiting hours. My father waved me over. I gulped as my feet began to move. I leaned down and whispered in her ear.

"I love you, Mom. I'm sorry. You were right about me. You were right about everything. Oh God, Mom, I'm truly sorry for the things I put you through." I bit back a sob as I watched her face for any sign of recognition.

Her eyes opened lazily. They were yellow. I also noticed she'd lost a lot of weight; she appeared as though she'd pretty much quit eating. Nevertheless, I was still in denial.

"Hey . . . Honey," she rasped in between breaths. Tears gathered in the corner of her eyes as she grabbed my hand. Her voice was even fainter due to the oxygen mask over her mouth.

"Hey, Mom," I replied. Tears spilled down my cheeks and dotted my shirt.

"Where . . . have you been?"

I gulped and watched the vapor from her breath fog the inside of the mask, then fade away. "In a small town in Georgia."

My mother nodded slowly. "The . . . baby?"

"I had a girl. Her name is Kyashira Star Davis."

A faint smile crossed her ravaged features. "A little . . . girl. Pretty." She paused to catch her breath, then asked, "The . . . father?"

I gritted my teeth. "He's not around," I said shortly.

"I'm . . . sorry." She sighed. "Honey, I know we've . . . had our ups and downs, but . . . it doesn't . . . matter." Her chest labored with the effort to talk.

I patted her hand. "Mom, don't push yourself to talk. You need your strength." She managed to squeeze my hand gently.

"It . . . doesn't . . . matter who was right . . . or wrong. I . . . I love you." She went into a coughing fit that had me looking for the nurse's call button in a panic. Dad got up and grabbed a plastic cup from the bedside table. He gently removed the mask and placed the straw in Mom's mouth as he supported her head. She took a few sips then lay back on the pillow in exhaustion. Dad replaced the mask then set the cup back on the table.

I began to sob as the extent of my mother's illness hit me in the gut. It was all too much. "I love you too, Mom! I'm sorry for all that I put you through. I'm so sorry. I truly mean it this time." I lay my head down on my mother's bed and just cried my heart out. I felt a faint touch and realized that it was my mother's hand on my head, stroking my hair. I raised my head and saw her looking down at me with love for the first time I could remember in a long time. I wiped my face clean with the back of my left hand.

"I had a drinking problem . . . for a long time," she started. "I have . . . cir . . . rhosis of . . . the liver."

My mother looked tired. Part of me wanted her to stop talking. The other part of me wanted her to continue.

"It started . . it started—" She coughed again, then started wheezing, struggling to breathe. Dad stood again and reached for the cup of water, but Mom shook her head. I rubbed the top of her hand, hoping to relax her.

"Can't you get a transplant? Why are you giving up hope? Maybe you can get better."

"I'm . . . dying. There's no use . . . in waiting . . . for a new liver, or . . . trying . . . alternative treatments. I'm in . . . stage four of cir . . . rhosis."

"Oh, God! I . . ." I shook my head in despair. My mother was dying.

"I just wanted . . . better for you, so I hid . . . it."

"Shh," I admonished her. "Rest, Mom. You look very tired."

I gently stroked her head, then kissed her cheek and let go of my mother's hand. I walked to the bathroom, closed the door, and just cried. I felt weak and lifeless as my mind flashed back to each time I called my mother a bitch, each horrible thought I had about her, each mean comment I made about her, and each time we fought. I felt terrible. There was nothing I could do to take back any ill words or harsh remarks. After about five minutes, I wiped my face and straightened my clothes.

When I exited the bathroom, I heard my mother call my name. "Honey." My father sat closer to the bed this time, holding her hand.

"Ma'am?" I answered as I held her other hand.

"Your . . . father," she whispered. My father looked at her, then at me, then stared down at where his hand was entwined with my mother's.

"What, Mom?"

She swallowed. "Your . . . father . . . ha . . ."

"I can't hear you." I leaned closer.

"Your . . . Dad had an . . . affair."

I stared at her in disbelief. She didn't say what I thought she said . . . did she? Maybe it was the medication. I looked over at Dad, and he was still staring down at their hands like he was trying to memorize them. My stomach did a slow roll.

"It tore our mar . . . riage apart. Then I had . . . one."

My dad had an affair. My mom, too. What was going on here? Why did this happen? Why was I finding out now?

"Mom, we can discuss this later, when you're better. Right now—"

" . . . Love you, Honey. I never stopped lov—"

All of a sudden, my mother's monitors blared, beeped, and whistled. I ran in the hall and yelled, "Nurse! We need a doctor in here!"

A nurse came in, pressed the emergency button, and shoved me aside rudely as she started checking the monitors. Soon a team of nurses and doctors rushed into the room with a cart, which held a machine with electric paddles. I saw something like it on TV, when I watched *ER*. My dad was pushed aside as well and he came to stand beside me as we watched the team fight to save my mother's life. A long, high beep sounded and seemed to go on forever. "She's flatlining! Let's get the paddles charged. Push some epi," a doctor ordered. Nurses scurried to inject something into my mother's IV while the cart was brought closer to the bed.

The oxygen mask was removed and a breathing bag was placed over her mouth, while her gown was lifted and the paddles were placed on her chest. "Charging," the doctor warned as the machine emitted a high whine. "Clear!" he yelled as he pressed the buttons on the paddles. My mother's torso jumped off the bed as the electric current raced through her in an attempt to restart her heart. All eyes turned toward the heart monitor; the line stayed straight and green. The doctor waited for the machine to charge again and my mother's torso jumped a second time when the paddle charge was released. The line still didn't change. One nurse injected more medicine into the IV while the other nurse continued to breathe for my mother using the bag. This went on for about fifteen minutes until the doctor finally removed his gloves and pronounced her dead. I looked at my mother's peaceful face and felt an instant void in my life.

Someone asked us to leave, but we stayed put. My father and I clung to each other as tears streamed down our faces. Valerie was gone. Our rock, our family glue, our common enemy was no more. Even in the midst of all this, I still heard my mother's last words. Not only had I heard some real heavy shit that rocked my world sideways, but my mother left this earth before she could completely explain the reason behind her drinking problem.

⟫※⟪

During the wake, I stood next to my mother's casket and thanked the mourners who came to pay their last respects. I did this for two reasons: one, I was upset that my father cheated on my mother, and two, my father was in such bad shape, he asked me to receive people who came to the wake. I greeted the constant stream of people and directed them to sign the guest book and view her body. As sad as I was, my crew got word and showed up, no questions asked. Because of Yolanda, and Pookie, it made it a little easier to accept that Dr. Valerie Davis was gone.

For some reason, I chose to ignore my mother's admittance of her own affair; in my mind, it was just a reaction to my Dad's affair, so he was really the one at fault. My head was still spinning from my mother's deathbed confessions. All this time, I thought I had been the one who'd been drinking my father's good liquor when I was acting wild.

My mother had been a self-professed alcoholic, but my father and I agreed that we would tell people who weren't aware of the truth that she died from cancer. It was easier that way, and it allowed her to keep her honor, just as she would've liked. I felt like a rug had been pulled from under my feet. Why add to my pain with the truth?

Mikaylo—yes, *that* Mikaylo—showed up at the funeral home and I literally scratched my head, trying to figure out why he was there. I couldn't believe my eyes; this was the first time I'd seen him in months. He laughed and joked with his boys, like nothing had ever happened back in Georgia and we weren't even in a funeral home. As soon as he saw me, all that stopped. Our eyes locked for just an instant and his smile faded away. He walked up to my mother's casket looking like a million bucks. He had two-carat diamond stud in each ear, and they didn't look fake. I couldn't help noticing how fly he looked, and how much nerve he had to show up and pay respects of any kind. I sat down with Pookie and Yolanda, pretending I hadn't even seen him.

He sighed and rubbed his forehead as he stood in front of me. "Look, I just wanted to extend my condolences." He hesitated. "I heard about . . . you know."

"No, I don't know," I snapped. Yolanda and Pookie looked at me, then at Mikaylo, then back at me, like they were following a tennis match. I didn't need them in my business right then; they didn't know about Kyashira.

I stomped away, but he followed me. I moved to a private corner, away from the rest of the mourners, where we could have some privacy since Mikaylo seemed determined to talk about Kyashira and what happened in Georgia.

"I wasn't sure if you'd be here or not," he began. "I know it was foul to leave you like that, and I didn't want to, but—""You didn't want to?" I balled my hands into fists; the urge to knock him into next week was strong, and it burned through my grief. "Don't come near me, ever again! We don't ever have anything to say to each other for the rest of our lives."

Mikaylo took a step backward. He looked a bit nervous. "Um . . . how's the baby, Honey?"

"None of your business, Kaylo!" I hissed. I looked around and saw a couple of people looking at us curiously. "And keep your voice down." I lowered my own and stepped closer to him. "You have no respect for my mother, showing up and bringing up that issue here. You could've stayed around to find out how your baby was doing. Why don't you call your aunt Paula and ask? You left her holding the bag, too.""You know?" His eyes clouded over in a way I had never seen, and then he stepped back some more. The distance between us was pretty big."You heard what the fuck I said."Mikaylo fidgeted and shoved his hands inside his pockets. "You said you needed and wanted me! Now you're cutting me down. Some appreciation for me just trying to—"

Before I thought about it, I hauled off and smacked him. A large, red handprint graced the side of his face and Mikaylo's head snapped back from the impact. He rubbed his face, then sighed. I knew he wouldn't hit me back. Mikaylo knew his disrespect was over the top, in more ways than one. My single act of hostility helped me gain some closure, although I surely could've done it in a far less violent manner. The action spoke for itself, though, and I turned and walked away from him for good. Mikaylo made himself scarce after that. I spotted someone signing the guest book and returned to my duties.

※※※

"Don't worry. I'll be at the funeral with you," a woman was telling my father. I walked into the house and found my dad with Reverend Daniels. His head was in her lap, and she was stroking his soft, curly hair. Spiritual advisor, my ass. My mother's intuition about that woman was correct, and mine told me that she and my father had already been intimate. All I could think of was my mother's suffering before she died. My father told me all about the liver function tests that led to her biopsy, and how he went to every single appointment with my mother until her hospitalization and eventual death. I was immediately disappointed in him for allowing Reverend Daniels to comfort him.

"Hi, Honey," he told me, lifting his head a little. "You know Reverend—"

I cut him off. "I know who that skank is. It's not her place to be here. We have family business to attend to, and a funeral to address, Dad. My mother's not even in the ground yet, and she's trying to get her claws in you."

"That's not true, Honey," my dad protested even as a reddish hue snuck across his face. He tried to sit up, but Reverend Daniels kept his head in her lap

"Don't lie about it, Dad. I know you've had sex! I can tell."

"Reverend Daniels has helped me through this while you were gone, and she has counseled me through many tough times over the years. She even volunteered to handle your mother's funeral to make it easier on me."

Pussy will sure change a man. I shook my head in disgust. "How blind can you be, Dad? Was the sex that good? Even Mom could tell that Reverend Daniels always wanted you for herself. I'm sure your money and prestige doesn't hurt." I turned on Reverend Daniels, who was staring at me with a smirk on her face. "Who the hell do you think you are? I don't appreciate you disrespecting my mother. Get the hell out of our house!"

Reverend Daniels pushed my father's head out of her lap and stood. The kindly reverend was gone and in her place was a woman ready to do battle over her man. "If you want to come at me like that, it's not really your place to be here, either. You think you're so special? You think you're something else? Well, let me tell you something, baby. You may not know what it feels like to want for anything, but you don't even know who you really are. You don't even appreciate the way someone took care of your alcoholic mother, and the baggage that didn't even belong to him," the minister said.

"And what is all that supposed to mean?" I glanced over at my dad, who sat with his head in his hands.

Reverend Daniels chuckled nastily. "Apparently, your mother didn't tell you during her little deathbed talk.""Darlene . . . Reverend . . ." My dad tried to interrupt her spiel."No, Jerome! She needs to hear this."I was confused. "Hear what?"Reverend Daniels pointed at my dad and said, "He isn't your father."

This woman was truly evil. "I don't know what kind of sick game you're playing, but you have crossed the line. Get the hell out of my father's house!" I screamed. "Dad, why are you even letting this happen, at a time like this? Mom is barely in her grave! This is sick."

His head dipped lower than it already was. Then he stood and exhaled deeply. "It's true, Honey." "What?" "Your mother and I agreed long ago that it was best if you didn't know until after one of us passed away. I was going to tell you after you had time to regroup after the funeral." He paused as if to gather his thoughts. "I had an affair with a patient years ago, and she threatened to report me. It got really ugly and I could've lost my medical license. You mother found out and started drinking. Then she decided to get back at me by having an affair of her own. We couldn't get a divorce. She was Catholic, and we had our images and careers to consider, so your mother retaliated and got pregnant with you."

Too many lies had been told. The truth had been hiding in the dark for too many years, tucked up under all of that proper behavior. I didn't know how to feel and I didn't know what to say. I began to cry uncontrollably. I ran upstairs to get my bag and ran down the long staircase.

My father looked at me with pain in his eyes. "Honey, don't leave. Please! I never meant to hurt you. There's a reason why I didn't explain all of that," he pleaded.

"I'll bet! Give me my money from my trust fund!"

"Now, everything will be tied up in your mother's estate," he hedged.

"What do you mean? I know there was money just for me." "Why do you think you had a trust fund in the first place?" Reverend Daniels asked. I could tell she wanted to add fuel to the fire and she did. "It was so you'd be taken care of, in case anything ever happened to *that* woman who defiled God's word and had a bastard child. Too bad for you, she didn't reinstate it before the inevitable happened."

She had to be lying. I looked at Dad for confirmation. "Dad?"

He shut his eyes. "It's true, Honey. Valerie never reinstated your trust fund after your last argument, despite my pleadings with her to do it." So now I was not only motherless and fatherless, but I was also broke? I couldn't take any more drama. "Thanks for nothing," I spat at my father. "To think that I came back here because I loved and respected you. You said you needed my support, but you really didn't." I eyeballed Reverend Daniels. "Had I known the truth—that you were posted up with some knock-off preacher—I never would've returned."

"You have until the end of the week to find somewhere else to live. By Saturday, we want you and everything you own out of here," the reverend told me with an evil grin.

I looked at her as if she'd lost her mind. "What authority do you have around here? It's not your place to tell me to go anywhere, spiritual advisor or not."

Reverend Daniels' grin widened. "We're engaged." She waggled her left hand at me; light glinted off the three-carat diamond ring perched on her ring finger.

I stared at them like I'd just walked in on them passing a crack pipe back and forth except instead of the drugs going up in smoke, it was my life evaporating into thin air. Dad looked like he wanted to say something to me, but he turned to Reverend Daniels instead.

"We've been talking about it, but you have no right to put words in my mouth," he snapped at her.

Talking about what? Why was my dad talking to this scheming bitch about anything involving me?

"It's best for all parties involved," Reverend Daniels insisted. "When is this girl going to learn responsibility?"

"I am responsible! I've been out here in these streets enough to peep your game!" I shook my head real slow. "He may not see it, but I do. You're going to burn in hell for the trouble you caused, and what you're out to do." I spun on my heel and walked away.

"You're a whore and a slut! I know all about you," Reverend Daniels retorted as she followed, hot on my heels.

Dad's face darkened with anger. "Get out!" my father shouted at her. "You have no right to talk to my daughter that way." "She's *not* your daughter." Reverend Daniels grabbed her oversized purse from a nearby chair. "I'll see *you* at the funeral."

She gave me a scornful look and headed toward the door. I was hurt and confused by everything that I'd learned in such a short period of time. No matter what the man I thought was my father tried to say to comfort me, none of his words mattered. My mind was in a far, far away place. Where was I supposed to go? What was I supposed to do? Who was my real father? I was tired of letting myself down, and I was tired of people letting me down at the worst times. I just wanted to crawl into a cave and not come out until all of this blew over.

PART TWO

WHAT'S LOVE GOT
TO DO WITH IT?

Chapter Eight

DAMAGED GOODS

When I returned to New York, I thought I was going to return to school and get my shit together, even if I had to go to summer school to do it. But after everything that went down, I couldn't even manage to go to my mother's funeral. It rained the day that Dr. Valerie Davis was laid to rest. I mourned for her in my own private way that day. I knew she would forgive me for not going to her funeral; at least I spent time with her during the wake. I cut Jerome—my "father"—off, cold turkey. The best I could do was not even think about the situation. I convinced myself that I was better off without him.

I turned to Ritchie, that old friend who was a tad bit older than I was, because I knew I could count on him to help me out in an emergency. I had helped Ritchie out of a jam not too long ago, and he was repaying the favor. My main concern was to find somewhere to live, although there was no way I could afford to pay rent. I had plenty of acquaintances who would loan me money, but letting me shack up with them was another story. I knew Ritchie would always have my back if I asked. We were two dropouts from two different words, an unlikely pair, but very good friends. One thing scared me about crashing with my friend, though, and that was fear of the police bringing me back home. I was still under eighteen and I knew that being granted an emancipation decree was extremely rare, and I didn't have Jerome's permission to live outside of his home.

"Home" became Ritchie's one-bedroom apartment on St. Nicholas Avenue. As soon as I got settled in to my new spot, Ritchie asked me where I wanted to sleep. "I don't know if you feelin' the couch, but I ain't got no other bed."

"I'll take your bed," I answered. "I think you know me a little better than to want the couch." We were unpacking my stuff when he just broke out laughing and shook his head. "Them niggas really kicked you out?"

"I wouldn't even be here, Ritchie, if my father hadn't. You know that. My ass would be comfortable in my own bed, but no, Dad—I mean, Jerome—was on some real bullshit!"

Ritchie caught me stumbling over Jerome's name and title but decided to let it ride—for now. He knew me well enough not to just take my word for it, that there was more to the story than I was telling. "Uh-huh. What did you do?" he asked with a smile.

I sucked my teeth and flopped down onto his bed. "*I* didn't do anything. Maybe, just maybe, someone else did."

"Yeah, right." He looked at me like, *hurry up and tell the whole story.*

I decided to stretch the truth. "A'ight. It was a lotta shit that led up to it, like . . . you know, what happened with me running away with Mikaylo. My daddy really wasn't feelin' that. When I came back after my mother got sick, he was acting like I was still wildin' out at parties. And I forgot to tell you the best part!" I reached for the Nerf football on the edge of his dresser. Ritchie tossed my now-empty luggage into his closet and moved to the other side of the bed, opening his hands in preparation for the game of catch.

He screwed up his face as if to say, *how could it get any worse?* "The best part? Wait, there's more?"

"This is the kicker right here. There's no trust fund." I sailed the football over the bed and he caught it in one hand, then tossed it back.

"Wait, what? What happened to the money you had coming?"

"All two hundred and fifty thousand of it will be wrapped up in my mother's estate. Every single dollar I thought I owned no longer belongs to me."

Ritchie looked dumbfounded. "Can your father do that?"

"He sure can. My mother revoked it before she died. She was pissed as hell about the time I snuck out to go to that party. She never set it back up. Now ain't that a kick in the fuckin' ass?"

Ritchie shook his head and flipped the football up in the air. I already knew what he was thinking. He was trying to figure out a way to help me get some money. He had completely abandoned our game of catch. He lay back on the bed and tossed the Nerf above his head.

"I have no way of surviving, but I refuse to go crawling back to my father like a crippled dog." I crawled into bed next to him and we both stared at the ceiling.

"Well, technically, this is kinda your fault," Ritchie admonished. "Plus, you did get pregnant." He winced, waiting for me to punch him. I didn't because as much as I hated to admit it, he was right. "You ain't stupid, developmentally challenged, physically impaired, or otherwise incapable of finding suitable employment. You're just spoiled."

"Thanks for nothing! Tell me something I don't know. Cut me some slack, though. My mom did just pass away, and I'm still just seventeen. I'll be eighteen soon, but still." My eyes teared up.

Ritchie sat up and gave me a hug. "What happened? You never did tell me what killed your mother."

"Cancer, that's what."

"Well, she's in a better place, I'm sure. You know what happened to my dad early on in life, so I know what it's like not to have two parents." Ritchie's father was a gangster who got caught on the wrong end of a drug deal, leaving Ritchie's mother—and eventually, just Ritchie— to care for Ritchie and his four sisters and brothers. I wanted to tell Ritchie the part of the story about my father not being my blood father, but I bit my tongue. Although it was Ritchie I was talking to, I still had my pride. "So what's the deal with school? Did you get enrolled again?"

"Screw that. I can study for my GED. I ain't going to college now, anyway."

"You?"

"Yeah, me. I know what kind of family I come from and everything, but I don't want to spend four years of my life chasing higher education. I'd only be thrown into the business world without any previous work experience, and inevitably end up in a dead-end job somewhere while I slaved away forty hours a week. Humph, even after all of that, I bet I'd only pull in a couple grand a month for my troubles. I'm destined to be a rich bitch, and I don't see hours and hours of studying at Howard as the way to do it."

Ritchie shook his head in disbelief. "So what options do you have left? Honey, you're seventeen and used to having a silver spoon hanging out of your mouth. I'm not hatin', I'm just sayin'."

"Let's be honest about something for a minute. Most of the real money in the world, albeit fleeting, comes from illegal means. Fear was put into our hearts by the government, and I bet more people would get their hustles on if it weren't illegal. I bet the majority of people would be selling drugs, carrying unlicensed weapons, murdering, stealing, raping, and generally doing whatever the law said they couldn't."

"Who you been talking to, Honey? Sounding like you about to start a revolution." He laughed. "You're talking some really heavyweight stuff, girl. I had no idea you were that deep."

"There's more," I said proudly.

Ritchie raised an eyebrow. "What would that be?"

"Get paid to get laid."

Ritchie burst out laughing. "That's prostitution!"

I shrugged. "If you wanna be technical about it, you can say that." I rose to my knees, my voice filled with excitement. "Come on! That shouldn't be shocking to you, considering what I just said."

"If you don't wanna be technical, then you pimpin' men who are out to hit some designated pussy," Ritchie smirked.

I laughed so hard, I almost rolled out of the bed. "I'd still be pimpin' myself!"

"You gettin' paid to fuck is prostitution, no matter how you slice it." Ritchie had a way of turning words into his own personal weapons, so he could use them to his own advantage. "And what do you know about trickin', anyway? You got knocked up by the first dude you fucked, so it's not like you have a whole lot of tricks, and that's what's gonna put you on as a pro. I'm not hatin', I'm just sayin'."

I punched Ritchie in the shoulder. Damn him. He always had a valid point.

Ritchie rubbed his shoulder. "Why you hittin' me? You know I'm right."

"Oh please, Ritchie!" I hit him upside the head with a pillow. "It can't be that hard. All I gotta do is watch a couple of good pornos, and do what them chicks do."

"Yeah, I guess that is true." Ritchie warmed up to the idea and then began making his own suggestions. "You got plenty of rich dudes that hang out in bars and stuff, all lonely, even if they are married. You cute, got a nice shape, and got some class about you. They'd pay for the pleasure of having you around—money, cars, trips, clothes, jewelry. It'd be like an ego stroke. Then, if you fuck 'em, that would just add more money to your pockets."

As we sat developing my idea, I grew more eager to execute my plan. That's when I reminded myself that I'd snapped back into shape after my pregnancy, with the added bonus of more lush curves. I could give those models on the cover of *Smooth* and *King* a run for their money. Even now, you couldn't even tell that I'd had a baby; I hardly even had any stretch marks.

"Think about it," I urged. "This could be my main shot to get paid and get laid, all without breaking a sweat."

"Oh ya ass gonna break a sweat," Ritchie joked.

Money and sex without effort. Sounded like a plan to me.

Chapter Nine

LIFE OF THE PARTY

Ritchie was born to steal. He found a way to get his hands on anything and everything. When I told him I wanted him to be my mentor, all he did was smile. Ritchie boosted because he could, and because he was good at it. It certainly wasn't because he didn't know where his next meal was coming from, although that's how he got his start. He just got so used to it that it sort of became his profession. He had an enviable client list which included movie stars and rappers. He wasn't one of those crackhead, TVs-for-twenty-five-dollars types of boosters. No, he was one of those brand-new-forty-inch-plasma-screen-TV-with-surround-sound-and-optional-DVD-hookup types of boosters.

If your lady wanted that new pair of Prada boots but every time she got near a Neiman Marcus, the price tag stared her back uptown, you could've called Ritchie. He'd have the boots *and* a matching outfit for you by the end of the week, and it would cost you half the retail price. If your man wanted to look spiffy with the new Mauris, Ritchie could've hooked you up with those too. If you gave him your inseam, you'd be good for a new pair of designer jeans as well.

"What you mean, you wanna boost?" he asked me when I first proposed the idea to him.

"I wanna do more than that. I wanna get the shit myself. Like, from the source."

"You wanna rob the manufacturers?" He shook his head in confusion. "I ain't followin' you."

"What do you do after you pay your bill in a restaurant, Ritch?"

He snorted. "That's easy: I leave a tip."

I nodded. "Exactly. And the better the service, the bigger the tip, right?" He nodded. "So I'm saying, why should I just be getting payment for services rendered, and payment that *they* think I should be receiving, at that? I might as well be working in an office, getting a salary."

It took Ritchie a minute to figure out what I was getting at but when he finally did, he grinned from ear to ear. "You wanna be on some Black Widow shit, huh?"

I laughed. "Kinda sorta. I won't be killin' anybody. I can't afford to get my hands that dirty. But you're on the right track, though. I just wanna rob them, and get my tip off the top."

"But how are you gonna get started? Where are you gonna go? Who's gonna be your first mark? Did you think about all this shit yet?"

"No, but that's why it's called planning, numbnut. I'm gonna figure out all that shit, test it out and if it works, I'mma be in business."

"I'd feel better if you told me you was finna be a cat burglar or some shit," he said with concern. "I don't like the idea that you gonna be out here alone with these niggas.

"You know how I am; once I make up my mind, it's a wrap. Plus, I need fast, untraceable money."

"True dat, but you're still underage and this is really a potentially dangerous way to get it."

I threw up my hands in exasperation. "Look, Ritchie, just living is dangerous. My mother seemed to have everything going for her, and she's no longer here. I can be scared to live, or live to scare niggas. I need money, and I need it now. I have to do something, Ritchie, or else I'm gonna be the next bitch standing on line for food stamps, and you already know what I'm about to say about that. And you know there's not a snowball's chance in hell of me going home, so get that thought outta your head right now. Either you with me on this, or not. So?"

He didn't hesitate. "Yeah, yeah, whatever. If you insist on this, don't ever get greedy with it. Just take what you need to tide you over, 'cause you never know when it's that little bit extra that'll get you caught. Get in and get out. And don't plan on doing it long, okay?" He grabbed my chin and forced me to look him in the eyes. "You got a lot more going for you than you think, Honey, and it's not between your legs," he said softly. "Don't throw it all away for some get-rich-quick scheme. You not built for this over the long term."

That's the advice Ritchie gave me when I first started my little scheme to rob men who had shit worth taking.

"Do your homework, Honey," Ritchie admonished. "A hundred percent of niggas get caught when they don't plan. You gotta know what you finna steal 'fore you steal it, and who you finna steal it from. Don't just be walkin' up in somewhere like, 'Hmm, I think I'mma just go crazy today and pick up whatever catches my eye, and maybe I'll pick it up from him.' Nah. That shit will get you caught or shot."

In addition to pickpocketing lessons, Ritchie also schooled me about forensic evidence. "Girl, don't you watch *CSI*?" he joked. "Fingerprints are the first thing they'll hang you with. Fibers and hair are next. That's why you need to get in and get out; the less time you're in a mark's place, the less time there is to leave a vital piece of evidence behind. DNA evidence is nothing to play with." He instructed me on how to wipe down a mark's place before I left, how to keep from touching surfaces beyond what was absolutely necessary, how to minimize the amount of hair that I left behind. He also discussed the removal of towels, washcloths, and sheets from the bed. "I told you, Honey, DNA evidence is no joke. They can check your pussy juice and track your ass from here to Alaska."

❧❧

"Your father kicked you out after your Mom died?" Yolanda asked, stuffing another handful of popcorn into her mouth. "Damn, what did you do?"

"I'm tired of repeating the same story over and over again. I don't want to talk about it, okay?"

"Damn, Honey! What the fuck did you do?" Pookie asked. She shook her head and frowned.

"That doesn't make any sense, at a time like this. I mean, your mom just died. I agree with Pookie," Yolanda said.

I cocked my head and threw popcorn at them. "Y'all supposed to be on my side! What you mean, it don't make sense?"

"Because, Honey, we know you. We know that you had to do something to really piss him off."

"Do you know my father? No! You don't know him, or what he's really like. I hate y'all both!" I folded my arms and pouted. "It was a lot of shit." My eyes teared up. "I just miss my mother," I said as the tears spilled down my cheeks.

"We're your homies. It's okay." Yolanda hugged me.

I hugged her back. "You're always so supportive, Yolanda. Thank you."

Pookie joined in. "I support you, too. Oh yeah, before I forget." Pookie slid off the bed and retrieved three colorful, glossy fliers from a bag and handed one to each of us. I skimmed it and a warm sensation overcame me. I knew it was a way I could connect the dots to the conversation I'd had with Ritchie before they arrived.

"What the fuck is this?" Yolanda asked.

"Some guys at City College are throwing a party. I think it would be good for Honey to get out and have some fun. It's next weekend, and they want a lot of girls there. They said the last time they threw a party, it was like a straight dickfest all night."

"That's because they gave out all the flyers right next to Rice University. Them niggas be thirsty to party," Yolanda remarked, flipping the card over.

"Dress code, casual and sexy," I read. Okay, I could do that. "Ladies free before eleven and ten dollars afterward. Must be eighteen to enter—twenty-one to drink."

"And they having a Flyy Girl contest, too! The best-dressed girl gets five hundred dollars," Pookie exclaimed.

She had my undivided attention. "Who said that?"

"Look right here, at the bottom. It says so, right on top of the address. You see it?"

I nodded and smiled to myself as I read the not-so-large script that mentioned the contest. If Ritchie could come through for me, I knew I'd have money in my pocket for the next week.

❈

"And this party is gonna be where?" Ritchie asked as he stared at the flyer.

"They rented out Club Avalon."

"How many people gonna be there?"

"I don't know, Ritchie. I guess enough to fill the club up."

"Hmm." Ritchie had come through the door about fifteen minutes after Yolanda and Pookie had said their goodbyes. I showed him the flyer and knew for a fact that he could help me win the contest. He had been studying it for about fifteen minutes, and I assumed he was sizing up its validity. "College niggas are usually broke, but it wouldn't hurt to put in work with them in the beginning, to get you started. Well, you know I can hook you up," he said at last.

"Yes!" I screamed, jumping into his arms. "Thank you, thank you, thank you!"

"Yeah, yeah, yeah. They got these new boots out that all the girls is goin' crazy for right now. You ever heard of Manolo Blahnik?"

"Yeah. Why?"

"Well, they got a new pair of boots out right now that look like Timberland stilettos. I can get you a pair of those, and then we can just work on the outfit from there."

A pair of Timberland stilettos? I had never heard of the idea, and until I saw them for myself, I would be skeptical. "See if you can get me a picture of them, or a pair to look at." Ritchie was already on his way out the door before I could finish the sentence. Whenever he got a request, he was on it that same day. He didn't like to waste time because in his words, "Time is money."

※

Ritchie got the boots and yes, I loved them. They were synonymous with sexy and fly. The minute I saw them, I knew I had to have them. I also I knew I was going to win the Flyy Girl contest at the party. "How much did they cost?"

"Enough," Ritchie answered with a smile. "Enough to make it worth it, if you win."

To go with the shoes, Ritchie hooked me up with a beige fitted jumpsuit, and a belt made of gold link that hung right on top of my hips. Sometimes I wondered if Ritchie was gay, because he was just a bit *too* on point with women's fashions. But I'd never seen him with another dude and hell, even if he was gay, that didn't change our mutually beneficial relationship. The jumpsuit enhanced all my young curves perfectly, and a diamond solitaire pendant sparkled around my neck. The day of the party, I got my hair blown bone straight, with bangs trimmed to fall just on top of my eyes. I had my nails painted an outrageous bright pink, neon green and yellow pattern because I wanted to stand out in any way possible. Ritchie drove me downtown to Sephora to pick up some lipstick, mascara, eyeliner, and perfume. Around ten o'clock that evening, I was finally ready.

Pookie and Yolanda wanted to get to Club Avalon early in order to scope things out, so I told them I would meet them there. I wasn't in any rush to get there because I wanted to make a grand entrance. I didn't want to be standing around for two hours while the other hatin' bitches scoped out my outfit; I wanted to walk in and have everyone look my way and just know that I looked the baddest. At least, I was truly hoping it would go that way, after all the effort it took to get ready.

At eleven forty-five PM, Ritchie and I made it to Club Avalon. He decided to come along because he wanted to see if all our hard work was going to pay off at the end of the night. I hoped that my fake ID would get me inside the club and luckily, it did. We checked our coats and walked into the main part of the club, searching for Yolanda and Pookie. I assumed they were able to pull off the ID scam, too.

A girl came up to us, looking rather excited, and shoved a clipboard in my face.

"Ma, you *gotta* sign up for the Flyy Girl contest!" She eyeballed my outfit like she wanted to wait outside for me when the club closed. "Where did you get them boots?" she squealed.

"They were a gift," I answered, smiling back. "You like them?" Since she had a clipboard, she obviously had something to do with the whole Flyy Girl process, so I was going to be as nice to her as possible.

"I love them! Oh my God, I am so jealous! What size you wear?"

"Seven."

She stomped her foot and sucked her teeth. "Damn it, girl, I was hopin' you'd say eight and a half. If you had said that, I was gonna rob you," she joked good-naturedly before she walked away. As Ritchie and I made out way to the bar so he could get a drink, I could feel eyes staring at me from all around the room. I got the feeling that homegirl was alerting people to my presence, which, at that point, was a good thing.

They started the contest at exactly midnight. As each contestant's name was called, she walked to the front of the club and showed off her outfit, then stood in a line by the bar. I wasn't really feelin' getting put on the spot like that, but I figured it was for a good cause; I could use the five hundred bucks. The girl in front of me had a lot of damn nerve, getting on the line, looking the way she looked. This ho had on a half a wife beater underneath a half jean jacket with red trim. I guess the red trim was supposed to match the huge plastic red-and-gold bamboo earrings she sported. She also wore a miniskirt with the same red trim, red fishnet tights, and a pair of denim high-heeled boots. She looked fucking ridiculous, like she was trying out for an LL Cool J video or something. She got a few half-hearted cheers from some dudes in the crowd, but the rest of us were busy trying to figure out what the hell had gone wrong.

"And next up is Honey, from uptown," the emcee said. I followed the light and smiled as I walked to my place at the end of the bar. A fine light-skinned something kept smiling at me every time our eyes locked. I kept my eyes on him the whole time I walked by. I saw that my shoes were getting stares and hoped that was a good thing. The music was so loud at first that I didn't even hear my name so by the time I got to the bar, there was already another girl approaching the front of the club. I was surprised to see Pookie walking toward the bar, because I didn't even know she'd entered the contest.

As close as Pookie and I were, she always felt the need to compete with me. Everything she did was focused on a move I'd already made. With my parents being able to buy me top-of-the-line everything, I know she assumed that little Miss Spoiled Honey struck gold again. We had a love/hate relationship, except that she never actually made her feelings known. When I turned and saw her behind me, I wasn't really surprised. She knew that when it came down to dressing, she was no match for me. She wore a pair of skintight Pepe jeans, knee-high hot pink-and-black boots, and a pink-and-black baby tee. She looked cute, but not Best-Dressed-contest cute. I also wasn't surprised when she rolled her eyes and ice-grilled me after I won the five hundred dollars. I knew Pookie's undercover jealousy was going to cause our friendship to end one day; I just didn't know when.

"Congratulations," she growled when I got back over to where she and Yolanda sat. Yolanda didn't sense the tension between the two of us because she was genuinely happy I had won. She gave me a big hug and passed me one of the drinks Ritchie had bought.

"I knew you was gonna win! I was like, my girl is so fly, these wack-ass bitches ain't gonna know what hit them. Right, Pookie?"

Pookie looked even more insulted because she was one of those "wack-ass bitches" to which Yolanda referred. Yolanda realized how her words came out and said, "Pookie, I'm sorry! I didn't mean that—"

Pookie cut her off as she glared at me and said, "No, you're right, Yolanda. Honey is the flyest." She downed the rest of her drink and brushed past me like I stole something from her.

Yolanda was embarrassed. "Honey, I didn't mean that she was wack. I didn't even know she was entering the contest until her name was called."

I shrugged because I could've cared less. Pookie was just being Pookie.

Ritchie hugged me and lifted me off the floor when he saw me. Then he pulled the money out of my hand and put it in his pocket. "Consider that your first month's rent," he laughed in my ear. I wanted to punch him in the chest, but I knew why he took it, so I smiled and hugged him again for making me so fly.

The light-skinned lovely who caught my eye earlier reappeared across the room and gave me serious eye contact, so I made my way over to him. He must have had the same thought in mind because he met me halfway.

"What's good wit' you?" he asked.

"Why don't you start by telling me your name?"

"My friends call me Meech. What's yours?"

"Wouldn't you like to know?" I teased. "So what do you do?"

"I'm in college."

"Meech the College Boy." I half laughed.

Although I wasn't even eighteen yet, attracting the opposite sex had never been a problem. Pulling a grown man was a normal thing for me. Plus, I had a feeling about Meech. I mean, he seemed like he actually had some sort of funds coming in, by the looks of his clothes. I could've been wrong, but it was worth a shot.

Since he was on the tall side, I put those boots to work and stood on my toes to talk in his ear. "What's good wit' you?"

"I'm a'ight, I'm a'ight. I just wanted to say congratulations. You do look like da bomb!" His eyes roamed up and down my body appreciatively. "You gonna ever tell me your name?"

Right then and there, I knew this wasn't going to progress any further. Anyone who still said "da bomb" was light years behind the rest of the world, and I couldn't spend or waste my time catching him up. But, as Ritchie had taught me during my pickpocket lesson, the fat wad in his back pocket just might come in handy later.

"Brenda."

"You wanna dance, Brenda?"

I nodded and took his hand as we walked out to the dance floor. The smell of his breath told me that he'd had more than a couple of drinks. Better him than me; I was glad my mind was clear. He started to grind against me and feel on my body as the music played. I wrapped my arms around his body too. When he stumbled a little bit, I realized just how intoxicated he really was, and I decided to take advantage of the situation. Putting my arms around his neck, I waited until his eyes closed to slip his chain from around his neck and put it around my own, then promptly stuff it down the front of my jumpsuit. Ritchie had long since caught on so when I slid Meech's wallet out of his back pocket, Ritchie was right there, gently moving through the crowd to put it in his own pocket.

"Thanks for the dance, cutie pie," I said. I didn't wait for Meech to respond. I quickly made my way toward the exit because I knew Ritchie was ready and waiting outside with my purse. I didn't look back when I heard Meech arguing and half-slurring his words. I looked back as the distance grew between us. He tried to push his way through the crowd in my direction, but his equilibrium was all fucked up. Once outside, Ritchie stood away from the curb, but in a nearby place where I could spot him.

"You picked the right one," Ritchie congratulated. "That dude was tore up. He won't even remember your name from the Flyy Girl Contest if he tries to find you. That shit was smooth, Honey. I think you might have a li'l potential after all. I'm impressed!"

"I told you I could do it," I answered, grinning from ear to ear.

When we got back to the house, I flipped on a movie and heated some leftovers in the microwave while Ritchie took a shower. He came out an hour later, dripping wet, steam nearly rising from his feet. He tossed something my way, grabbed some clothes out of his dresser, then walked back into the bathroom.

"What's this?" I asked.

By then, he had already shut the door behind him. I looked down and saw my five hundred dollars and College Boy's wallet sitting in my lap. I clutched my winnings and smiled harder than I ever had. I suddenly felt like I had the potential to fast talk and hustle niggas in the streets. Despite my privileged background, I did have a few tricks to my advantage. I knew how to play the sweet, innocent role all too well. I didn't even realize it back then, but sucking wallets dry served two purposes: It helped numb the pain of what went down with my mother, and it also helped me to achieve my goal of financially getting back on my feet without working hard. Pickpocketing was good practice for increasing my skills and level of confidence. Before long, it was time to move on to bigger and better things.

Chapter Ten

GROWN WOMAN

Five years later . . .

By the time I'd turned twenty-one, I was deep in the game of conning men out of their loot. Despite the fact that I was in dire straits for some years, a spoiled diva couldn't resort to wallet snatching for long. That was bottom-of-the-barrel shit that was okay to do back when I was seventeen. I could sashay in any club my cold little heart desired to meet my victims, or do typical things like boost clothes. By eighteen, I was out to have fun, and I had no interest in seriously interacting with men. I guess you can say I did turn out to be a modern-day Black Widow. The only difference was, I didn't kill my prey, but stole from them.

At twenty-one, my game got serious. My first big win was snatching over $50,000 worth of goods from some investment banker who looked like he needed a hair replacement. I met him at a night club when I was wearing a real hot and tight Versace mini-dress. He did far too much bragging to the wrong girl, and his short dick did the thinking for him at the worst possible time. He made the mistake of inviting me up for a nightcap at his condo, without a security camera to keep an eye on my ass. Dumb, dumb, dumb!

That night, Mr. Wall Street wore a pinstriped suit, power tie, and expensive shoes as if he couldn't—or was too important to—change before coming to the club; everything about him had the classic Wall Street look.

We chatted it up for over an hour about things I'd mostly made up. When he suddenly put his clammy hand on my thigh and leaned close to my ear, I decided he would be my guinea pig. I made a bet to myself: if I bungled my plan, I'd rethink the whole snatch-and-grab-from-wealthy-men plan. If I pulled it off, I'd take it as a signal that I should move forward.

Mr. Wall Street—whose name was actually Fred—was already drunk by the time I arrived, compliments of scotch and Yuengling lager. I had the same number of drinks as he did—a shot and two beers—but all I had to do was piss. Although I never had been a hardcore shot-glass diva, despite my best intentions, my tolerance was far higher than his. I tended to drink just enough to relax men and myself, and that's how things stayed—more or less—so I could run game on them. With my mother passing away from an alcohol-related illness, I guess the hardcore drinking was something I didn't feel the need to do.

"So what do you say me and you go back to my place, you African queen?" Fred slurred.

It was all I could do not to burst into uncontrollable laughter in his ear. African queen? Was that supposed to be a compliment? A turn-on? What the fuck? I leaned back and said, "Okay, Daddy, let me freshen up before we go."

He clutched my hand tightly. "You can freshen up at my place. It's not that far from here."

Jack-motherfucking-pot. He had said the magic words. I grabbed my purse, ran a hand over the long, curly, black wig that I had donned for the evening, slid off the barstool, and followed him outside. I had never slept with a white man because I felt that fucking outside of my race would be a strange thing to do. I decided to take my chances with this one, though.

"D'ya mind if we take a cab?" Fred laughed stupidly. He was walking into the street in a diagonal line. "I'm so loaded." He ran a finger through his brown hair and stepped off the curb, waving down a yellow cab. Almost immediately, a cab stopped for him. He held the door open and helped me in, which was a gesture I wasn't used to on a consistent basis, other than in my parents' social circles when I was growing up.

"Uh, where the fuck do I live?" He laughed again while leaning against me. I smelled the alcohol on his breath and wrinkled my nose. I'd just finished drinking too, but I knew my breath wasn't kicking like his. That's what mints were for! "We're going to . . . we're going to . . . uh, 72nd Street, between York and FDR," he managed to tell the driver. I thought about all the buildings that were downtown and wondered which one he was referring to. The only buildings up there were the high-rise condos, which meant big money to me!

Fred drunkenly felt me up in the back of the cab, and I actually let him. He sloppily kissed my neck and face, reminding me of a dog. I took his slobbering personally and it made me want to rob him real good for getting whiffs of his stinking breath. He ran his hands over my breasts and tried to get his fingers inside my thong. As particular as I was, I briefly wondered if his hands were clean. But I was a big girl, playing big games, so I let that wolf-breath sucker rub and grope me until the cab stopped. After all, he was going to pay for all of the foreplay. We got out and there was no turning back when the cabbie pulled away from the curb and drove up the street. Fred started singing Frank Sinatra's "My Way" in a terrible pitch with half-closed eyes, dancing across the street like we had just come from a karaoke spot.

Fred waved me into the building as the doorman held the door open. Fred was so drunk, I wondered if he was going to do something extreme to attract attention to us but fortunately, he didn't. In the elevator, he went back to feeling me up, only this time, he whispered dumb shit to me as well; I guess he thought it would get me moist.

We finally made it to his apartment on the 32nd floor. Fred dug through his pants pockets and found the keys to the apartment. I followed him inside when he turned to me and said, "Welcome to *mi casa, senorita*." First, I was his African queen, then I was his Spanish *mamacita*. I guess we all did look alike, bless his drunken heart.

He tried to passionately kiss me, his breath still reeking of expensive liquor. The more I gave him, the more he wanted. Fred grabbed a remote control and his stereo system was soon playing "The Girl From Ipanema." Everything about his place spelled money. Sweet.

"You are so sexy. D'ya know that? You're so fuckin' sexy," he said, still slurring his words. He dropped his pants and began to jerk off. I was so disgusted! By then, I knew his hands weren't clean, the dirty-ass pervert.

"Come here, sexy. I wanna pop that black cherry," he moaned, still stroking his dick like he was in an Olympic jack-off contest. He was making me nauseous with that shit, and I thought of those women I watched in porn movies. Surely they couldn't have had good chemistry with all of their on-screen sex partners! I took a deep breath and figured, when in Rome, do what the Romans do. I swallowed my nausea and shimmied toward him.

"You want some of this, Big Daddy? You want some of this juicy cherry? Hmm?"

"Oh God, yes! Come give it to me. You're such a beautiful girl."

I stopped in front of him, peeling off each piece of clothing as I tried to block my actions from my mind.

"How about a drink first, though? It helps me to relax." I grinned in what I hoped was a convincing way. I stood completely nude. By the way he looked at me, his blue eyes glazed over, I could tell Fred had never seen black pussy before.

"The bar is over there." He pointed to a nearby corner. He was still staring at the bush between my legs and suddenly reached out to touch it cautiously. I guessed that was okay because had he done something I didn't like, I probably would've tried to break his hand.

"Fix me a drink too, baby," he said. "And dance for me when you come back. You like to dance, don't ya?"

Of course; all black people like to dance. I managed not to roll my eyes. "Yes, Daddy," I answered. Fred was making this entirely too easy for me. He closed his eyes and leaned way back in his chair, waiting to suck up another drink.

My mind raced through the next part of my trap. To the average observer, I was a neurotic female, obsessed with smelling one hundred percent fresh at all times; I carried a perfume spritzer in my purse for that very reason. That spritzer was really more like a vial, and its contents were the key to my success in robbing men. One of Ritchie's biggest clients was a veterinarian's assistant. As long as Ritchie kept a good discount running for him, I stayed supplied with Special K, otherwise known as ketamine. I liked like using the date rape drug because it worked quickly and effectively. Ketamine came in liquid or powder form, and I preferred using liquid because it had no smell or taste. It was pretty much untraceable, unless a physician specifically looked for it in your system. A couple of drops into almost any drink would have a victim knocked out for a couple of hours. The best part was that they wouldn't remember shit when they woke up. The important part was getting the dosage just right. Too much could kill someone, and I wasn't trying to do anything that deep.

I plucked the spritzer out of my purse and went to the bar. I plucked a glass off the shelf above the bar then poured a double shot from whatever was in the nearest crystal decanter. I sniffed the liquid: cognac. Four drops fell into the glass, and the magic spell was about to go to work.

By then I was slowly dancing to the sensual jazz music piping from his stereo. *I'm your private dancer, Fred, a dancer for your money,* I thought. I was actually starting to enjoy myself. I felt free and powerful as my hips moved and I charmed Fred. His eyes followed me again as he sipped his drink, like I was the best thing since sliced bread.

"God, you're so fuckin' sexy. I swear to God," he mumbled. He was such a clown. I wanted to laugh at him, but I kept my hips moving. I must admit, he hung in there like a champ. I wondered what was taking him so long to drop the glass and pass out. I stalled a little while longer, waiting for the spell to work. I played with my titties, rubbed my belly, thighs, and shoulders, then went back to my titties. I tugged on my nipples as he watched, transfixed. After he unbuttoned the top two buttons of his dress shirt, I suggested that he get cleaned up. I turned around, spread my legs and stuck a finger inside my pussy. I looked over my shoulder and watched Fred's eyes glaze over with lust.

"If you want some of this juicy, wet pussy, get ready to have some fun. I love to ride, *and* I'm sweet." I knew I was going to break Fred's heart when he realized that I didn't have sex with him, but I didn't feel one bit guilty. I plunged another finger into my wetness and winked. "Can you imagine how good I could fuck your brains out with all of this?" I arched my back like a cat ready to pounce, showing off my bubble butt. There was nothing not to love about the Brooklyn Bridge I was selling him. I instructed him to take a shower while I played with myself, to get our little party started.

When he stumbled out of the bedroom, I sent Ritchie a text and it was on. The biggest takes were usually more dangerous, and I had little time to waste. By the time Fred had managed to wrap a towel around his hairy butt, he fell out cold on the bed. I worked fast. I started with his wallet, which was packed with credit cards—including a Black American Express Card—and dropped it into my handbag. Next, I grabbed his wristwatch, a beautiful gold-and-diamond Rolex, and dropped it in the bag as well. Looking around the apartment, I figured I would have to quickly survey everything and take the most valuable items because frankly, Fred had a lot of shit. I wasn't interested in snagging the sculptures or the paintings; I didn't have enough time to plan for that move. Plus, I couldn't get all that shit out of the main doors without the doorman getting awfully suspicious. For scores like that, I called in my boy Ritchie.

I cleared all of the jewelry out of his bedroom, and all the cash my eyes could find. I felt a little guilty leaving Fred in his bed in his current state, but I couldn't indulge in a guilt trip. I had already wasted enough time in his condo, and I couldn't wait to get home and see what I had gotten away with. I quickly pulled a towel from my bag and wiped down every surface I may have touched in the apartment, including Fred's glass, the decanter, and the doorknob. I left the condo, threw a smile at the doorman, and left the building.

Ritchie scooped me up, calm, cool and collected. Since I left my car at the bar when we left, I had to go back and get it. One hour later, Ritchie and I were on an incredible high, so we decided to go back to his spot, pop some bottles, and smoke a little something to get even higher. I had never revealed to Pookie and Yolanda just how I made my money. They knew I liked to go out in the evening, and they still assumed I was living off of Ritchie's boundless generosity. That's how I was able to cover my ass for a long time. Inviting them over to celebrate my big catch was a no-no. It was just Ritchie and I, counting up our stash, dividing up our shares, and straight celebrating the rotten shit we'd done.

"A'ight, I got the wine," Ritchie said after I came out of the shower. I was wearing sweat pants and a T-shirt, the green-colored contact lenses I'd worn resting safely in their saline solution-filled case. I couldn't wait to clean my own ass after those men touched me in any way shape or form.

"Eew!" I grabbed the Pinot Grigio from Ritchie and examined the label. "Wine? They ain't have no Henny or nothin' in there?"

He popped me upside my head. "You little ghetto bunny. You know you gon' be twisted by the time we get to the bottom of that shit, so don't complain. You shoulda stolen some liquor too, you thief." He chuckled. "You ain't shit! You robbed that man blind."

"You ain't shit either, Ritchie."

We both laughed.

"If I was such a ghetto bunny, I couldn't have picked out a gullible motherfucker with class and cash," I bragged.

"Yeah, I guess your background did come in handy."

He pressed two twenties into my palm. I immediately held them up to my nose, inhaling the scent of the bills. "What's this for?"

"Save these. If you ever need an incentive to keep pimping these men, think of the way you put it down tonight."

He handed me two Dutches. I walked over to the couch and sat down while Ritchie looked for some matches. I joined him on the living room floor after he found them. Ritchie turned on the TV and his PS2 and started up *NBA Live*.

"Is that all you ever play, nigga? I mean, really."

He shrugged and poured me a glass of wine. "It's either this or *Mortal Kombat*. And you ain't nicer than me in that shit."

I sucked my teeth. "You wanna bet?" Ritchie smiled and handed me a controller.

Two-thirds of the Pinot Grigio, a pepperoni pizza, and two blunts later, I was using the very last of my lives to try to finish off Ritchie. Honestly, he was busting my ass, but I refused to give up and have him call me a loser. I put all my faith into what was left of Jade's strength, drop-kicked Jarek, then twisted him until I broke his neck. It was a lucky win, but a win regardless.

"Yes! Yes!" I screamed, jumping up in the air like a twelfth-grade cheerleader. Because I was a female who had just beaten a dude at a video game, I got the typical reaction from Ritchie.

"What! You can't be fuckin' serious!" He flung the controller across the room and tackled me into the couch, then started beating me over the head with the pillows while shouting, "You can't be fuckin' serious!" I laughed so hard, I thought I was going to have a heart attack.

We were having so much fun that we didn't peep Ritchie's new girl-friend, Tatiana, watching us have our innocent fun. I hadn't cared much for Tatiana since I first laid eyes on her, nor did she care for me. She was one of those bitches with eye, mouth and hand problems, and I was the type of bitch who had just the remedy for them. She eyeballed the liquor, and blunts, added our wrestling match, and let her imagination get the best of her insecure ass.

"What's this shit all about?" she snapped.

"Same shit, different toilet," Ritchie replied. "We're just chilling. How'd you get in?"

"I see that you're chilling, plus some extra shit . . . obviously!" She threw a key at Ritchie. "Don't worry about how I got in. I'm your girl-friend. I knocked and got no answer, so I let myself if."

"You took my key?" Ritchie frowned, looked at me, then back at Tatiana. "I told you when we met that I had a roommate. I don't under-stand why you gotta be all like this now."

"Did you neglect to mention the sex of your roommate when we had this discussion?" Tatiana knew that Ritchie had a habit of leaving out information *he* didn't think was particularly important.

Ritchie shrugged. "I didn't think it was gonna be no big deal. Now you tryna act like I'm tryna play you or somethin'."

Tatiana put her hands on her hips and glared at him. "Leaving out the fact that your roommate is a female, and y'all up in here getting high and drunk and wrestling and shit . . . I might have been born early, but I stayed up all night."

I sat back, slit open another Dutch, removed the tobacco, and added some weed. I was content to let the drama unfold around me. It was better than a soap opera.

"You ain't my mama," Ritchie snarled at Tatiana. She started swelling up like a toad and I chuckled a little at the sight. "You ain't gonna spoil my night."

I shook my head and fired up the blunt. Tatiana had to be trained. Ritchie had to teach the bitch that just because she was his girl, that the world didn't revolve around or stop for her. In the grand scheme of things, she didn't fucking matter. What I *did* mind, though, was how this bitch was acting like I didn't belong in my own house. Well, technically it was Ritchie's house, but I made my contribution in other ways than rent, so I could call it my house too.

Tatiana kept it going. "Why you ain't call me?"

I saw Ritchie's body tense up and knew the arguing was going to start soon. It was only a matter of time, and I was ready to see what the cause was going to be this time.

"What the *fuck*, Tatiana!" he shouted. He stood and loomed over Tatiana's 5'4" frame. "Um, because I was planning on callin' you at the end of the night, like I always do."

Tatiana sucked her teeth and cut her eyes at me. "I see you got time for everybody *but* me."

Ritchie looked down and bit his bottom lip. He was trying hard not to let her shake him and ruin our celebration. I wanted to tell her to shut the fuck up for him, but I took another puff of the blunt and stayed out of business that wasn't mine.

"Tati," he said.

"Yes?"

"You here, right?"

"I am now, but not 'cause you called me to come over."

Ritchie ignored that part. "So if you here, why you complaining? You actin' like I told you not to come. As a matter of fact, you cutting into Honey's time, because we was just chillin' tonight. So if you gonna be here, be here. If you not, you not, a'ight?"

Ooh! What did he say that for? Tatiana sucked her teeth so hard, I thought they were going to come out of her gums. "I wanna talk to you in the other room, please."

He passed the last of the older blunt to me. "Do you mind, ma, while I go . . ." he trailed off.

I acted as nonchalant as possible. "Nah, go right ahead. Give me some time to practice my moves." I smiled my biggest smile at him. Tatiana knew what would happen to her if them eyes rolled, so they stayed in her head properly as they walked into the bedroom. As soon as the door shut, I heard her go off.

"You knew I was fuckin' comin'! I been tellin' you all week I was comin' on Friday! So why that bitch gotta be here?"

"First of all, her name ain't 'that bitch.' Her name is Honey. She don't disrespect you, so I would appreciate it if you didn't disrespect her. She's also my business partner."

"Just her bein' here is disrespectful! What the fuck is wrong with her that she gotta be livin' with you? She can't get no apartment?"

I laughed to myself because I could see Ritchie in my mind, waving his hands above his head to get her attention. "Hello! I live with her too! We roommates. What the fuck is wrong with you, yo?"

Meanwhile, I cracked my knuckles, hoping Tatiana called me a bitch one more time. It was amazing to me how much shit she popped when she was out of my eyesight, yet silence reigned when I entered a room. That was one of my main problems with her. She was as fake as that horse hair on her head.

"Why she can't move out? Huh? Why she can't move out? That's why the fuck you be tellin' me I can't spend the night here? You be fuckin' that bitch regular, huh?"

"I'm sick of playing all of these games! How many times I got to tell you that me and Honey don't roll like that? She does her thing, I do mine. All we do is live and make some moves together. I ain't gonna keep explaining this shit to you, Tatiana, and I ain't gonna keep defendin' my best friend every time you feel like being insecure. You got a problem with her, take it up with her."

"Good idea. Maybe I will," she retorted. The door swung open. Tatiana could've stood to lose the twenty pounds that jiggled as she moved. I had finished the last of the blunt and was working my way through a Newport when she stomped back out to the living room. She stood directly in front of the screen and only instinct made me press pause. Otherwise, the judo kick on the screen—directed at my head—would have killed me. I leaned to the side to continue my game around her oddly-shaped hips. "Uh, do you mind?" I asked sweetly.

"Can I ask you something?" The hood rat in her made "ask" sound like *aks*, and I knew this was going to be the first and last conversation we ever had.

I shrugged. "It's a free country." I still played around her body. She finally got the hint that she wasn't going to get eye contact and moved the fuck over. *Thank you very fucking much, bitch.*

"Is you and Ritchie sleeping together?"

"Nah. He got his own bed, the last time I checked," I replied.

I saw her fold her arms through my peripheral vision. "So y'all ain't never fucked? That's what you tellin' me?"

"Is that what you're asking?"

"Don't play games with me," Tatiana threatened in the most menacing voice she could muster. It took the greater majority of my strength and willpower not to get up and lay her ass out, so I took it out on my opponent in the game. I wanted to do one of those uppercuts on her that had the game opponents flipping backward through the air. Then I would've added a combo kick, or some crazy shit like that. At that point, our conversation would have been over.

"As you've been told time and time again, out relationship is strictly platonic. To sleep with him would be like sleeping my own brother, if I had one. Since you don't believe what your man is telling you, *I* don't know what to tell you," I said.

Ritchie reappeared and had calmed down a bit. Then he put it plain and simple to Tatiana, as only Ritchie could. "See, this is why Honey is the only female I ever *could* live with. She doesn't put me through all of this lip like you do."

Lord, why did he tell her that?

"What the fuck you mean, the only bitch you could live with?" Tatiana's neck started rolling and she waved her finger in the air accordingly. "What the fuck you tryna say? I'm good enough for you to fuck, but I ain't good enough to live with you? Fuck you and that bitch!" She stomped around and grabbed her handbag, muttering all kinds of "bitches" and "hoes" under her breath. She had yet to say "fuck you" to my face, because she knew it would be straight to the Laundromat for her ass if she ever did.

What I didn't get about Tatiana was the fact that she was *sooo* fucking stupid. I hadn't liked her from the day we'd met, granted, but since Ritchie liked her on some crazy level, I decided to pretend for his sake. I tried to be polite, respectful, and to give her some breathing room, but nothing I did mattered. It got to the point where I would leave the apartment before she came over, so neither one of us would have to see each other. She had to act like a junior high school bitch. And to top it off, I guess she got my number out of Ritchie's phone one day because suddenly I was getting prank calls on my cell. I wasn't too pleased about it, but I dealt with it because I wasn't entirely sure it was her. Every time I answered, I got a hang-up.

Ritchie sat back down next to me and grabbed his controller, starting us up a fresh game. "You finished embarrassing yourself for one night?" he asked Tatiana.

"We ain't done! If y'all are just friends, how come you let her disrespect me? If you don't tell her to go right now, I'mma walk. I'm tired of this bitch flirting with you in front of my face, too."

Oh, no she didn't. "Let's not go there," I snapped. "Do you think he's rich? You get what you get, partly because of me. The fake nails, the fake hair, the money it takes to feed your ass, is partially compliments of yours truly. Ritchie and I make it do what it do together, so get your panties out of your funky crack and shut the fuck up!"

Ritchie added, "If you feel like stayin', then stay but if you do, I ain't gonna be listening to that nagging shit all night. I was in a good mood until you showed up."

Tatiana was appalled that he dared speak to her that way. She grabbed her jacket and left, making sure to slam the door loudly behind her. We hadn't officially scrapped yet, but I knew that if something didn't give, it would be just a matter of time. That's when I decided it would be best if I got my own place. Not because Tatiana said so, but just because it was

time.

Chapter Eleven

CAUGHT ME BY SURPRISE

When Tatiana realized that I'd moved into my own apartment, it enabled Ritchie and I to get more business done for a minute. She wasn't crying no rivers over me relocating, no doubt. She felt like she'd won and did everything but click her cheap-ass heels. That chick was small potatoes, so I just rolled my eyes and kept things moving. The first order of business was, well, more business. As a side hustle, to bring in a little extra profit each month, Ritchie started dealing weed and coke. He usually traveled only within the tri-state area but every now and then, he got an offer to go to California that he couldn't refuse. When the extra money began to pique my interest, he began teaching me the finer ways of transporting and not so long after that, a very large, lucrative deal came our way. I smuggled some product just one time. I was scared as hell, and it really wasn't my thing, although I did make $20,000 off the deal. It was probably for the best that my new endeavor got cut short. There was an opportunity to make more with some heavy hitters but a certain someone went running her mouth, so the next opportunity to make bigger money went flying down the drain.

Ritchie's spot got hot because of that God damned Tatiana. When they had one of their infamous fights, all of a sudden police showed up at his door with a warrant. I was glad my ass was long gone, and I also was glad he didn't have any hot shit or drugs stashed in his apartment at the time. Ritchie decided to lay low after that and. I decided to lay off after that, although I did have some weed stashed at my place. If Tatiana would jeopardize her cash flow, she sure as hell would fuck up mine. Had Ritchie been arrested, that could've been just the thing to get some real foul shit popping, for real. And worse than that, even if he broke up with Tatiana for good, she knew too many trade secrets. The left hand should never let the right hand know what it was doing, especially if it involved breaking the law! To make matters worse, since she hated me, Tatiana would've put my name at the front of everything.

≈※≈

When Yolanda told first told me the news about her baby, I didn't say anything because I couldn't believe what I had heard. I looked down at the phone to make sure I wasn't dreaming and then said, "Come again?"

"Oh God, Honey, you're gonna make me repeat myself? I know you heard me."

"Oh, I heard it. I just don't believe it."

"Well, it's true. The doctor confirmed it on Wednesday. He said my due date should be January 12th."

"You're really not shittin' me, Yo?"

"Would I lie about something like this, Honey? Seriously."

"Congratulations then, skank! Whose is it?"

"Carlos's. He's so happy."

I managed to refrain from sucking my teeth when I heard that. I had a feeling, no, I fucking *knew* that dumb-ass nigga was gonna get her knocked up. Carlos was the latest in a series of Yolanda's boy toys, but she felt that he was "The One." I didn't bother to tell her he was a scumbag that was using her for her apartment and her pussy because she wouldn't believe me if I did. I know I had a nerve to talk about relationships after my history, but if getting a hot meal at Wendy's and some good dick every other night equaled love, Carlos and Yo should have gotten married.

Despite all of that, Yolanda still had a man. For the first time in a long time, I felt a twinge of jealousy, and I almost wanted to have someone in my life, for real. I had to check myself because I was sure I was hating a little something extra since Mikaylo didn't want our child, and it just didn't seem fair. I did want Yo to be happy and if the baby did it for her, then more power to her. I wasn't going to talk down about my friend in her time of joy. She was my sister in spirit and it wasn't in my nature to judge her. I just hoped she didn't have a repeat episode of what happened to me.

"I'm happy for you, ma," I lied. "I hope this works out better than what happened with Justice."

"Why are you bringing up Justice? Yeah, he beat the shit out of me on a regular basis and caused me to end up miscarrying three months later, but things will be different this time. Carlos is not Justice," she defended.

"I'm sorry. You're right." She had more faith in Carlos than I did. The last time Justice acted a fool with Yolanda, Ritchie found out and got one of his boys to help him dole out a little justice of his own. After that, a sucker named Jihad got Yolanda pregnant and his constant lying and cheating stressed her to the point of dehydration and insomnia, so that poor little baby gave up the ghost as well. I really hoped the third time would the charm, plus Ritchie was not in the market to give no more ass whippings.

I listened to her rave about that damned Carlos, as usual. Hearing Yolanda tell me about the baby forced my mind back to a house in Georgia, where two lesbians were raising my baby girl. I thought briefly about Kyashira and then tried my hardest to get her out of my mind. I had written and forwarded a brief letter to the pair, but I just hadn't gathered enough courage to call to follow up, after I didn't hear anything in return. I informed them of my move and also sent updated contact information. Although I still had the number, I felt a call was inappropriate under the circumstances. I never ever bothered to get my GED, I never returned to visit, and I chewed Mikaylo the hell out when my mother died. I didn't exactly deserve any Mother of the Year awards. Part of the reason I didn't return to school was shame, part of it was just because I was chicken. I had become the woman who didn't take care of her own child. I never purchased clothes or toys to send to my daughter. I never sent money, or asked for a single picture of her. Plus, given my current "occupation," it was hard to consider cleaning all the mess in my personal life. Nevertheless, I considered reaching out. I'd written a few letters over the years, but not many.

After thinking about Yo and her baby, I decided to call Jessie and Paula to check on my own child. My palms suddenly felt clammy, and my heart began to race. In fact, I had to take a few deep breaths to calm myself down. Not knowing what to expect scared me. I didn't know if Jessie and Paula would be angry at me for not taking an active role in Kyashira's life, or if I'd find out that Kyashira didn't remember me at all. The longer I waited, the more scenarios made me even more nervous than I already was. I finally stopped stalling and managed to place the call.

An automated message came on. "We're sorry, but the number you dialed has been disconnected or is no longer in service. Please try your call again. Thank you."

Maybe I didn't dial it right, I told myself. *Let me try again.*

With shaky hands, I redialed the numbers. The same message came on.

"What!" I yelled, alarmed. I felt angry and confused. "Where is my baby? What's happened?" I sat down in a chair and dropped my head. "Oh God, please let Kyashira be okay," I prayed aloud, rubbing my temples.

I felt the weight of my actions—or non-actions—fall onto my shoulders. As usual, avoidance became my way to cope. I didn't know what to do. I decided I'd deal with issue later, because I just wasn't ready to face the truth just yet, whatever the truth was. I was both stressed out and angry with myself. Instead of club hopping and robbing niggas, I did try to hang out with Ritchie one more time. I just wanted to be with someone who would understand, but of course, bad got worse.

Chapter Twelve

DIAMONDS ARE A GIRL'S BEST FRIEND

Tatiana and Ritchie were beefing again, and that drove me to toss more liquor back than I'd intended. It turned out that they didn't break up for good after all. Trying to spend time with my friend only threw me right in the middle of more shit. The way I felt, I needed that like I needed a hole in the head.

Ritchie called to ask if I wanted to come over and hang out with the crew. I was in his kitchen, marinating chicken and rolling up ground beef for the burgers. Yolanda had come over to help me, so were both in the kitchen rolling meat balls.

"That skank ain't got nowhere else to eat?" Tatiana said, as soon as she appeared and saw me.

"Now, what's your problem? She's just visiting," Ritchie explained.

"You always do this shit to me, Ritchie! You never said she was going to be here."

I motioned to Yolanda that I was done. It was time to go. I was not trying to swing on Ritchie's hood rat that night. I swear, I could have killed Ritchie with my bare hands for keeping her around.

"I can't go through this anymore," I told Ritchie. "I'm out. Peace."

Yolanda followed me in silence.

"No, Honey. You don't have to go," Ritchie insisted. "You don't either, Yolanda."

"Only a dog wants a bone! No skinny skank is going to shake my self-esteem, thinking she can push up on my man! Fuckin' skinny-ass bitch," Tatiana commented.

It was all I needed. Yolanda must've known what I was about to do because she quickly backed up, out of the line of fire. I pulled my fist back as far as I could and launched it into Tatiana's face. The first hit was like the first shot of whisky after a long week of work. I wanted another. My left fist took over for my right, and then they took turns as Tatiana collapsed to the ground. I fell on top of her, punching as hard as I could. I saw blood, and that was all I needed. Ritchie tried to drag me off her so I let him, but not without a handful of the bitch's store-bought hair in my fist. It wouldn't come out of her head, so he ended up dragging both of us. Reggie, another friend, pried her weave out of my hands and helped lift me off Tatiana. Well, I thought it was a weave but she happened to be sporting a wig that day and the entire thing came right off, revealing her short, dry dome. Yolanda stood in the background, chuckling.

"Honey!" Ritchie shouted at me. My chest heaved up and down and I was shaking from the adrenaline rush. I looked down at my hands; they, too, were shaking, and bloody to boot. I looked down at my victim and felt a sickening sense of satisfaction.

Tatiana lay in a bloody heap at Ritchie's feet. He helped her wipe the blood off her face. He made her hold her head back and shoved about fifty napkins under her bleeding nose.

Yolanda couldn't hold her laughter in any longer and laughed out loud. "Stop laughing, Yolanda. This ain't funny!" Ritchie snapped. Tatiana continued to lay on the ground, bloody, bald, and moaning in pain.

"I'm not in it. I'm just an innocent bystander." She chuckled and walked to the door. "You comin', Honey?"

"My wig! Get my wig, Ritchie," Tatiana told him.

For the first time ever, she actually sounded humble. I watched him retrieve it from Reggie and put it back on for her, but she got no sympathy votes from me. The way I saw it, everyone should've been standing on my side of the fight. She had had it coming for a long time and now that it had happened, it felt *so* good.

"Now I can leave too," I said. I just shook my head. I was going to keep it moving, but guess who took up for her?

"I'm just so glad you felt the need to do that shit," Ritchie said harshly. "Hitting my girl wasn't right."

I just looked at him like he was crazy. "Oh, so this is my fault now?"

"Hell yeah, it's your fault! All you had to do was exercise a little self-control, and you couldn't even do that for me."

Now I was *really* getting mad.

"A little self-control? What the fuck you think I been exercising since I met that bitch? Every move I made has been out of self-control. She's fucking lucky it took this long."

He shook his head. "Why does everything always have to be about you, Honey? Why you can't ever make sacrifices for anybody else?"

I walked out of the door. Ritchie followed me into the hallway. I turned around and gave him some more food for thought.

"Me putting up with her and her bullshit has been a sacrifice enough. When that bitch comes here, I'm not even welcome. I even moved out. I been walkin' on eggshells since the first day she came here, and now she's getting her just desserts. Now why is that my fault?"

Ritchie shook his head like he didn't want to hear it. "What the fuck did she say, huh? What did she say to you?"

Was he deaf, or just stupid? "You didn't hear her?"

"No, I didn't hear her. If I'da heard her, I'da checked her myself, don't you think? I been checkin' her this long. Do you think I'm just gonna stand there and let her play you in front of me? What the fuck did she say?"

I rolled my eyes toward the ceiling. "She called me a skinny-ass bitch who was trying to push up on her man."

Ritchie's look was incredulous. "That's all she said?"

"Yeah."

He glowered and I cringed for a second because I really thought that he was gonna hit me. "Honey, I call you a bitch every day!"

"So? That's you. Me and you go way back. She don't have that right."

Ritchie threw his hands in the air, exasperated. "Look how y'all was treatin' her! Y'all ain't even bother to make her feel comfortable. Did y'all even give her a chance?"

"A chance to what, Ritchie? Open her mouth and put her fuckin' foot in it, like she always do? Don't none of us like the stupid ho."

He just leaned forward and said very quietly, "Fuck you."

I stepped back because the words hit me like one of my fists had hit Tatiana earlier. "Excuse me?" I asked. Ritchie had never said those words to me seriously, and never in that utterly final tone.

"You heard me, Honey. Fuck you!" He turned around and walked back into his apartment. He slammed the door shut behind him.

It was close to midnight when my cell phone rang. I didn't answer it, nor did I ever feel the same about my boy again. Our business ventures were over. I was getting ready to paint the town instead. Fuck the dumb shit. It was time to go hard again, and focus on making money. I decided Ritchie was pussy whipped, and I moved the hell on with my own operation. He knew I'd always love him like a brother, but when it came to business, I wasn't going to let anyone or anything stand in my way.

❈

I knew that if I kept hitting men on a robbery tip, my luck would run out way too fast. I wasn't sure how I was going to upgrade my game until the solution fell right my lap, compliments of a sugar daddy named Sammie Lee. Successful and generous men who wanted to treat me like a princess were more my speed. At some point, I revised my plan to make money, although the clubs and bars were still good places for good pickings. I perched on various barstools around the city as a means of starting up conversation. I got free dinners and flattened some wallets in the process.

I worked out a deal with Larry, the owner of a spot called Club Deep: I got him good weed, and he got me the inside scoop on regulars he knew something about. Club Deep became my home base. I never stood in line, had a table at the club any time I wanted it, and broke Larry off with a little sumthin' sumthin' every time I made a score on one of the cats he told me about. It was a perfect solution for getting rid of what I had at my apartment. Larry liked to relax by taking a smoke or two, so he was happy to agree to the deal. Fucking him was out of the question, though. The last thing I wanted was static from him, when I was out to get with other men. I mainly used my table when I was looking to snag a new target.

That night, it was early still, only eleven-thirty, which was more than enough time to plan my entrance and exit for the evening festivities. Before long I met the mark, who turned out to be more than my usual grab-and-dash victim.

There was a line almost around the corner when I got to the club. I parked down the street, knowing the clubgoers had a habit of leaning up against whatever car they could find and I wasn't having it, even if my shiny pearl white 2007 Infiniti G35 wasn't the new car I really did want. I set my alarm and slung my purse over my shoulder, as I walked down the street toward the club.

I could hear the music blaring loudly from the street and I smiled, inhaling deeply. I psyched myself up for the thrill of another night at work. I walked right up to Jamal the bouncer and held out my hand for him to shake.

He chuckled. "Girl, you're a mess."

"Hey." I gave him a hug and kiss.

"You ready to party tonight?"

"Hell yeah!" I winked at Jamal. "You still got me, right?"

"Get your fine ass through the door."

I discreetly slipped a $100 thank-you package into his jacket pocket. He moved the velvet rope out of my way and directed me inside, much to the chagrin of those still in the line. I heard some girls suck their teeth and mutter something about a "stupid bitch." I couldn't resist turning to the girl; I stuck out my tongue before disappearing into the club.

My first stop was the bar. I gently shoved my way through the crowd before I found empty seats at the end of the bar.

"Hey, ma," someone said. "What you sippin' on? I got you."

I acted like I didn't hear the guy. I sucked my teeth, irritated that it was that crowded. Too many fake rappers, producers, baby daddies who snuck out, and chickenheads with cheap shoes and scary weaves. I planned to order a drink and head to my special table. I knew that the bartenders and waitresses were working overtime, and I wanted a damn drink fast. Just after I'd ordered a Shotgun, a man stood close to me. He watched me knock half of it off in one swig. Then I asked for a Heineken chaser. He was impressed and intimidated at the same time.

"You got a strong stomach there, huh?" he asked.

I resisted the urge to ask him who the fuck he thought he was talking to. Then he turned in the light and I got a good chance to size him up. The chocolate brown Lothario at my right-hand side was about as perfect a mark as I was going to make tonight. It meant I didn't have to spend most of the evening scanning the club. Yes, he had come directly to me.

"Cast iron. What about it, baby?" I replied, taking another sip of my beer.

The man held his hand out. "I'm Sammie."

"Honey," I answered, shaking his hand.

"You've got beautiful fingers. You play piano?"

I smiled and blushed softly. That question reminded me of my childhood, and of my mother saying that I needed to practice my piano before my lesson. I pushed the memories aside. "No. No, I don't."

"So what brings you out here tonight, Honey?" Sammie Lee leaned closer so I could hear him over the roar of the crowd. That was sexy, since most men tried to yell above the music and conversations. Up close, I noticed his smooth skin and neatly maintained dreads. Sexy wasn't the word. I wasn't sure about that damn name Sammie Lee, but the brother was very easy on the eyes.

"Just relaxing. It's been a long week." By that time, I had also scoped out his high-top Prada sneakers, True Religion jeans, Sean John chocolate brown velvet blazer, and a beautiful TechnoMaster watch on his left hand. The conversation was worth continuing. I had a feeling he wouldn't be a waste of time.

"It's been pretty rough for me, too."

"So what is it that you do?

I shrugged and swirled a finger around in my scotch. "It depends on what mood I'm in. I'm sometimes an independent retailer, sometimes

I'm a masseuse, other times I just lay back and let my roommate pay the bills."

You know they say there's much truth found in a joke. I thought it would break the ice, and Sammie Lee did seem to find it funny, although he asked me an odd question.

"Don't you have dreams and aspirations?"

"Of course I do." I pulled my finger out of my drink and sucked it seductively. Sammie Lee laughed again, then rubbed his chin.

By the time the last call for alcohol came, Sammie Lee made his move.

"What do you say we finish these drinks and get out of here?" he said.

It sounded good to me. He moved quickly but the faster he went, the faster I could get paid. Sammie Lee slipped some cash onto the bar to pay for our drinks. I winked at him then followed him out of the club. He was driving a silver Mercedes. When he slipped behind the wheel, he motioned for me to follow him. I don't know what happened, but I had a change of heart. I got that empty feeling again, and I wanted to try something a little different. Experience taught me that I didn't want to come off too easy or too scandalous, so I slowed my roll just a little bit. I got out of my car and went to talk to him.

"You know what? I think I'd like to take a rain check. We just met, and I don't want to give you the wrong impression."

Sammie Lee got out of his car when he realized that I wouldn't be tagging along.

"I understand," Sammie Lee replied. "It's just that you seemed different. I mean, you have a different air about you than any woman I've ever met. Every little thing about you intrigues me. I don't know anything about you, of course, but I plan on spending the better part of my future days trying to figure you out."

To take my mind off how quickly and easily I was becoming attracted to him, I kept trying to figure out his yearly salary. Oddly enough, for the very first time, I didn't want to steal any of it. I didn't know what to do. I stood in front of the perfect target, and I didn't rob him. I actually liked him. What the hell was going on?

"I'm sorry to back out, and I'm not trying to assume you wanted to have sex with me. Just in case, though, I'm not into one-night stands." I shrugged, then smiled sweetly. "I'm very picky. I guess I just got caught up in the moment. Don't get me wrong though, I think you're a very sexy man."

Sammie Lee stared deeply into my eyes. "I'm not into one-night stands either. I know this may sound like a line, but it's not what you think. I want to get to know you beyond tonight, if that's what you want. I know you don't know me, but all I can say is the choice will be yours. I'm not into games."

Sammie Lee sounded real good, but he also sounded real smooth. Too smooth.

He must have sensed my apprehension because he said, "How about I visit at a decent hour, in a neutral place? That will keep us both out of trouble."

I reached in my purse and scribbled down my number and name. I was playing hard to get, and I was waiting to find out if my next line would be a turn on, or a turn off. "Call me. I would love to hear from you."

He took my hand and kissed it. "It's been a pleasure."

I tried to ignore the tingle on the back of my hand where he kissed me, so I turned around to walk back to my car.

"Honey, please don't leave. We can just sit up and talk if you want to. I really would love to have your company. Please," Sammie Lee said.

I paused, and Sammie Lee grabbed me abruptly and kissed me on the cheek. He took the piece of paper out of my hand and ripped up my number.

"Say yes," he urged. "Now, I have no way of getting in touch with you, and I have a business proposition for you too."

"I don't know what all of that means, but you win, Sammie," I said, smiling.

He grinned. "Good. You won't regret it."

Our conversation took about twenty minutes, but I felt the time investment was worth it. I didn't want to seem too easy or too eager to get with Sammie. As I started up my car, I was sure he got the message. Curiosity got the best of me, too. I wondered what business proposition Sammie Lee had in store for me.

Sammie Lee invited me to his condo on the Upper East Side. It was a relatively new building— the type with a concierge who eyeballed everyone who entered until they either came correct or left. Apparently Sammie Lee was loaded, and I drank in my surroundings as we stepped onto the elevator. As soon as the polished doors shut out the world around us, his hands were all over me.

"Slow down," I told him.

"I'm sorry, baby. You're right."

The elevator pinged at his floor. He picked me up and carried me. I laughed, surprised at how strong he was.

"You better not drop me!" I joked as he stumbled a little near the front door. Sammie Lee put me down and stuck his key into the lock. We made it inside and slammed the door behind us.

"Wait, wait, hold on!" Sammie Lee picked me up again, which began to feel like some sort of erotic foreplay.

"Will you stop playing? Put me down!" I insisted, laughing again. "I need another drink."

"We can talk over drinks," he agreed. "Make yourself comfortable."

We sat in the living room and I did my best to get comfortable on one of the plush suede couches. When Sammie Lee returned with two glasses and a bottle of Chardonnay, I thought of all of the times I'd drugged men. I was glad the bottle of wine was sealed. It was all good!

We drank some wine before he finally started talking.

"You seem like my kind of girl."

"Maybe, maybe not," I flirted.

"I'm sure you probably get this a lot," he started as he took my hand, "but you are absolutely stunning. You're beautiful. To be honest, I think you may be the most beautiful woman I've ever met."

Even though it sounded like some of the biggest bullshit I'd ever heard, this man had me fucking blushing, and I didn't blush over men. I made *them* blush. "I do get that lot. But none of them have ever meant it. So, thank you," I answered shyly. What the hell was he doing to me?

Sammie Lee sat back and made himself comfortable. "I guess this is a good time to get to the point. Like I told you before, I'm not interested in a one-night stand. This may sound strange, but I'm looking for a mistress. I want what I want, and I'm willing to compensate well for it."

Wow. He certainly didn't waste any time. "You're married?"

"Yeah, I'm married." Sammie Lee sighed. "It's not what you may think, though. My wife and I don't have a quality relationship. I'm working my way out of the situation but for the time being, I'd like to have someone special who can understand."

He sure could shovel the bullshit. "Let's get straight to the point. What would be in it for me?"

"What wouldn't be in it for you? I've thought this out well, and I can afford the luxury. If I couldn't, I wouldn't try it."

Sammie Lee popped the cork of the wine bottle as he went on to explain that he was a high-profile investment broker for a prominent investment banking firm. He also told me that he'd graduated *summa cum laude* from Harvard Business School. He loved football and basketball, and his favorite teams were the Giants and the Lakers, respectively. His favorite food was shrimp Parmesan and his favorite beer was Guinness.

"I hate to interrupt, but I need to use the bathroom," I told Sammie, grabbing my purse.

"It's the first door on the left."

"Okay. I'll be right back." I smiled. I knew that Sammie Lee was watching me walk away. I could feel his eyes studying my body, so I put a little extra dip in my hips.

Once inside the bathroom, I turned on the water for effect. I whipped out my cell phone and sent Larry a text. I sat on top of the toilet lid and waited. I hoped he wouldn't take too long replying, all depending on what was going on at Club Deep.

DO U KNOW THAT GUY SAMMIE LEE I WAS WITH? ANSWR ASAP!

About five minutes later, I heard back from him.

A LITTLE.

IS HE LEGIT?

WRKS 4 INVSTMT FIRM. MARRIED. NVR SEEN WIFEY.

WORTH MY TIME?

DON'T KNOW. SPENDS WELL HERE. ALWYS ALONE. ALL I KNOW.

THNKS! C U SOON.

PEACE.

I shoved my cell phone in my purse, flushed the toilet, and turned off the water. I also remembered to plaster a smile on my face.

"I'm back," I told Sammie.

After we talked a while, Sammie Lee mentioned that his Mercedes was paid for. So far, his story was matching up with Larry's, although Larry couldn't tell me much about him. I decided to stay and take my chances. Plus, a part of me was attracted to him anyway.

"What does an investment broker do?" I asked.

"I work in the Global Wealth Management division."

"Doing what, exactly?"

"I provide advisory services and assist buyers and sellers of stocks. I periodically fly to other countries and help our investors manage their funds. Sometimes we do webcam and conference calls, but clients feel more secure to see my face every now and then. On the upside, it's so much more fun to say 'I flew to Tokyo today' than 'I called Tokyo today.'"

Hmm. A world traveler. I could travel with him and he could write it off as a business expense. Sammie's proposition was looking sweeter and sweeter. "Well, if you're gone so much, then where does this leave us?"

"Let's talk details. I prefer that you live here, so that I can have full access to you. No company, under any circumstances. When I want to see you, I expect that you would make yourself available to me, although you would be free to come and go as you please. Discretion is a must. I'm big on loyalty. Keep this to yourself, and never come looking for my family. No stress from you, no drama." He paused. "Sex is a must, of course."

"I don't know. This sounds like a job. I'm not sure it's beneficial to get involved with a man who can't commit," I hedged. Big fish must be reeled in slowly. I couldn't rush it.

"That's why you will get paid. I'll make sure it is beneficial for you . . . if I get what I want."

My interest piqued at the sound of "get paid." "So, what's this job of yours pay?"

"That's a good question." He nodded in approval. "I see you're a businesswoman at heart. I like that. I'll be right back, Honey."

He left the room. I sat and pondered his proposition. I'd never been a kept woman, and that's exactly what I would be for Sammie Lee should I accept his proposal. On one hand, I wouldn't mind not having to hustle for my next score. On the other hand, giving up my freedom to be with whoever I chose, whenever I chose, was not something I took lightly.

Sammie Lee returned and placed a manila envelope in my hands. I looked at it, then him curiously. "Open it," he urged. I did so and my eyes almost popped out of my head as I stared at the banded stacks of $100 bills. There were ten stacks in all.

"If you accept my business proposition, this is all yours. Consider it advance pay to prove that I'm serious. I'll take care of your living expenses, and you'll earn the rest as we go along. If you want to verify my employment status, Google me. I'm not hard to find. Don't worry; I can afford you."

I held the $10,000 in my hands, trying not to seem impressed. Of course, he could have just banded a $100 bill along with cut-up stacks of paper to make it look like $10,000.

As if reading my mind, he confirmed, "There's $10,000 there. If you don't believe me, count it. That's just a start." He leaned forward and stared at me earnestly. "You will have the time of your life, if you agree to the arrangement. So, is your answer to this yes or no?"

Valerie didn't raise a fool. "Yes," I replied. A rush of excitement invaded my body.

"Great."

I was soon butt naked on the couch.

With the first touch of Sammie's wanting fingertips, I shuddered. He gripped my naked shoulders as he studied my frame. His hands wandered down the length of my arms, right down to my fingertips. Then he gently stroked my right thigh as a single finger from his left hand crept into my pussy. He moved it back and forth a while until I shuddered again. My hard nipples tingled, begging for attention. I let my eyes close as Sammie Lee suckled my breast like a newborn baby. I'd be lying if I said I didn't like it. While the few men I'd been with didn't waste time plunging straight into my ocean, Sammie Lee took his time. That delicious piece of chocolate started licking between my breasts, then his slow, precise tongue stopped at my belly button. He moved his head back and forth as he gently nipped at my skin with his teeth, then he started licking my skin again.

"Goddamn, Honey! You taste so good. I love the way you smell," he moaned. I could see his arousal through his boxer shorts.

"Mmmmm!" I moaned in agreement.

It was usually against my new rule to let him know that I was enjoying anything, but fuck that rule! My legs slid open and his lips tickled the top of my clit. Sammie Lee placed my hand on his erection. It was stiff and big and I bit my lip as I explored the warm, hard rod with my hands. I had a grown man on my hands; his ass was no Mikaylo, which was a good thing.

"Come here, Papa. You're my new Daddy," I purred in a silky voice. I pushed him back onto the couch and slid off his boxers so I could cradle his dick in my hands, studying its length and girth. I rubbed it tenderly and patiently, my hands moving up and down the length of his ten inches. I watched his body relax and the tension in his face vanish. I could tell a fresh wave of pleasure took hold of him as his hands fell to his side. Sammie's chest moved up and down slowly as I sat up and rubbed his dick against my cheeks and lips.

"Suck it," he instructed.

Instead, I gave him three slow and torturous pecks—one between his balls and shaft, one in the middle of the shaft, and one on the head of his dick.

"Oh damn! Suck it, baby. Do it," he begged in a softer tone.

I grinned as I took my time. Sammie Lee was like putty in my greedy little hands. I proved to him that I was in control. I would not mount, ride, and fuck his mind numb until *I* said it was time. I wanted to make it clear that he would always have to walk a tightrope of self-control with me, never expecting to get what he wanted on the spot. Even if I was going to be his mistress, he would have to be trained Honey's way. He was in my web, and I took advantage of it.

I squeezed his dick gently one final time before letting go. I walked away from the couch, got on all fours, and crooked my index finger. "If you're serious, you'll eat this." I turned and lay on my back, then opened my legs. "Ladies always come first. I'll take care of you, but you've got to take care of me. Go get a rubber so we can get the party started after you do."

Sammie Lee got up and walked down a hall, returning with a box of condoms. Without speaking, he massaged my feet until my juices flowed steadily. My head tilted back on the imported rug near the fireplace; I imagined a fire burning as another woman's husband made me woozy when his long tongue swirled in all the right places. His touch felt good. I made up my mind that before we were through, I'd have that man suck on all ten toes.

"There's your proof that I'm serious," he told me. Pussy juice dripped from his mouth.

My icy demeanor melted into something beautiful and soft. Sammie Lee rolled a condom over his rock-hard dick. Maintaining control, I pushed him backward.

"Don't miss out on the best fun. I like to ride, and I think you'll enjoy the trip."

I eased down onto his tool, persuading my sweet walls to receive him.

"Oh shit, baby! Ooooh shit! This feels good," he moaned. "It's so juicy and tight. Niiiiice . . ."

My knees dug into the carpet as I gently rocked back and forth. I sang a lullaby to him with my body. I squeezed my muscles, working up a nice, steady rhythm. Then I caught myself and slipped out of my tender fantasy. I forced myself back to reality and called on my icy demeanor once again. I was fucking for money, not for love.

"I'm just getting warmed up," I cooed, wildly bouncing up and down on top of Sammie. At some point, I planted my feet on the floor and gripped his solid arms to anchor myself. When I steadied myself perfectly, I studied his face. It had a look of sweet pain. That got me and wetter and made me talk dirtier.

"Do you like this? Does your wife do it like me?" While I contracted my pussy muscles, I rode him like a champ.

"No," Sammie Lee panted. "Oh, my God! Goddamn!"

"And she never will. Welcome to magnificence," I bragged.

"Get up," Sammie Lee ordered.

"What?"

"Just get up for a second."

Confused, I climbed off Sammie. He took my hand and pulled me into the kitchen.

"Have you ever been fucked in a kitchen?"

"No."

"I knew it! I know what to do with you. I'm ready to hit that sweet pussy from the back. Bend over the countertop and spread your legs wide," Sammie Lee instructed. "This is my pussy now. Let me hear you say it."

"This is your pussy, Sammie."

I smacked my own ass several times. Sammie Lee was nearly drooling at the mouth, eager to entertain the fantasy of being the first man to fuck me in the kitchen. He pushed his dick back inside me but by then, he was getting used to my pussy. He was no longer afraid to make my booty cheeks bounce as his hardness throbbed. Balls of sweat rolled down both of our faces. We did it slow, we did it fast. He taught me how to get a quick nut off with him, and he also taught me how to take his time that night. I wanted to make sure he remembered how I felt, so I didn't mind Sammie Lee letting me know that he was in charge. Marathon sex gave me a wicked power I didn't realize I held between my legs. I knew I had it in me to leave a man struggling to keep up with me, but I just didn't understand exactly how much it could add to my worth, if the right one came along. Although Sammie Lee told me that I had great pussy; not average, or even just good. It was great.

※》《※

When the light of day filled the bedroom, I unlocked my arms from around a snoring and drooling Sammie Lee and headed for the bathroom. He had barely gotten it in for a third round of the get down before he fell over on my shoulder, went straight to sleep, and didn't get back up. I wanted to prove to him that he picked a winner, and I felt pretty confident that I had! I was suddenly happy that I hadn't fucked too many men, and that I wasn't all stretched out and used up. It apparently made a difference. Had that been that case, I would've been slinging fries in a greasy ol' fast food joint. And of course, I was too spoiled to even consider getting dirt on one of my manicured nails. When I returned from the bathroom, Sammie Lee was still snoring. I looked down at him.

"Bastard," I said softly. As I climbed back into bed, I was thinking that Sammie Lee was about to get everything that he deserved. In my eyes, dear Sammie Lee was about to get taken the ride of his life!

Chapter Thirteen

JUST CALL ME THE JUMP-OFF

One month later, I was laid up in that same bed, enjoying the softness of the plush sheets and feather pillows with silk pillow cases. I'd been to the Guggenheim Museum with Sammie Lee, the Garment District, the infamous Apollo Theater, and I'd even seen a Broadway musical. I didn't have the heart to tell Sammie Lee that I'd been to all of those places, some more than once. I pretended it was new to me, just to make him feel good. It was nice to be treated as more than just a booty call. Sammie Lee never stopped by, coldly expecting me to open my legs wide, so he could drop a load and then move on. He was considerate and respectful, and even when a quickie was on the menu, I felt special. As I said before, I quickly trained him to spoil me beyond reason. In return, I let him have his space. I let him call when he wanted to talk to me. I made it a point not to nag or stress him out. Fun was what Sammie Lee got with me, although he knew he was paying to play.

I was sexy and whorish behind closed doors and a lady when Sammie Lee needed one in public. To make being a mistress work, a woman needed to have both tight sex and mind games. I started giving Sammie Lee head to make his toes curl. Some hot porn did teach me a few noteworthy tips, and I wasn't afraid to implement them. Good head was worth as much as good pussy to many men, and Sammie Lee was one of them. All I had to do was screw him, listen to his jokes and complaints about his wife, then top the whole unofficial shrink session with a little "physical therapy." Yes, Sammie Lee actually did enjoy conversation and my willingness to listen to him. The way I saw it, most women spoiled their men, putting up with their shenanigans freely, but there I was, not even twenty-one years old, and already hip the game.

I wanted to give Sammie Lee my undivided attention, at least in the first month and lead him to believe that I was on point at all times. One day, he arrived while I was exiting the shower. It was after eleven in the morning.

"You're just rolling out of bed? Now that's a shame!" Sammie Lee teased.

I kissed him passionately, like I really felt connected to him.

"That's what you pay me to do, roll around in bed. That's why I'm still here," I joked.

"I knew you were something special. Here." He gave me a bright red Cartier box.

"What's this?" I asked. I wiped some crust from my eyes. I opened the box and was blinded by the sparkle.

"Diamonds! Oh, Sammie! Thank you."

I was animated and motivated by those nicely cut beauties. I hugged him hard and gave him a passionate kiss. Mistress duties were looking lovely . . . yes!

"You would only notice the diamonds, Honey," Sammie Lee chuckled. "This necklace is from Cartier's new collection. It's also made of platinum and rubies. You've got matching earrings as well. I did a little shopping today because you've been playing your part so well," he gloated.

That's when I did take the time to admire the craftsmanship of the jewelry. Two teardrop-shaped rubies hung from several diamond links that were attached to a sparkling diamond orchid. A large burgundy ruby sat on top of the lower flower petal. The earrings were smaller replicas of the same design.

As much as I hated to admit it, I was blown away. Never in my life had I received anything so beautiful—or expensive, even from my parents. "It's all so beautiful. Could you put the necklace on me?"

"I'm glad you like it. Sure."

I kissed him again and his dreads swung from the movement. I rolled over onto my stomach so he could fasten the necklace around my neck. The diamonds and rubies rested with a comfortable weight around my collarbone.

"I'll keep your certificate so I can insure your jewelry," he said, handing me the paperwork.

Sammie Lee wasn't done, though. Next, he dropped many thousands of dollars worth of merchandise out onto his California king-sized bed, and it was all for me. There was bag after bag after bag from La Perla, Prada, Tiffany, and Manolo Blahnik. I rooted through a bag from Neiman Marcus while I sat, Indian style, and squealed at my first-rate treasures. He dumped the contents of the shopping bag onto the bed and I plucked out a black-and-pink Juicy Couture mini-bag. How he found the black-and-pink stilettos to match was beyond me. The final touch was my pink baby tee that which showed off my belly button and decent waistline, considering I'd had a baby. I'd thought of having some excess baby fat removed, but Sammie Lee never complained. I decided that I'd ask him to pay for my surgery, if he ever pressured me about working on it. It truly wasn't that bad, though.

When he left the room, I lay back on the bed with my arms stretched above my head, watching the sparkle of the diamonds hit the bedroom lights. The kaleidoscope of colors danced across my face and pillows, casting triangular shapes onto my skin and the fabric. My mother always taught me to love every piece of expensive jewelry. I loved my diamonds, and they made me happy. Then again, so did fur, shoes, purses, clothes, jewelry, and exotic vacations. Most of all, I loved money because it made all of those things possible.

My entire life revolved around money: the pursuit of it, spending it, and taking it from others. I felt that I could soon be a self-made millionaire without doing a day of legitimate work, if I kept fucking with men like Sammie Lee and then investing my hush money correctly. I decided I was going to treat him like gold in order to take all that I could—or earn all that I could, depending on how you saw it.

"Well, baby, I've got to run back to the office. I'll be back for my dinner later, though."

"Don't you mean dessert?" I teased.

Sammie Lee smiled wickedly.

I knew what that meant, and I smiled back. As soon as he left the house, I took a shower and smoothed a layer of Johnson's Baby Oil gel into my skin, following each stroke with a spritz of Issey Miyake. When my entire body was moisturized and smelling good, I retrieved a set of black lace La Perla underwear out of the La Perla shopping bag and walked over to the mirror, watching myself as I stepped into the panties. I adjusted my breasts so that they sat just right in my bra then pulled on my jeans, baby pink tee, and a new pair of pink-and-black Via Spigas. I brushed my hair back into a bun and swept my bangs down over my forehead. I looked at myself in the mirror one more time, watching my sexy reflection staring back at me.

"You're one bad bitch," I told myself aloud.

I rode the elevator to the lobby and walked outside, chirping the alarm on my brand spanking new, 2008 BMW. I loved my Z4. It was

navy blue with a creamy tan leather interior and a wood grain dash-
board. The black-tinted windows were just one notch above illegal. I
drove to get something to eat—I had a taste for Manhattan clam chow-
der and grilled Atlantic salmon from Aquagrill.

Two hours later, I returned home with a full stomach. I looked like I
had a fake baby bump, and I felt like I was going to pop at any moment.
My face was covered by stunner shades, and I was looking forward to
chilling because I surely wasn't going to work any of that food off! My
hustle allowed me to enjoy the finer things because Sammie Lee kept
offering me things worth considering. I walked away with a weekly
deposit, the car my parents were supposed to buy for my eighteenth
birthday, a monthly allowance, and an apartment for my use. Sammie
Lee insisted that I move to his penthouse, since it was more convenient
for him. I decided not to argue. I simply rented out my place, which
turned out to be more income for yours truly.

Of course, there was a catch. He was a married man, and the unexpected catch turned out to be the other woman in his life: his wife.

❈

When I made it inside the condo, I kicked off my shoes and peeled
off my clothes as I walked over to the stereo, trying to catch a song
that I'd heard on the radio in the car. After I turned it on, I twirled and
danced around naked, doing a booty dance in a jolly old mood. You
know how you acted silly when you thought no one was watching you?
I boogied my way to the shower, since I expected my payday to blow
through a bit later, but someone interrupted me in the midst of my
personal party.

"Well, well . . . aren't you the life of the party! A certain person we
have in common says he'd rather see a woman wake up happy than
wake up grouchy, so I guess you've learned that much so far." I followed

the voice and saw a tall, light-skinned woman with a pained expression and tightly drawn jaws standing in the door of the master bedroom. She was classily dressed in a charcoal gray pencil skirt, cream silk blouse and simple yet expensive black pumps. In fact, she looked like a former model. Her reddish-brown hair was in a neat chignon and she looked well kept. The only flaw I noticed was dark circles under her eyes. She looked stressed the hell out, like she hadn't been getting enough sleep.

I nearly jumped out of my skin at her appearance. I patted my chest, my heartbeat fluttering wildly underneath. The woman calmly examined her French manicured nails.

"Who the fuck are you?" I snapped.

"If you want to play this game, be prepared to enjoy the spotlight. Believe me, I've been waiting to tell you *exactly* who I am." She walked toward me. "My name is Lola Lee, and I'm Sammie's wife. He told me about you, and I wanted to meet the one who got him hooked. I wanted to see what the cat dragged in this time." She looked me up and down dismissively. You're cute, I'll give you that, but you're no more than a flavor of the month."

I bristled at the condescension in her tone. "Well, Sammie Lee spends a lot of money on this flavor of the month—and has done so for the past few months—so I think you need to get your facts straight."

Lola chuckled. "Sammie Lee is very generous with his women, as he is with me." She cocked her head and looked at me with pity in her hazel eyes. "I hope you don't think you're anything special. He will trade you in for a newer model soon enough, so don't get too comfortable."

"I can get as comfortable as I damn well please," I shot back. "Maybe you're the one that shouldn't get too comfortable, since your husband spends a lot of time here with me—and did I mention money?" I sounded big and bad, but I was really unsettled by Lola's appearance and he calm demeanor, and by the fact that we were having this conversation while I was buck naked. If the tables were turned, I'd be wildin' the fuck out and furniture would be moving. I grabbed a towel and wrapped it around myself.

"Oh, you poor dear!" Lola grinned. "He can't just walk out on me, because I'm the one who has this," she flashed the rock on her finger, "and will continue to for some time."

I had to admit that she had me there. When all was said and done, Mrs. Lola Lee had the legal right to do whatever the fuck she wanted; I was just the sidepiece, here at Sammie's whim. I wished I could say she was frumpy and plain, but she wasn't. She was cute. And yes, she was a trophy wife type. I was shocked that Sammie Lee was cheating on someone who looked like she did. My eyes fell on a coffee cup next to her chair.

"Look sweetie, I appreciate you saying hello, but I really don't have anything to say to you. I think about what I want for fucking men, and I get it. You may have the ring, but—"

"What do you mean, you don't have anything to say to me? You've been sleeping with my husband!" Lola took another step toward me. Instinctively, I backed up a step. A curly tendril fell on top of her right eye. Her jaws began to loosen. It seemed like the caffeine in that coffee cup was beginning to work.

"I didn't pursue Sammie, he pursued me." *Woman up, Honey!* I told myself. *Don't let her punk you!* "I ain't scared of you, Lola. Since you had the courage to show up like this, bring it, baby," I taunted. "Now that you've seen me, if you have something on your heart, let me know. It seems like you need to do this for yourself, so your mind can be free."

She put her hands on her slender hips, drawing attention to her small waist. "I hear that you're hugely popular for your talents in bed, but that comes with a price. If no one's told you, that makes you a prostitute, sweetie. Don't think it doesn't, just because you're not standing on some street corner." She flicked the tendril out of her eye and hooked it behind her ear. "My husband told me everything. I know about the little arrangement, and I know about you living here. I know that women—I mean, *girls* like you—have an expiration date. When the thrill is gone, he'll be home full-time again." She stepped even closer. "I just wanted to let you know that my husband had enough respect for me to put it all out there. You're not getting away with anything. All you've done is put a price tag on *that*." She pointed to my rather shapely, towel-covered ass.

This woman had me shook, but I tried to play it off. I knew I was wrong for messing with a married man—especially considering my family history with affairs—but I wasn't going to admit it. No, fuck that: I earned everything I worked hard for. If you left a man in the desert, would you not expect him to search for a drink? Some people had the good stuff, and some didn't. Lola was a damn looker, but I wasn't giving her any props.

"You can't touch the likes of me," I shot back. "Look at me, and look at you. I can see why he prefers someone with a little meat on her bones." I went straight for the ego and won. At least, I hoped I won.

"You're a bold one. I'll give you that as well." Lola nodded her head in acknowledgment. "Well, while you're shooting off your mouth, remember that this could happen to you too, one day. What goes around, and all that."

"Yeah, yeah." I waved off her comments. "Since you didn't just come here to experience my sparkling wit, I figure that you came to tell me to move on with my life and let you two be, right?" I rolled my eyes. "How typical."

Lola walked over to her Birkin bag, removed a pack of cigarettes, and lit one. Funny, I would have never pegged her as a smoker. She shook her head at my assumption. "Wrong." She sat gracefully down on the couch, turned her knees to the side and crossed her ankles. My mother and her cronies used to sit the exact same way; it was the mark of an old-school debutante, which reinforced my impression that Lola Lee was no dumb wifey sitting at home with a pack of squalling brats, dependent upon her man for survival. She came from something, from a good background. The same kind of background I came from.

"Then what do you want? Why are you here?" I asked.

Lola blew a perfect smoke ring and looked at me. "Look, I know he likes them young and dumb, but you've got to go."

Boy, she was something! And again, she had a point, but I couldn't go out like a sucker.

"I'm not leaving, unless Sammie Lee asks me to. I'm his guest, not yours. Maybe you and Sammie Lee had something great at one point in time but obviously, you no longer are the queen on his throne. Do you believe this is the man you should still be married to? If you did, you wouldn't have to check up on him." I strutted to the front door and opened it. "I think it's time for you to go, in more ways than one."

Lola shook her head. "Honey—that's your name, right? Well, Honey, you seem like a somewhat smart girl despite your current activities, so I'm going to remind you again: I am Sammie's wife. I'm also the joint owner of this property, which means that you will leave when I tell you to leave, no matter what Sammie Lee says." A malicious smile crossed her face.

The thought of being bounced out on my ass in broad daylight was embarrassing. I tried to stall for time and intensified my attack. "What do you do as his wife? Nothing! You sit on that bottom and live off a rich man. I guess you don't want anyone to beat you doing nothin'." I snorted. "Play your part or get lost. You know these niggas are no good. If you forgot that, then don't shoot the messenger." I shrugged. "Men cheat: deal with it. If you were really sure that Sammie Lee was the man you should be married to, you wouldn't have to be here, beefing with me."

Lola's smile never dropped. "Little girl, please. I'm above you. I'm too much of a lady to beef with you. And in case you were wondering, I have a master's degree, and I'm a real estate agent with upscale celebrity clients." She looked around the living room with a practiced eye. "In fact, I'm the one who picked out this investment property. My house was paid for when I met him. I had my own money, and my own things. When I saw the great, big light bill on this investment property, I knew he was at it again." She rose, again with grace. "Now, what I asked you to do is just leave. Need I remind you that my name is on the deed?" Lola ground a cigarette butt into one of my designer shoes, which lay on the floor.

I started toward the burnt shoe. "Hey! Hey! Excuse me!" I protested, eying the damaged kicks.

Lola reached into a drawer and removed pictures of their family: her, Sammie, their two kids. She placed them on an end table.

I didn't even know those pictures—or those kids—existed. Yet another bitch slap from reality. "Damn, bitch! Get a grip."

Lola snorted. "I know you think you're at the center of Sammie's world, but these are the people who mean the most to him." She ran a loving finger over the edge of one of the sterling silver frames. "Whatever he says to you is not our reality. You don't live with us to see the truth. He's telling you what you want to hear." She looked at me and the smile finally dropped; she looked tired. "For the last time, I'm asking you to leave."

"And for the last time, I'm telling you that I'm not leaving until Sammie Lee tells me to leave!" I grabbed one of the pictures and threw it onto the floor. The glass shattered, leaving shards of glass on the expensive Persian rug.

Oh God, why did I have to do that?

Lola's nostrils flared as two spots of red appeared on her cheeks. "Okay. Fine. Have it your way. Since you want a ribbon for being a first-class whore, I'll give you one!" She reached into her purse and grabbed her cell phone. "I'm calling 911."

As dumb as it was for me to do, I jumped on her back. She twirled around in a circle before she collapsed from my weight. I had to stop that loon from destroying everything I worked hard for, in my own way.

When the cell phone fell, we both scrambled for it, but I beat Lola to the punch. I ran to a window and threw it outside as fast as I could. Lola didn't even try to fight me. Like the lady she was, she simply headed toward the landline. It wasn't the best idea, but I was desperate. I snatched the receiver from her hands and quickly slammed the phone down then I charged at the at her.

Lola danced out of my range and scurried around to the other side of a massive mahogany table. "You're out of line. Don't put your hands on me!" she screamed.

"Maybe so, but until Sammie Lee says it's over, it ain't over!"

I crawled across the table, pushing a crystal vase full of wildflowers to the floor. The crashing sound was just a soundtrack to my assault on Lola. My towel came undone and I was once again naked. I lost my temper and pushed her. Her skinny ass went flying into a China cabinet. Doors flew open and expensive Waterford china, crystal, and other knickknacks fell to the floor, shattering upon impact. A shard of glass bounced up and cut her leg. Blood started pouring from the wound. Despite the glass and crystal slivers, we rolled around on the floor like two kids on a playground. Since she took it there, I grabbed Lola by the hair and stuffed her face into the carpet until she screamed, "I can't breathe!" I let her hair go and allowed her to turn her head to the side and take great, big gulps of air. I wasn't trying to kill her, I just wanted her to back off. I sat on her back, my chest heaving from the exertion.

"You are one pathetic, desperate broad, coming over here to fight over a man," I panted. "I would never lower myself to do something like this. Maybe Sammie Lee doesn't love you, or maybe he doesn't know what love is."

I hoped she was finished showing her ass. When I noticed her bleeding leg, I got Lola some tissue from the dresser and held a wad of it on the gash. I poured myself a drink, since a bottle of the good stuff managed to remain unbroken on a wet bar in the corner. I was surprised that Lola didn't try to clobber me with the bottle. I just stood there and let the sweat dry on my face before I gingerly tiptoed over the broken glass to retrieve my towel.

"Give me thirty days, and I'll decide what I feel like doing about it," I told her. I drained my glass. "You can change the players, but the game will always remain the same. It's obvious that you don't understand that your role is not to change Sammie. He will be who he is, twenty-four hours day, whether I'm in his life, or another woman is. I just dropped a jewel in your ear, so get it right, baby." I set the glass down on the table. Lola sat up and straightened her clothes as she sucked in a deep breath, then sighed again as she contemplated me with newfound respect.

"You are trouble."

I nodded. "Yes, I am. Aren't we all? I bet you've been trouble at some point in your life, and still may be today." I plopped down on the couch and made sure my towel remained in place. "And I don't live in fear. I'm not scared of you, nor am I shook by you coming here to face me," I lied. "Right now, I'm having a good time."

Lola redid her disheveled chignon. "A great pity—that's what you are, Honey. I tried to reason with you." She shook her head. "To even suggest that I should share my husband tells me that you have the IQ of a rock! I call the shots, and don't you ever forget it."

"Sure you do," I said sarcastically. "Look, Lola, I'm tired of rumbling with you, and I'm even more tired of trying to reason with someone I don't respect. Since you don't get the picture, didn't you smell your husband's balls on my breath?" Lola's shocked look spurred me on. "He wants me, and enjoys everything I do to him. So why don't you just limp on out of here, and hurry up about it? If you don't mind, I need to take a nap. You're interrupting my beauty rest." I rose and carefully walked to the bedroom, trying to avoid all of the broken glass and china. I turned and said, "I think you need to take all of this up with your husband, not me. Marriage is a serious commitment, but I'm not the one who's married. There's a certain organ that caused you to get dragged into this with me. If he loved you as much as you say, he never would've invited me here. Obviously, I have no sympathy for you. If I did, the only two pieces of advice I could offer is for you to ask your husband to go get a vasectomy, or turn up the heat when you and Sammie Lee bounce back under the sheets so he won't beat his meat and think of me when he's with you."

I heard a knock at the door. Despite Lola's hurt leg, she swiftly moved toward it without shooting insults back to me. When I followed Lola down the hall, I saw two policemen standing in the doorway, hands on their holstered guns.

"Did someone call 911?" One of the policemen asked. The other looked at me with suspicion.

"I did, Officer," Lola acknowledged. "I have a trespasser on my property who refused to leave." She pointed at me.

"Do you live here, ma'am?" The officer asked me.

"Well . . . not really. I mean, I stay here as her husband's guest, and this is his place."

"You mean you stay here as his mistress, you home-wrecking rat."

Lola smiled sweetly. "My name is Lola Lee and I can prove that I'm the joint owner of this property, Officer, along with my husband, Sammie Lee."

The officer turned to his partner. "Check it out," he ordered. The second officer spoke into the radio on his shoulder and gave the address of the property."

"Don't bother. I'll leave." I'd been humiliated enough for one day. I knew when I'd lost.

Lola grinned. "That's a good idea, unless you'd like me to press assault charges, too."

Assault charges? I was scared as hell. I only managed to pull on my clothes that I'd just taken off, got my damaged shoes, purse, and keys, and got out of there! I glared back at Lola after I walked out of the condo door and swiftly moved down the hall.

"It was nice meeting you. When you see Sammie, do tell him that I said hello," Lola called out in my wake, waving goodbye.

"Yeah, bitch! I will."

I pressed the elevator button. When I made it to my car, it was resting on four flat tires. Lola probably had someone to do it while we were chitchatting. I dialed Sammie Lee with shaking hands. I was so mad, all I could see was red. I didn't know why he put me in a crazy position like that, but I sure as hell was gonna tear his ear up.

PART THREE
THE CLEAN-UP WOMAN

Chapter Fourteen

THE SETUP

Lola's unexpected eviction reminded me that I was playing with fire. Plus, I had a tenant in my apartment for the next week, so I couldn't go there.

"What's wrong? Are you all right, Honey?" Sammie Lee answered his cell phone.

"Hell to the no! Are you listening? Are you sure you're listening?"

"Yes! Yes. What is wrong with you?"

"Your wife is crazy as hell, Sammie, that's what's wrong with me! I'm beginning to wonder if you're crazy too. She said you told her all about us, and she kicked me out of the condo after calling the police. As a matter of fact, I'm standing outside next to my car—which has four flat tires, might I add—looking dumb as hell right now." Looking at the tires made me mad all over again. "Is there something you want to tell me? She said you told her what was going on between us."

I paced back and forth in the parking lot, feeling the stress build up in my head. Of course, I skipped over the dirt I'd done.

"Calm down, Honey," Sammie Lee tried to soothe me. "I'll take care of this, but you've got to stay calm and—"

"Did you hear what I said?" I screamed. "Calm down, my ass! I don't need this fuckin' shit, Sammie. What kind of crazy games are you playing? You told me to never bother your family, then you turn around and tell your wife our business!"

"I can't get into this right now. I've got an emergency with a blue-chip client in Boston."

"Great, Sammie. Just great. You're in Boston now?"

"I'm sorry, Honey. Yes, I'm already here. I'll take care of everything, though. The first thing I can do is make arrangements for a limo to pick you up. I promise, the driver will take excellent care of you."

"He'd better!"

"I'll have him take you to Saks to get you some clothes. Charge them to my store account. I'll notify my personal shopper that you are coming by."

"And?"

"I'll book you a room at the Waldorf Astoria for the next couple of days."

"*And?*" I was determined to milk this incident for all it was worth.

"I'll deposit an extra $10,000 into your bank account."

I got quiet. Saks, the Waldorf, and an extra $10K wasn't a bad haul. It almost made the altercation with Lola worthwhile.

"I really want to make this up to you," Sammie Lee crooned. "I don't want to argue. Will you accept my apology?"

I sighed. "I don't know. Maybe. I'm just disappointed that you didn't handle your business right. I had to leave all of my new presents behind, including my jewelry. Do you know how humiliating it was to get kicked out, with the police standing there? I could've gotten in big trouble."

"I can't apologize enough for that, Honey. How you feel is important to me. I told you that I would take care of you, and that hasn't changed. I need you to turn that 'maybe' into a yes. How does a trip sound?"

"A trip where?" I wiped my teary eyes with the back of my hand. I really was behaving like an obnoxious brat.

"Hawaii. I can meet you there in a few days. I was going to surprise you and take you anyway. I have some business I have to tend to there. We can talk about this then. *Please*," he said in the cutest voice.

I sighed again. "Okay. I'll go, but just hurry up and get me out of here, Sammie."

"Great. Leave your keys with the limo driver, so he can take care of your car repairs. You're going to love Hawaii."

I was excited to be going to Hawaii on such a whim, but I didn't want to seem overenthusiastic. I figured that downplaying my reaction would inspire Sammie Lee to keep my makeup "trinkets" coming. As soon as I hung up, I jumped up and down all over the parking lot. I suddenly felt refreshed.

"Yeah, baby! I'm going to Hawaii," I exclaimed.

The limo driver did take me to Saks to pick out some clothes, some swimsuits and beach wraps, and a new set of luggage. After that, we were off to Citibank, where I checked my account balance to make sure that Sammie Lee wired the $10,000 to my account, then I made a small withdrawal to tide me over until Sammie Lee arrived in Hawaii. I relaxed in my luxurious room at the Waldorf Astoria and ordered room service, spa treatments—the works, all on Sammie's dime. Hours later, I was eating shrimp cocktail in first class, headed for the other side of the United States. I looked around the cabin and saw that I was surrounded by white-collar movers and shakers at the top of their game. It gave me a rush, and I halfheartedly sized them up, in case Sammie Lee needed to be replaced quickly. Sammie's extravagance explained why Lola was willing to fight for him. He had access to a wealthy life that even surpassed my parents', and that was saying a lot.

I wasn't exactly thrilled about flying over water for so many hours and I slept as much as I could. When I wasn't eating and sleeping, I found out all I could about my fellow cabinmates. My hustle never stopped . . . *never*. I drank, ate, and joked with the men on the plane. When I got up to go to the bathroom, I let them salivate over my backside without chewing them out. We made corny toasts with champagne.

"Well, all right, now. It's official! I have been waiting all day for this," Bob happily said. His belly was as fat as a Buddha's, but I was sure he already knew that. He was a group director at Young and Rubicam and was celebrating that he and his team had landed an exclusive advertising account.

"Come on, Honey. You've got to have a toast with us," he urged. The rest of his team backed him up and added their urgings. "Come on, sweetie. I won't take no for an answer." We waved the flight attendant over. I think she hesitated, wondering if I was old enough to drink, but she didn't question me. I think Bob was too much of a heavy hitter, and she didn't want to make him mad, so she just handed me some top-of-the-line bubbly.

"I usually don't drink, but I'll make this one exception," I lied. "I think I can handle that."

"Good, good." He laughed.

Before long, he was bright pink, running his mouth about things he should've kept quiet. Ego—he was all ego! I bet his wife was miserable. I didn't let the chance to taste fine liquor pass me by, but I watched them drink until they were drunk. It wasn't the time or place to be that lit. With my faculties fully in place, I was sharp enough to periodically eavesdrop on their conversations. I was trying to figure out who was just talking shit, and who could back it up the most.

Just as Lola reminded me, I wasn't the one cooking Sammie Lee eggs and grits in the morning, and a married man who was creeping was still married. I never understood why a woman on the side fully committed herself to a man who had someone full time. Dumb.

"Call me some time," Scott said. He was a neurosurgeon at Beth Israel Hospital and was on his way to a medical conference in Hawaii. He passed me his business card, which launched a pissing contest among the other men in first class.

"You've got to come out for lunch on my yacht," Gerald said. He handed me his business card, and had his cell phone scribbled on the back of it.

"Can you keep a secret?" Andrew asked, doing a terrible job of whispering. He was an attorney that specialized in white-collar crime.

"Of course I can," I flirted, smiling.

"I'm throwing a little get together for a cosmetics and perfume mogul at an exclusive and private location in Manhattan. I'd love for you to come. I think you'd have a real nice time." He handed me *his* business card. "Call me. My cell number is on the back. And don't tell any of those guys!" He chuckled.

Even the ones who had forgotten to remove their rings before flirting were trying to get at me! It was comical but energizing, to say the least. I just had to be sure to guard my insurance policies well. I didn't want Sammie Lee to be all up in my business.

As the plane touched down in Hawaii, I smiled and looked out of the small window. I was anxious to get off the plane. I pushed my way into the airport, looking for the driver who would take me to my destination. I spotted an older Hawaiian gentleman holding a sign with my name on it. I started to walk toward him but was intercepted by a young woman in a bra and grass skirt, who draped a fresh lei around my neck.

"Aloha," she greeted me with a smile. "Aloha," I replied with a grin.

It was a thirty-minute ride from Kahului Airport to my hotel. Maui was everything that I hoped it would be. Even more than that, the hotel where I stayed was nothing short of a beachfront paradise. After I got settled in, I walked out onto the private balcony and inhaled deeply. I took in the sights as I enjoyed being a guest at the Ritz-Carlton. I gripped the balcony with both hands as I thought about my life, and how much it had changed. Only time would tell if it was for the better or for the worse.

I heard a knock at my door. I answered it and was greeted by a hotel employee holding a dozen roses. The card read:

I'LL BE IN THE LOUNGE DOWNSTAIRS IN ABOUT AN HOUR. WHICH ONE OF YOUR ADMIRERS FROM THE FLIGHT AM I? I HOPE YOU'LL JOIN ME AND FIND OUT. A GIRL'S GOT TO EAT. HOW ABOUT DINNER ON ME? IT WOULD MEAN THE WORLD TO ME IF YOU INDULGED ME AT LEAST ONCE.

I'd planned to shower, eat, and then sleep. Sammie Lee wouldn't be in Hawaii for a few more days, so hanging out with a new friend wouldn't hurt. I decided to go shopping in town and purchase something especially for this occasion. I took a cab to Whaler's Village, which was about fifteen minutes away. I stopped at the first boutique I spotted and found a nice dress to wear. I made it to the lounge only a few minutes late. My admirer turned out to be David, a junior member of Bob's advertising team. He was fresh out of Wharton, making $60,000 in his first real job. Nice, but not quite nice enough for me. Interesting, almost cute, but still very wet behind the ears. I knew he was on my never-to-be-called-list when he told me he preferred serious relationships, and only wanted to date one woman at a time. Then he actually admitted that he was on a strict budget because of his student loan payments. I received more bad news when he mentioned that he preferred to stick with his used Honda Accord for the next year, before buying a new whip, probably another Accord, or maybe even a Lexus if he could get a good deal. He may as well have told me he drove a go-cart! He continued to explain that he did not party due to his obligations with his job. *Yuck!*

"There are many ways to measure success. The car I drive isn't one of them," he explained. I couldn't handle being in the presence of a man who was waiting to step up. He had no game, and I hated him for it. I made up a reason to leave immediately—after he paid the bill for dinner, of course. There was no way he'd get one fingertip in my pussy!

"Nice seeing you again, David. Thanks for the dinner, but I gotta go," I said abruptly.

He looked concerned. "So soon? Are you sure?"

"Yeah, I'm sure. I have cramps," I lied.

"Oh." He got that uncomfortable look that most men did at any mention of a woman's menstrual cycle. "Well, do you think we can do this again before you leave?"

"I'm not sure, David. We'll see." I kissed him on the cheek and left, clutching my abdomen for effect. I knew it was wrong to shoot him down so rudely but he just didn't seem to take the hint that I wasn't interested. Still, I didn't want to completely burn my bridges; David might turn out to be a serious baller someday, and I wanted to lay the groundwork before he blew up and skanks started coming out of the woodwork. I went back to my room, undressed, and crawled under the wickedly soft cotton sheets. I just wanted to get a little shut-eye so I could get some real shopping done before Sammie's arrival.

Shopping was exactly what I did. I went back to Whaler's Village and took my time perusing all seventy-five shops. I also snagged some mosquito repellant and sunscreen. I topped off my shopping day with a yoga class, to keep my mind off my mother's death. Although a little more than four years had passed, I still missed her. Her passing began to set in, along with the drama of Lola's visit and fleeting thoughts of my daughter. I even thought about Jerome, and how much I missed him being my father. By the afternoon, all of my negative thoughts flew out of the window as I hit the pool and swam up to the bar to get my drink on.

❋

A few days later, Sammie Lee and I attended a real Hawaiian luau. Talk about a feast! There was live entertainment, an all-you-can-eat buffet, and an open bar, where I drank several delicious Mai Tais. I had to try the baked Molokai sweet potatoes with coconut glaze, tropical fruit salad with toasted coconut, and Lomi Lomi salmon. It all called me. Main course or not, I was a little scared of eating that pig cooked in an underground oven, but there was more than enough for me to eat otherwise. The fire dancers were off the chain, and seeing a traditional hula was cool too. The Hawaiian music and dance was something I'd remember forever.

After gorging myself, I needed to stretch my legs. I was worried about my weight getting out of control, but Sammie Lee just laughed and told me they had a gym in the hotel, if I really thought one huge meal would make a big difference.

"Come on, Honey." He grabbed my hand and pulled me up.

"I am so full," I said, rubbing my belly. "Where are we going now?"

"A walk on the beach."

It was just after sunset, and it looked like a fairytale. His hand felt so big and strong, and I admired the sheen on the water.

"Would you like to scuba dive or snorkel tomorrow?" Sammie Lee asked.

"I hear there are lots of dolphins here. I don't think I could handle that. I'm a bit squeamish." I shuddered at the thought of big fish swimming anywhere near me. And didn't I read somewhere that dolphins had teeth?

He laughed. "If you say so. Every time I'm here, I do it. They won't hurt you."

"Great. With my luck, it could turn into a real mess," I said.

Sammie Lee frowned. "Aren't you having a nice time?"

I shook my head. "That's not what I'm talking about. You know I've been waiting to have a conversation with you about what happened, and you know I'm capable of a tantrum. I'm trying to stay calm about it all, but I've got to tell you how I feel." I turned to Sammie Lee as a breeze blew across my face. I held both of his hands in mine. "Our agreement is too much pressure. I assumed you'd be careful and discreet, but you weren't. Why did you tell your wife about us?" I sighed as I stared out at the ocean. "I never wanted to know details about your personal life, but it turns out that you exposed ours to her. Now what, Sammie? My confrontation with her changed things so much."

"You're not just my mistress, Honey, you're becoming my best friend." He pulled me close to him.

I drew away and looked in his eyes. "Are you still sleeping with your wife? You told me you weren't." I examined Sammie's face for any sign of lying, but he maintained a neutral expression. Either he wasn't sleeping with Lola, or he was one of the best liars I'd ever encountered. I stepped completely away from him. "I can't be myself in this situation.

Maybe you do this to enjoy the chase. Maybe you will dump me and go back to your wife and children." I knew my behavior lately had been deplorable. I started to feel guilty about the woman he was letting down so badly, but Sammie Lee boosted me right back up.

"Lola was an aspiring model in the city when I met her. Over time, and after the kids, our mutual aspirations changed and we grew apart. And no, we don't have sex anymore." He gave a heartfelt sigh. "All I hear is nagging. Don't think I didn't try to make the marriage work, because I did, although she had a child with me to persuade me to commit. I knew Lola was not the one for me, but I stepped up to the plate and gave my daughter my last name." He shook his head, took my hand, and continued our walk along the beach. "All I've gotten was a bunch of complaints and misery in return. I only started looking outside of home for happiness when it became clear I would never get it there." He stopped and turned to face me. "I somehow thought I was doing the right things at the time. I now see that was wrong. Communication has been a chore with Lola for many years now, Honey. You see how she is. It's only gotten worse in the last few months. She got suspicious because she found out about a balance on my credit card that she knew I paid off. A lot of things I'd purchased for you were on the statement. Although the credit card is in my name, I just didn't feel like lying to Lola any longer. Yeah, she invaded my privacy by opening my mail, but what she saw spoke for itself. I wanted her to understand that she drove me to this point. I couldn't build a relationship with you through lies and secrecy. Plus, everyone gets caught eventually."

Interesting; Lola told me that she noticed the huge light bill on the condo, and that's what tipped her off about me. But I didn't call Sammie Lee out on his lie. "You know I enjoy your company, but we weren't supposed to be building anything in particular! Why are you suddenly trying to change the game here? I thought you were only interested in a discreet sexual relationship, for fun and money. I'm used to saying and doing whatever I want."

Sammie Lee placed a kiss on my forehead. "You stay on my mind so much, I would miss everything that we've built with each other. I need you. How do you think I feel to be attached to Lola, when the right one for me came along?"

He was really laying it on thick. Guilt is a motherfucker. "Our time together would be too difficult. This is my very first time trying to be anyone's mistress. Quite frankly, I can get all of the things you're giving me from some other man, with fewer complications."

Sammie Lee nodded. "You're words couldn't be truer, but what if I need you? I'm sorry I had a lapse in judgment. Please trust me."

Sammie Lee bent down and kissed my lips. I wanted to tell him to stop it, but I didn't. I kept my feelings to myself. Sammie Lee was cool for picking up tabs and keeping the sex coming all night long, but I would never fall in love with a man who treated his wife and kids like shit. I never wanted anything of lasting value from dealing with him. Plus, I met him at a club and he sexed me in the blink of an eye.

When our lips parted I said, "I don't know what to say to all of that, Sammie. I really don't." I shook my head and we began walking again. "I will never chase you. You have a lot to work out on your own. Maybe this was not the best idea after all, at least the part of moving into your place." I paused. "What did I really expect from a married man? How am I going to survive Christmas and the holidays?"

I did my best to lay the guilt trip on thick.

"What if I want to be with you? I feel like we're in this together, and I've already grown attached to you." Sammie Lee sounded flustered. "I've been contemplating a separation, which is why I spent so much time at the condo with you. Do I need to file for divorce to prove it? I'll start the paperwork, if that's what you want."

"You've got kids," I protested. Deep down, I danced for joy at his words. "Don't leave Lola because of me, or because of this, Sammie. If you do leave your wife and kids, you may lose me for sure. Make things right with her, just as you're trying to make things right with me," I advised.

Although I shot off my mouth to his wife, it was true that I didn't set out to intentionally hurt her. On the other hand, I felt that if she put up with things after knowing about me, it spoke volumes about her lack of self-esteem. Speaking of self-esteem, Sammie Lee suddenly enveloped me securely in his arms and broke down crying. To see a wealthy, grown man behave that way made me feel like queen of the world.

After we talked things over, we ended up in bed again for some excellent makeup sex.

"You're my superstar," Sammie Lee murmured as he nibbled on my earlobe, pushing me backward toward the bed. "Damn, you get me through the day!" He ground on top of me with that hard package of his. Soon, we were into round two, with the patio doors of the hotel balcony thrown open.

The next morning we ordered room service, dressed, and rented a convertible to go sightseeing: a volcano, a waterfall, and parks. I guessed Sammie Lee had been to Hawaii a few times before because he didn't need a guided tour. We had a blast, and even took some pictures. Sammie Lee kept me from getting bored, and that was another thing I liked about him.

After we got back to the hotel, the pool attendant spritzed my tanned skin with Evian until I cooled down. Sammie Lee arranged massages by the beach under a crystalline sky. He was putting in extra work to make sure that I wouldn't call off my mistress duties. His actions put him way up on my keepers list; he was becoming pretty valuable. His wife had a lot to protect, but so did I.

I decided to drag out my final answer about our situation until after we got back to New York and I made sure he came through on at least one of the many promises he made me, two of which were payment of my college education and setting up a nest egg for my future. I could get with that. I didn't tell Sammie Lee I didn't have my GED, or that I hadn't even finished high school, but he never asked. I figured I could still do what I had to do and catch up, on his tab. Sammie Lee also tried to throw in a stock portfolio to keep me around. It sounded good, so I told him I'd think about it. At least he was offering me a chance to look out for myself, and that made me want to trust him.

When the time came for our massages, we both lay under a thatched hut. Sheets were draped over two massage tables. Two beautiful Hawaiian girls spoiled us with their hands and fingers.

I was so relaxed, I had nearly drifted off to sleep when I heard a cell phone ring. My eyes popped open. I knew it wasn't mine; mine was back in the hotel room. The phone was closest to me, and I looked at Sammie. He knew he still had a lot of things to prove to me after all that mess he talked, so he told me I could answer it if I wanted to.

"Are you sure?"

"I have nothing to hide from you," he assured.

I pressed the green button. Before I could utter one consonant, I heard, "Sammie, where are you?" It was Lola.

"This isn't Sammie, but we're getting massages in Hawaii," I replied.

"What! Put him on the phone," she demanded.

"Okay, Lola," I calmly said. "Nice to hear from you again." She was cursing a mile a minute.

"You have some brass balls! You are jobless, shameless, and you are hoping my marriage fails so you can get what you want. Didn't you learn anything from what happened?"

Her voice was shrill, but it didn't move me. I just didn't reply; I simply closed my eyes again after handing Sammie Lee the phone. Never back down. Never say you're wrong. Never apologize. That's how I was living.

"I'm away on business. I'll be home when I get there," I heard Sammie Lee tell her firmly.

At that moment, I decided that virtually all married people were miserable and kept secrets. My parents set the stage for my pessimistic attitude, Mikaylo was the middle of my dissatisfaction, and the situation I was in with Sammie Lee was the icing on the cake. As promised, Sammie Lee and I took our time returning to The Big Apple. We stayed in Hawaii for almost two weeks and he only had one business meeting that I noticed. I thought we'd be there for a weekend or something, but Sammie Lee really spread it on thick. I never questioned anything. I just took what I could get. It wasn't like he was some undesirable man who was bald, fat, or hard up. In return, he got the fantasy and excitement of having a mistress.

Yeah, sure. What a fool believed, and Lola wasn't the only fool. My time to read the writing on the wall had finally come. After the plane touched down in New York, Sammie Lee had the limo driver drop me off at my old place. My tenant was long gone as of last week. We sat in front of my building as the driver gathered my packages and suitcases.

"I'll call you later. If I can slip out to see you tomorrow, I'll come by. In the meantime, get some rest," Sammie Lee said.

"Only bother to come by if you have cash."

Sammie Lee just gave me a half-cocked smile, as if I'd told a joke. I was dead serious.

"We'll talk about your portfolio, and I'll bring you some money for your living expenses, including your rent for the next three months."

"You can just deposit into my account, like you've been doing." I was thinking that now was a good time to put a bit of distance between me and Sammie. I had some serious thinking to do.

"No, I'll bring it by personally. I want to see you, Honey."

I shrugged. Whatever, man. "It sounds like a plan, then. I guess you'll be getting what you want."

Sammie Lee gave me a stern look. "I told you, you're not going anywhere. Whatever it takes to keep you in my life, I'm willing to do it."

"Okay then, Sammie." I folded my arms and gave him a serious look. "What happened in Hawaii, stays in Hawaii. Don't dish up the details to your wife this time." I hesitated. "I want to stay in your life, too," I lied.

Sammie Lee beamed. "Fantastic! I was hoping you'd finally say that."

I sealed our deal with a kiss and moaned softly as his tongue slid into my mouth. My hand slid to the crotch of his jeans. I massaged his hard dick until I realized that the driver was holding the door open for me. I smiled one final time as I walked up the steps toward my place.

I slept the remainder of the afternoon away, thinking that things in my life had been a bit rocky, but they were finally looking up. In the middle of my peaceful sleep, I was awakened by a knock at my door. I thought maybe Sammie Lee had had issues with Lola and came back. I sighed, wondering what went wrong again. I threw on my robe and looked through the peep hole. It wasn't Sammie; it was Ritchie.

I managed to recover from the shock of seeing Ritchie, whom I hadn't seen in almost a year, when I realized he was talking to me.

"Honey, where have you been?" Ritchie asked me through the cracked door.

"I don't think that's any of your business. I think you need to get back home to Tatiana before she objects. If you don't mind, I need to get my beauty rest. I'm not in the mood for drama, Ritchie." I started to shut the door but Ritchie stuck the toe of his shoe in the crack and kept it open.

"Stop trippin' and take the chain off the door! I need to talk to you about something important."

Why me, Lord? "I'm not in the mood for this, Ritchie. Please give me my space. Go home."

"It's about Kyashira."

My heart began to pound when I heard my daughter's name. I fumbled to unfasten the chain and unlock the door. Ritchie walked in, agitated and with a serious expression on his face.

"I've been looking everywhere for you! You need to go see about your young'un, Honey. One of my boys told me he was in Georgia not long ago, and he heard that Kyashira was not doing so well."

"What's wrong with her?" I said with fear in my voice and widened eyes.

"She's in foster care. That's all I was told."

"Foster care?" My heart stopped.

"Yeah, foster care."

I shook my head. "No, that's not right. Kyashira has two people caring for her." I frowned. "If this person knows so much, what town was she in?"

"I think some place called Barnesville. You need to check into this as soon as possible. Maybe it's a rumor, but I heard this from a pretty reliable source. I thought you'd want to know." He turned to leave. I grabbed Ritchie to stop him; I didn't realize until then how much I missed his friendship, and how much I missed him having my back. Ritchie must have seen the confusion, fear, and desperation on my face because he put his arms around me and acted like our beef was irrelevant. I clung to him as I began to cry.

"Be strong, ma. Hold it together," Ritchie murmured. When my sobs subsided to a whimper, he lifted my chin and looked me in the eyes. "Let me know how you make out when you get back. Don't cry, Honey. Be a soldier like I taught you, okay?"

"Kaylo doesn't even care. I've got to do this all by myself," I wailed. "I'm scared, Ritchie. I did leave her in Barnesville. Now I'm really afraid that the bad news about my daughter is true."

Ritchie gave me a small shake. "Look, you gotta pull it together. Fuck him! That's your daughter. You need to be strong for her."

The shake brought me back to my senses. I had to get it together for Kyashira. "You're right. Thanks, Ritchie," I said, sniffling.

"Anytime, ma. You got my cell number, so call me and let me know what's what, a'ight?"

I took a deep breath and the sense of urgency kicked in. As soon as Ritchie left I rushed to pack, leaving some things in my largest suitcase while stuffing other items in it. I had a hard time thinking clearly. In fact, I almost forgot to order a plane ticket. Sammie Lee had given me a credit card while we were in Hawaii, to use in case of emergency. It was a part of his "Get Honey to Forgive Me" incentive plan. I broke it in by finding a ticket on Priceline.com. I printed out the information and grabbed my luggage and purse. I ran down the steps of my apartment building, stuffed my luggage in my car, and was about to drive off when I was interrupted by someone.

Chapter Fifteen

A DOUBLE DOSE OF KARMA

"Honey Davis?" a stern voice asked.

"Yes?" I was startled to find a balding, dour-faced man standing an arm's length away from me. His tall yet stocky body was encased in an ill-fitting navy blue suit, and his blue-and-gray striped tie threatened to choke him. Another man silently approached and stood sentinel on the other side; he was shorter, younger, and dressed in a similar manner, except he had a thatch of thick, brown hair that complemented the shades of brown in his tie and his tan-colored suit. I had been so preoccupied with my upcoming trip that I hadn't heard them approach. I wanted to step back and reclaim my personal space, but I couldn't. There was simply nowhere to go.

"What's going on?" I didn't recognize these men, but their sudden presence gave me a bad feeling.

They studied me intently as they flashed their badges. "I'm Detective First Grade George Mayer, Homicide, 34th Precinct," the balding man said. "This is my partner, Detective Second Grade Joshua Bingham."

My body felt frozen. Detectives? Homicide? "What . . . what can

I do for you, detectives?" I stammered. Homicide meant someone was dead, and apparently it was someone I knew, or knew of. This was not good. This was not good at all.

"We're investigating the murder of Lola Lee."

Oh shit, I thought. "Murder!" I exclaimed. "I don't know anyone by that name. Who's Lola Lee?"

"We were told that you were pretty good friends with her husband, Sammie. Is that correct?"

My eyebrows rose as my mouth fell open in horror. Lola Lee? They were talking about *that* Lola, as in Sammie's wife? Blood drained from my face as the frozen feeling extended all the way down to my toes. *Lola's dead?*

"Well, I . . . ya . . . yes," I stuttered. I couldn't think; my usual fast talk had gone missing in action. I was shook! Lola Lee was dead, and two homicide detectives were asking me questions. Did they know about me and Sammie, I wondered?

"Do you mind if we ask you a few questions?" Mayer was obviously the alpha dog in this duo; Detective Bingham remained silent, though his sharp green eyes remained in motion. The phrase "still waters run deep" sprang to mind.

"Um, well, is it going to take long? I have to catch a flight; it's a family emergency."

"We won't take long, Ms. Davis." Mayer's tone implied that I didn't have much of a choice. "Let's go to your apartment, shall we? Or, if you'd like, we can go down to the precinct."

Go down to the precinct? Oh hell no! That was not an option, so what else could I say? If I didn't agree, it would make me look bad. Kyashira's newborn face flashed in my mind, but I had to push it away. I had to answer these questions so that I could focus on her with no distractions. Nausea surged in my stomach; I forced myself to swallow as I led the way, praying I wouldn't throw up, reluctance evident in every step I made.

I knew that I had to choose my words carefully. As Sammie's mistress, no one had to tell me that things could get real ugly for me, real fast. The detectives' eyes roamed around my small, one-bedroom apartment, taking in every little detail, including all of the expensive gifts that I'd thrown around in a hurry. I followed Bingham's gaze to a stack of big bills on an end table. *Damn!*

Mayer continued the questioning. He perched himself on the edge of my cream suede loveseat and removed a small notebook and ink pen from the inside pocket of his suit jacket. "How did you meet Lola Lee?"

I sighed in resignation. Lying would be futile. "I am Sammie's mistress." I took a deep breath, exhaled. "I only met her once. Apparently, Sammie told her about us; she came to confront me about it at the condo where I usually stayed with him, and we exchanged words about it." I refused to mention what happened after that.

"You only met her once?"

"Yes. Most mistresses don't make a habit of socializing with the wives of their lovers," I retorted.

Mayer shot me a disapproving look. I had to remember to hold my sharp tongue if I wanted to get to Kyashira.

"And you met her at Mr. Lee's condo?"

I raised an eyebrow. "I didn't *meet* her. We didn't have an appointment. She just showed up, unannounced."

"And when was the last time you saw Mr. Lee?"

"Earlier today. We just returned from a week in Hawaii, and he dropped me off."

"What was the purpose of the trip?"

I gave Mayer a "come on, now" look. "What do you think?"

Mayer continued to grill me: my whereabouts before and after Lola's visit, who I saw, who I spoke to. I thought I was home free when Mayer tucked his notebook back into his pocket. Then he blindsided me.

"Ms. Davis, we understand that you had an altercation with Mrs. Lee, shortly before her death."

Great. Of course they knew about the fight, and I had been really hoping to avoid that topic. I may have been a high-school dropout, but I watched enough TV to know that a mistress was usually a prime suspect in the death of her lover's wife, and a fight prior to the wife's death was not a good look. "Well, yes. I mean, like I said, she confronted me about my affair with her husband, Sammie. We exchanged words, and then things got a little *heated*. But right after that I left for Hawaii. All this is verifiable."

A little heated. That was like saying someone was a little pregnant.

"How bad was that altercation, Ms. Davis?"

Uh-oh. *Careful, Honey*, I told myself. "Uh, well, we got into it a little bit. Some slapping, rumbling on the floor. You know, a girl fight."

"Were either of you injured?"

"A few scratches. And my pride, I guess." I lowered my eyes as I remembered the humiliation of being tossed out on the street, with nothing but the clothes on my back—and there being nothing I could do about it. Not right then, anyway.

Bingham examined my face and spoke for the first time. "You seem to have healed pretty well."

"Well, a week in Hawaii does wonders for the healing process," I said nervously. My smile was falsely bright and had no effect on the jaded demeanors of the detectives.

Mayer and Bingham looked at each other in an unspoken signal, and rose to leave. "Thank you for your time, Ms. Davis. We'll be in touch. Please call us if you think of anything else." They each removed a business card from their respective wallets and handed them to me. I took them, ashamed to see that my hands shook slightly. As they walked out the door, Mayer turned and said, "Oh yeah. If you don't mind, we'd like for you to stay within the state of New York for the time being."

Hmm. It seemed like they didn't buy my story of a family emergency, or didn't care. Either way, I watched them walk away as fear gnawed a hole in my belly. Fuck what they minded; I had to get to Georgia. I had to get to Kyashira.

As I sped down the highway toward LaGuardia Airport, I knew that I would probably miss my scheduled flight to Georgia and would have to beg my way onto the next one; a family emergency just might bump me to the top of the standby list. I wondered if the detectives tailed me to the airport. I looked in my rearview mirror but couldn't see anything suspicious. The movies always showed a tail following three car lengths behind, but traffic was heavy and the only thing I noticed that distance behind me was a burgundy Ford Focus. If there was a tail, my amateur eyes couldn't spot it.

Would my flight plans be misconstrued? Would I look as if I were running because I was guilty? All I could do was hope that Detectives Mayer and Bingham did not follow me to the airport, and that I would be able to do what I had to do. The fairytale and fun of being a silver-tongued thief, spoiled mistress, and veteran party girl came to a screeching halt. Everything seemed to fall apart suddenly. When I was thrown in the hot seat, I could honestly say that I deserved everything that I got. Whatever the consequences that arose from my affiliation with a married man, I still had to accept the final result.

※※※

When I saw Paula, she looked broken and worn. I couldn't figure out what the deal was with her. She was not her usual jolly self, and just sat there as I studied her solemn expression. The once-lively house now looked dark and colorless. The furniture was sparse and the place looked like someone had just moved in, or moved out. Nevertheless, it was clean. The vibe I was getting was spooky. When I tried to talk to Paula, she seemed like she was alone in her own world. Jessie hadn't shown up yet, so I couldn't get any answers until she did, or Paula started talking.

"What happened to Kyashira, Paula?"

"She's gone."

Gone? A chill ran down my spine. "Gone where, Paula?"

She shrugged. A tear ran down her cheek.

"How could you let that happen to her? I left her with you and Jessie because I trusted the both of you." I looked around. "And where is Jessie, anyway?"

"Please don't fuss, Honey," Paula rasped. "It's not that I didn't love that little girl." She lowered her head. The panic I tried to keep at bay was threatening to spiral out of my control. Kyashira's gone, Paula acted like she had a deep, dark, secret, and I still had no idea where Jessie was.

"Paula," I said as calmly as I could, "I am just trying to find out what happened to Kyashira. A friend of a friend told me that she was down here in foster care, and I am trying to see if that's true or not, so I can know what to do." I stared at Paula. "Is Kyashira in foster care?"

I saw teardrops drip onto Paula's blouse. "The Division of Family and Children Services took the child from me. They took her downtown to be placed in foster care."

My fists clenched. Ritchie's source was on point. "But why? What happened? Where was Jessie?"

"After Jessie died, I just couldn't make it alone."

The room tilted as I struggled to process Paula's words. "Jessie died?

When?" I couldn't believe it.

"Yeah—not quite six months back. Cancer." The tears flowed more freely. "She'd been sick a long time."

I felt like I'd been sucker punched. "Shit. I didn't know."

"I miss Jessie, and I will always miss her. She was so lovely and sweet," Paula said with dreamy eyes. She hugged herself, as if she were cold and would never be warm again. "I let her down too. She told me to be responsible, for Kyashira's sake, and I blew it."

Paula confessed everything about that difficult time, how she cared for Jessie when she started going downhill, and how Kyashira fell through the cracks. When Jessie died, Paula fell apart and couldn't handle her own grief plus being a mother to Kyashira. She went on to explain that the neighbors reported my child being left alone after they heard Kyashira crying and a neighbor knocked on the door. Finding no adult home, she reported it to the juvenile authorities. After several interviews with Kyashira, a pattern of neglect was substantiated after Jessie died. Paula claimed she had been at work and couldn't afford a babysitter. I didn't know if that was true or not.

"Right after they took Kyashira, things got real tight for me financially," Paula continued. "Jessie's retirement check helped keep us afloat and when she died, well . . . we weren't married, and we never got around to formally adopting Kyashira, so the checks stopped." She sighed. "My brother bailed me out, but I had to put the house in his name in return." She looked at the staircase reflectively. "I rent from him now, and live upstairs. Some other people rent your old apartment."

I really didn't care at that moment about what Paula had gone through. Anger took over my senses. I tried to stay as calm as I could, but it grew more difficult by the second. I took a deep breath, but I still took a light jab at her.

"I can't believe I'm hearing this. I left my daughter in your care, and you allowed the authorities to take her away!"

"I did the best I could," Paula said defensively. She plucked at her blouse as she looked around the house, as if searching for an escape. Knowing Paula, she may have also been looking for some weed to calm her nerves.

"The best you could?" I looked at her like she'd lost her mind. "How the hell did you do the best you could, when you left a five-year-old alone in a house by herself! You knew better, Paula, grief or no grief! And even if you didn't, Jessie did, which is why she told you to get it together for Kyashira's sake. But you still couldn't, and now my child is in foster care!" My chest heaved with righteous anger. Paula's self-serving excuses were getting real old, real quick.

She stopped fidgeting and looked at me. "You're in no position to judge me, Honey. You haven't been responsible in your life, either. That's the reason you left Kyashira with me and Jessie in the first place, remember? You're her mother and at the end of the day, it was your responsibility to make sure that she was taken care of." She swallowed, then said in a calmer tone, "I swear to you that I made my best effort to make the arrangement work. I love that little girl, and would never want to see any hurt come her way."

As much as I wanted to tell Paula she was full of shit, I had to admit that she was right. I should've taken care of my own child, but I didn't. I couldn't manage to say much more to Paula after that; there really wasn't much left to say. I told Paula that I hoped things got better for her, then headed down to DFCS.

I became stuck in a land of red tape. When I finally explained why I was there, my next step was signing my name into a log and waiting to speak to someone in charge of Kyashira's case. I sat in a black plastic institutional chair during my long and torturous wait. A security guard was posted in the corner by a desk, flipping through a magazine. If I had come in there waving an Uzi, he probably wouldn't have paid attention. On top of that, other mothers were in the office with their children, who were making noise like they were outside on the playground. My eyes began to burn after I thought of all the dirt I'd done, and how Kyashira got caught in the crossfire, and I felt like it was killing me.

"Davis!" someone finally called.

I sprang to my feet and was guided to a small, cramped room, where a case manager, Mrs. Merrick, met with me. I explained that I was Kyashira's biological mother, and that I wanted to see her. I had to go through the entire gruesome story, explaining that I left her with her father's family several years ago. "I didn't come here to play games," I added.

Mrs. Merrick stared at me like I was something that crawled from under a rock. "You can't just show up and expect everyone to respond to your demands, Ms. Davis. There are procedures that must be followed." She picked up her pen and made a notation in the file in front of her. "Your daughter is in foster care. We'd have to contact the family that she is living with and ask when a good time would be for you to come and visit. Even though I've told you who she has been placed with, you must go through our agency to see her."

"But she's my daughter," I explained desperately. "I need to see her, to make sure she's all right!"

"As I explained," Mrs. Merrick said coldly, "a judge must decide if a valid reason has been established for the visit to be granted in the first place. From what you've told me, I'm not sure I can justify why even supervised contact should happen."

"How can you say that? I told you that I left her with family." I took a deep breath. Acting like I didn't have any home training was not going to help me see Kyashira any sooner. "I was unaware that she was not being cared for properly. I tried to get in contact with the people who were caring for her, but my letters went unanswered and when I tried to call, the phone had been disconnected. I tried!"

"I'm sorry, Ms. Davis, but we do have to follow procedure here." Mrs. Merrick closed the file and stood to leave.

"My daughter is just a defenseless little girl, and that's the best you can manage to say?" I banged my hand on the table, making us both jump. "How would you feel if this happened to your daughter?" I stood in indignation. "Why is it that my child is being treated like property? None of this is her fault! I'm here out of concern for her. No, I didn't choose my circumstances, but I was young and scared. Don't judge me for what happened. Don't judge me for the way I lived. I thought I was doing the right thing at the time when my family refused to help me, or let me keep her. I carried Kyashira, I gave birth to her, and I miss her. I am her mother, and no one else will ever be. Please help me," I begged. "You don't own her. I'm her mother! I can't speak to or see my own daughter?"

Mrs. Merrick sighed. "I'll look into it and follow up with the judge. But it's not going to happen overnight," she warned. "I've got sixty-five cases to handle, and I'm one person."

I wanted to reach out and smack the shit out of her, but I didn't want to give her the pleasure of seeing me screw up my chances to see my daughter. The whole situation felt like it was legal kidnapping. Fuck all that.

As soon as I left DCFS, I called Ritchie and asked him to find out if any of his contacts in Georgia could locate an address for a woman named Candace Jones, the woman with whom Kyashira had been placed in foster care. If he couldn't locate her I'm sure it would be easy enough to try myself via the Internet. Luckily, he got back to me with the information I needed. I scribbled the address on a piece of paper and went to see my child.

❊

I knew I was breaking the law by making an unannounced visit to the home where my child lived, but I had to know if Kyashira was in dire straights or not. If the streets were talking about my child being in harm's way, I refused to leave Georgia without seeing what was what for myself.

From what I could see, the home was not habitable, safe, or sane. I could hear music pouring out into the street. When the door opened, a chill came over me. A woman answered and she looked at me like she wasn't sure if I was there for business or pleasure.

"May I speak with Candace Jones?" I asked.

"Who the fuck is you?" she asked, smacking her gum.

"Are you Candace?"

"I said, who the fuck is you?" the woman repeated with an attitude. She propped a hand on her hips and dared me to say something.

I smelled weed and craned my neck around her. The place looked dirty as hell. I even spotted a crack pipe on a beat-up coffee table. People walked around in all types of dress and undress. The woman who was supposed to be supervising my baby deserved the Dumb Ass of the Year award. It was more than obvious that she wasn't the responsible type, either.

"Is a child named Kyashira here?"

Candace's eyes narrowed. "What about her?"

"We need to talk. Could I come in?"

"Hell, naw! I don't know who you are. I done asked you that two times and until I get an answer, we ain't talking about shit."

"I'm her mother," I finally explained. "My name is Honey Davis. I need to see my child."

Candace folded her arms across her small chest. "You not coming in here."

"I never terminated my rights as a parent," I informed her. "I need to see my child! Please, let me in."

Candace looked me up and down, noting the one-carat diamond studs in my ears, the matching diamond tennis bracelet and rings, the Donna Karan red silk baby tee, the Lucky 7 jeans, the snakeskin Jimmy Choo sandals, the Kate Spade red leather bag on my arm. My entire outfit probably cost more than the shack she lived in. "I heard that you abandoned her five years ago and left her with them dykes on the other side of town, when both of them was living." She shook her head and scratched her ass. "Anyway, I done fed her and put her to sleep." She gave my rings another look. "You seem to be doing good for yourself. Forget about her and go on living as you have, *bitch!*"

"Who the hell do you think you are?" I exploded. "I want my child! I want my baby!"

Candace merely sneered at me. "You expect me to pity you? You walk up in here like yo' shit don't stink, like everybody gotta jump just because you decided to come down here and act like you had a child. Yeah, I already got a call from Mrs. Merrick," she said as she saw the surprise on my face. "Let the courts decide if you should be able to come up in here. I ain't gon' stand here and argue with your stupid ass." She moved to slam the door in my race.

"My child is coming with me!" I blocked the door and pushed past this low-class bitch who stood between me and my daughter. She stumbled backward, off-balance, and I plowed into a hard, male body that reeked of weed and unwashed balls.

"Hey, ma. You want some of dis?" the thug asked, half high. He puffed on his blunt, held the smoke for about ten seconds, and blew it out. His eyes looked sleepy. "This is some bomb muthafucking shit!" he said, taking another puff.

I looked around in horror. In addition to the crack pipes and roach papers I'd seen when I peeped through the door, the room was filled with crackhead-looking broads who were hugged up on men. More people lined the walls, dirty dancing to the bass of the gangsta rap that rattled the windows. My blood really boiled when Candace turned and yelled at a child for accidentally dropping a cereal box. When I saw those eyes and that face, I knew it was my baby who'd come down the hall.

It was clear that my daughter was just there because of the check Candace received as a foster parent. Kyashira wore crumpled, dirty clothes and she looked very small and underweight for her age. Her hair was uncombed, and it didn't look like it had been washed for at least a month. Seeing that made me lose complete faith in the legal system. I thought of the privileged childhood I had and felt guilty and broken. My daughter deserved far better.

"Get your ass back in that room!" Candace yelled.

I called out her name. "Kyashira!"

She looked at me, startled.

"It's Mommy. Oh baby, Momma's here." My bottom lip began to tremble. I wanted to put my arms around her and moved toward her. People were too caught up in their madness to care what was happening.

"You hate your mother, don't you?" Candace said cruelly.

"She doesn't hate me!" I yelled. I finally touched my sweet little angel. I hugged my little girl tightly; she shook and smelled like fresh urine. "I'm going to get you out of here. I promise," I told her. I felt so selfish; I should have been in her life to love her each and every night.

"She doesn't even know you," Candace said.

"Mommy?" Kyashira finally said. She looked at me with shell-shocked, empty eyes. "Are you really my mommy?"

She started crying. I knew she was scared and didn't know what to believe. I couldn't blame her. I could tell that living in such a hellhole affected her self-esteem. She was scared, and I hated that Kyashira was with strangers of such a low caliber.

"Yes, I really am your mother, Kyashira. You're coming with me!"

I picked Kyashira up and walked toward the door. Candace grabbed one of her arms and pulled her in the opposite direction.

"Let go of her!" I yelled. We engaged in a human game of tug-o-war. Finally, the music stopped, I gave one final tug, and Candace fell to the floor the floor. I got an eyeful of stank, naked pussy. Her nasty ass didn't even wear any drawers.

"Somebody call the got damn police!" she yelled at the top of her lungs.

I never saw people scatter so fast. I began to realize that I'd made a terrible mistake, showing up like that. If I was going to roll up on Kyashira's foster home outside of DFSC approval, I should have been ready to find her, grab her, and get the hell out of Barnesville. I was going to pay for thinking with my heart, and not my head. The shit I stepped in only got deeper.

Chapter Sixteen

RAINY DAYS

A police cruiser with wailing sirens pulled up to the house. Two officers got out of the car, hands on their guns, and looked at me, then Kyashira, then Candace. "Someone here called the police?" one officer asked.

"Now look, this is what happened. I was minding my own business. *She* comes up on my property, unwanted, unannounced, yelling, pushing and screaming." Candace was bug-eyed as she pointed at me for dramatic emphasis. "The next thing I know, she is beating me up. I was down on the floor, trying to keep her from acting a fool in front of my child."

"That's not how it happened," I chimed in.

"Yes, it did!"

"No it didn't. You better recognize. I didn't beat you up in front of *my* child. Why not tell the officer about me being Kyashira's biological mother? Why not tell the officer how you had weed, crack pipes, crack rocks, and ex-con-looking crackheads up in your house while my baby came out of the back carrying a box of damn cereal, because your trifling ass wasn't feeding her right?"

The first officer looked at Candace. "Ma'am, are you the foster parent of this child?"

"Yes, I am." Candace snatched Kyashira out of my grasp and hugged her to her bony frame.

He looked at me. "And you are the biological mother of this child?"

"Yes sir, I am."

"Has the court granted you visitation of your child, Ms.—?"

"Davis. Honey Davis. And no," I sighed, "I didn't have court-approved visitation."

"See!" Candace screeched. "She just rolled up here for no reason, starting trouble, getting this child all upset and making me look bad."

The officers stepped to the side and had a quick conference. One got on the radio, spoke into it, waited for an answer, then signed off with "Ten-four." They both walked back toward Candace, Kyashira, and me.

I was arrested for disorderly conduct and trespassing. While I was detained in the car, the officers went into the house. Shortly thereafter, a green, state-issued car pulled to the curb and Kyashira was led away with a social worker. She was shaking, and I was screaming. We were driven away in two separate cars, headed for two different destinations.

What did it take to rectify past ugly deeds? That's what I asked myself as I sat in back of the patrol car, my heart breaking into thousands of tiny pieces. I finally realized that I needed to step up for the sake of my daughter. I began to thank Ritchie in my head for his true friendship. Had he not tracked me down, she would probably have fared far worse.

Little Kyashira was once again taken into custody by DFCS. This time, the abuse was clear and real, and the social worker documented that she was being treated as a meal ticket by someone who preyed on innocent children for a monthly check. I hated that I brought Kyashira more pain, and yet another home that was not with me. I only meant to make things better for her.

Drowning myself in material things could not make up for missing out on being in her life. At the time I gave her up, I was young and scared, but I had no excuse now. I had plenty of time to take custody of her again, especially when I started making good money. It was time to stop being promiscuous, to stop being a shot-glass diva. I wanted to break the cycle of pain in my own life, but first I had to deal with the situation I created in Georgia.

"Where are you living?" an officer asked as I was being processed into the county jail.

"New York," I mumbled.

"Could you be more specific?"

"I'm sorry. It's been a helluva trip." I sniffled and gave them my address.

When my name was run through the Bureau of Criminal Investigation database, I shortly found out that I was wanted for murder in New York!

"What!" I shrieked after I heard the news.

I didn't stay behind bars in Georgia much longer. The New York Sheriff's Department was waiting to extradite me back to the state of the initial crime.

"Now what?" I asked after I heard the news. By that time, I had calmed down some. Still, I choked back tears with an unstable mind. "I didn't kill that woman! I didn't! My child needs me," I insisted.

"Your child will be taken care of," I was told. "There are procedures in place for her welfare."

"That's what I was told last time," I snapped. But what else could I do? I just had to take my licks like a big girl.

※

Things started moving quickly after I was extradited back to New York. The prospect of being charged with murder was scary, but I still felt confident that the whole thing would blow over. What could they have on me, aside from being Sammie's feisty jump-off? Okay, fine. Maybe in their eyes, I had a motive to get Lola out of the way, but since I didn't do it, I told the police that I would talk to them without a lawyer.

Dumb move. I ended up having my street clothes traded for jail attire. When the guards gave me the basic jail essentials that included soap, toothpaste, and toilet paper, the reality of the matter set in even more. Terrified didn't begin to describe how I was feeling.

Within a day, I stood in front of a judge for a hearing, led there by police escorts. When the judge asked if I could afford a lawyer, I said yes. I figured I'd call Sammie Lee since this entire situation with Lola was his fault, and he did promise to do whatever it took to keep me in his life. Getting me a very good, very expensive lawyer certainly qualified. I was going to call Ritchie, but then I remembered I couldn't place a collect call to a cell phone. Plus, Ritchie didn't have that kind of money for a high-priced lawyer, anyway.

When it was time for my phone call, I called Sammie Lee at his office, and he accepted the charges.

"Sammie!" I almost cried with relief. "Thank God I reached you! Look, I don't know how this happened, but I'm in big trouble. Can you help me get a lawyer, because I really don't know—"

He cut me off abruptly. "Are you kidding me? You have a nerve to call me collect and ask for my help, after the trouble you've caused? You killed my wife! You killed Lola! Don't ever contact me again; I have nothing to say to you, except that you deserve to be punished!" *Click.*

He hung up on me before I could utter another word. I went through a whole lot of drama just to be able to use the phone, and the bastard hung up on me. He fucking hung up on me, then had the nerve to treat me like some criminal trash! It became clear that Sammie Lee only accepted the collect charges long enough to chew me out. But something wasn't right with him. Why would Sammie Lee think *I* killed his wife?

I stood there in a daze, still holding the phone, until I was moved along.

I was offered a court-appointed attorney, but I said that I would hire my own. I ended up not being able to do that after all. Who else was I going to call that seemed to give a real damn about me, but actually had not only a landline, but enough money to post my bail? I'd burned so many bridges, and I didn't have any financial reserves left since my accounts had been frozen. I was used to asking men for everything. I hadn't even stayed in touch with my friends Yolanda and Pookie. It wasn't looking good for me. In fact, things were looking kind of shabby. Real shabby.

By the time I stood in front of the Honorable Judge Harrington a second time, I made a plea for the public defender I once turned down.

"You again? Are you sure you made up your mind about counsel this time?" he asked harshly.

"Yes, Your Honor. I would like a public defender to represent me," I answered humbly.

As I was led out of the courtroom by the guards, my optimism faded and I felt like a nobody. All of the fun and games I played flashed through my mind. Room service, popping bottles, VIP rooms, first-class flights, designer clothes . . . all gone. Poof!

Later that day, the court-appointed defense lawyer did come to see me. Attorney Anthony Grant talked to me for two hours. I didn't like him. He seemed to have all the book smarts in the world, but that was it. I couldn't help but to envision him bungling my case. I felt like I was dangling off a cliff and my entire life and future was all up to him. I hated that helpless feeling, and I clasped my hands as my shoulders slumped. I knew I was in extra deep shit.

Despite that, I tried my best to bite my tongue since it was not the time to show off and give anyone else a reason to be completely turned off by my attitude.

"What did you do for a living?" the lawyer asked.

"I told you thirty minutes ago that I was a mistress to a wealthy investment broker. What do you think I did for a living?" I snapped.

"Oh," he answered, finally writing my reply down.

I answered all of his questions as straightforwardly as I could, but I had to insist that he take notes and act as if he took my life being on the line seriously. Maybe he wasn't dumb. Maybe he was apathetic. All I knew was that Grant didn't seem to respect the urgency of my circumstances. By the end of the interview, he told me he'd return after finding out some things from the district attorney.

❖

Upon Grant's return I found out that a search warrant of my apartment had been granted and my apartment had been searched. Although Grant didn't have billable hours working in his favor as a high-powered criminal attorney, at least I did get some light shed on the situation.

"The police found a weapon in your closet," he told me in a monotone. My eyes were fixed on his lips. He cleared his throat, but I didn't want to interrupt him. "The reports state the weapon was found in a box underneath a hat."

"You mean a hat box? I never put a gun in my hat box. I didn't do it," I interjected. I bounced my knee in an effort to calm my nerves.

"Yes, well, how did the gun get there?"

"I don't know!"

"That's where it was found, Ms. Davis. The gun was consistent with the wounds of the murder victim."

"But I'm just a suspect, right?"

"Well, there is sufficient evidence to keep you in custody now. In addition to finding the weapon, there's more," he told me with a dead-pan face. "The victim's husband stated that he wanted to end the affair he was having with you, but you insisted on continuing your relationship. He said he wanted to try and make it work with his wife. He said that they had no real problems. He had a fling after trying to ease some pressure in his work life. He does admit to the affair he had with you, but he says that he realized the value of his family. He stated that the relationship with his was great and regrets to have cheated on her just that once."

"That's a lie!" I shouted. Beads of sweat formed on my forehead. "He told me he couldn't stand her, and they didn't have sex!"

"Are you finished? May I continue now?"

"Yeah, yeah, yeah. What else?" I asked impatiently, a large lump growing in my throat.

"He also presented records: credit card statements showing gifts that were for you, phone bills showing calls to and from your cell phone number, hotel stays, bank deposits to your account, and other miscellaneous items. Clearly, he spent a lot of money on you, Ms. Davis. He stated that you didn't want to end the relationship because of the benefits you received from the relationship. You had no job, Mr. Lee paid your living expenses, and his wife's family was interviewed and stated that they had been told that you had an altercation with her. A police-man corroborated everything they said with a written report, something about an altercation at the couple's condo.

I started to shiver as Grant continued. "Your friends agreed that you didn't get along with others. It was stated that you ran away from home and had quite a checkered past with a young man named Mikaylo Jones. Because of your arrest in Georgia, information led the authorities to him because he is the father of a Kyashira Star Davis. The young man is not interested in guardianship, although the situation was explained to him. The detectives are still conducting their investigation, of course."

In nervous rage, I cracked my knuckles then stuck my fist into my mouth. I sighed with disbelief. I expected the streets were talking about me like a dog. Forget all of the public ridicule; it was Sammie's betrayal that hurt the most. I couldn't believe he implied that I was capable of murder, simply because of all of the things he'd done for me. He offered and came up with the initial plan to take care of me. It wasn't even my idea, although I did go along with it! Sure, Sammie. Sure. I was the jealous mistress on the fringe of upper-class society, who was kicked out by a man I once believed was my father, as I grieved over my mother's death. Then my temper was so bad, I became angry, frustrated and jealous enough to kill his wife myself or have one of my thug friends do it for me, because I survived off your generosity. The facts were all twisted and fucked up. Damn—what a theory!

I stood up, full of nervous, furious energy. "I can't believe Sammie Lee said those things! He did mention divorce once. I was the one who told him to stay with his wife."

"Please slow down, Ms. Davis. We're going to talk about that in just a moment." He waited for me to calm down and sit down before he continued. "Before I leave today, I will need you to make a list of your whereabouts on the following dates." He handed me a list. I looked at it and placed it back on the table.

"He's got to be setting me up! Now that I think about it, I'm sure that he is the one behind this." I bit my lip. Things were not looking good for me at all. The thought of never seeing Kyashira again, or at least not seeing her for the next twenty-five years, made me nauseous.

Grant shook his head. "According to him, Mrs. Lee was well loved, with no enemies. She was settled in her career, and loved her children. Mr. Lee was looking forward to sharing a long life with her. Given the turn of events, he wants justice served. He told the detectives that he would cooperate in any and all possible manners."

"I didn't always try to do the right thing, but that's a bunch of bull! This is getting ridiculous. I can hardly believe what I am hearing. The man is sounding real shady."

Grant shrugged. "In any event, the state needs to prove its case. They have solid evidence."

"The man is telling straight lies. How is that solid anything? He pursued me in a night club and propositioned me to have the arrangement we had. He manipulated me!"

"He has an alibi. You don't."

When Grant said those words, I felt like he didn't believe I had even one little redeeming quality about me. Though it may have been true, I was very offended by his comment.

"Am I being judged more because I'm a woman who was sleeping with a married man? What about Sammie? He didn't respect his vows. Why isn't anyone questioning him? Why is his version of the truth being accepted at face value? I don't understand why the authorities are skeptical of me, but not the spouse, who happens to be Sammie."

Grant sighed. Clearly, he hadn't signed on for anyone like me. "He is being investigated, Ms. Davis. As your attorney, I am simply telling you the facts of *your* case. That fight you had with his wife is very problematic here. That and finding the gun, of course."

"Like I told you, I was his mistress but I did not kill his wife. Do you even believe me?" I asked.

Instead of answering the question, my lawyer said, "It would help if you tell me if you know anything about this murder. If you help the police, we can try for a plea bargain."

I broke down crying. He had to believe me. If he didn't believe me, they might as well stick a needle in my arm now, even though New York didn't have the death penalty.

"I am sure you've worked on hundreds of murder cases, and mostly every one of the people sitting where I am today claimed they didn't do it," I sobbed. "Well, I didn't. I am a victim in this. I am no Mother Theresa, but I am not the villain either. I know you have too many cases, but I will not request that you make a deal just so you can go on to the next one." I shook my head in refusal. I took a deep breath to help myself continue as I cried. "No, I was not in the wrong place at the wrong time. I chose to be with Sammie, and Sammie Lee said he wanted to be together. He was willing to leave his wife for me. I did cross the line and deal with a married man, but I will not apologize for something I did not do. It's sad that a woman died, but I won't take the blame for a murder I didn't commit. My daughter needs me. She has no one." I began to sob again. "None of this is right! She may never see me again because of this."

Grant closed his briefcase and stood to leave. "That's all for today. I'll be back."

Everything became somewhat of a blur in my world of chains and steel bars. The nightmares of prison life were only something one could experience and never fully explain. I adjusted because I had to. No visitors came to see me at first. I started calling my girls because they had land lines as well as cell phones. Although Pookie did act jealous of me at times, she was still one of my best friends. I felt that she'd be there for me when it counted most, so I called her first. Also, a part of me didn't want to burden Yolanda. I knew she was busy with her baby. The last thing I wanted to do was upset her.

"Oh! I-uh . . . hi, Honey," Pookie stuttered after she accepted the collect call.

"Please come see me, Pookie! I'm sure you heard what happened. I can't get in touch with Ritchie because he only has a cell phone; could you please tell him to come too?"

"Yeah, girl. I understand completely how you must feel. We'll all be there," Pookie assured me.

While I waited, I thought about my friendships, which led to the choices that I'd made, and the bad karma that I would have to face. I found myself analyzing everything that had ever happened in my past. I thought of every warning my mother and father gave me, every cuss word I doled out when I was misbehaving, and every time I wanted to run the streets of Harlem.

I tossed and turned all night long, then got up at four-thirty the next morning. I dealt with issues of jailhouse informants trying to break me, and also the authorities trying to sweet talk me into taped confessions. I could trust no one in jail; I could barely trust myself.

Would I have to sit through a trial? Would I rot in jail, all because my wild days led to greed? Would I have to endure the press turning this into a media circus? I didn't know. On top of all of this drama, I learned that the DA was out to make a name for himself off the case. He was new in the position and needed a feather in his cap.

Every news channel began to cover Lola's tragic death, and yes, the media had dubbed me the "Scorned Mistress Murderer." Lola had been shown on TV, wheeled out of her home in a body bag.

"Lola Lee, wife of global investment broker Samuel Lee, was found dead in her home. The body of the forty-year-old real estate agent and former model was found by police after a neighbor called and expressed concern that the mother had not picked up her children from school. When police entered the home, the victim was found dead, with two bullet wounds in the head. School counselors have been speaking with students who mourn the loss of a favorite neighborhood mom. Her children are left to grieve, in the care of their father, aunts, and grandparents. Her husband's mistress, Honorina "Honey" Davis, has been charged with her murder. More to come on this breaking story at eleven."

One of Lola's aunts stood in front of her home and spoke to the camera. "I can never get my niece back. That woman should get the death penalty for murdering her, but since they don't offer that in New York, she should stay behind bars and never get to see the light of day again. The family is offering a $30,000 reward to anyone who provides information that leads to the killer's conviction. Please call the New York State police if you know anything."

❈

After that happened, whatever civil rights I thought I had were violated. Even the guards tried to force me to confess to a crime that I didn't commit.

"She made you shoot her, didn't she? You know, if you just admit to what you did, you can probably work something out," one guard said.

They alternated between the nice "friend" approach and a nasty, harassing one. When they were nasty, I was reminded that if I didn't accept a plea bargain, and if I did go to prison, those cat-calling women would eat me alive—literally—because I wasn't so tough. It became clear that I wouldn't go to some yuppie prison. Thoughts of places like

Sing-Sing shot through my head. I was just being held in a special isolated cell due to the media sensation of the case, but if and when I was transferred, bad would become worse. Hell, life in prison without possibility of parole would be the upside, though.

"Wake up and smell the coffee, Davis! You could get the death penalty for this," I was constantly reminded. I wasn't sure if the guards felt as though they were helping to eliminate evil in the world, or they were just mad because the pay was shitty, the hours were long, and the only thing that made them feel good was the power that they held over people like me. All I did know for sure is that they were fishing for information.

"My lawyer isn't present. I don't want to talk about this without consulting Mr. Grant," I answered. For that response, my food and water was withheld. These little pressuring sessions took place whenever and wherever. I soon found out that some guards were as shady as people they guarded; everyone was in cahoots.

When they couldn't do anything with me, I was pushed, slammed up against walls, screamed at, ridiculed, and even roughed up a little bit. Imagine what it's like to be stared at while you take a shower or use the restroom. Nothing was off limits—I mean *nothing*. I was stripped of every human decency that one could imagine. All I did was cry in a dark cell at night, pleading to be saved by anyone who would listen. No one came, of course. I sat alone on a mattress that smelled of mildew, in a small concrete cell. After a while, I accepted that no one would save me and let the numbness wash over me as I waited for the next opportunity to hear how the case was shaping up.

The next time I saw my lawyer, I was depressed and worn. I mentioned the corruption and coercion, and even showed him a fresh bruise on my arm, but my counsel just glossed over it. Maybe he thought I deserved all of that harsh treatment . Maybe it was for the best, as official complaints would've only made things worse for me. Forget reporting anything to the warden. That's all I had to say about jailhouse politics.

"There's a few things that came up," Grant began.

"Now what?" I let out a groan.

"A car was seen swerving in the area, the day of Lola's murder."

"I told you!" I said happily, my face breaking out in a big smile.

"Things haven't turned your way just yet. In fact, that's made matters worse, along with some other things from your past that came forward."

The happy look on my face soon left. "Do you even comprehend how I'm being treated in here? Everyone's on me! I'm stuck with some serious charges. What are you doing to sort this out?" I snapped.

Grant told me that comments were being made about me from various angles. Included were statements made by men that I'd hustled and drugged, who claimed to have been vulnerable and duped. I was said to have been a cold woman who wronged others without emotion or concern. Maybe some of that was right, if I was to be judged by my past, but a part of that just wasn't fair. If the case went to trial, the jurors would've already judged me before I even sat down to tell my version on the witness stand. I was a spectacle for all the world to see, and I hated how that felt. I was being railroaded, and no one seemed to care that my life was on the line and that I did *not* kill Sammie's wife. Then again, something happened to make me think twice about that.

Chapter Seventeen

WHAT'S DONE IN THE DARK

"Pookie! Girl, thanks so much for coming to see me." It had been over two weeks since I called her and asked her to come.

"Of course I'd come to see you," she told me. I noticed her half smile. Pookie seemed a little cold, but she'd always been moody.

"I need you now more than I ever have. This is really breaking me down emotionally. Where is everyone else?"

"They're here and there. You know how it is. Don't worry about it. Mikaylo said to tell you good luck with everything."

"Wow. How nice of him," I said with heavy sarcasm. "Is he aware that his daughter is in foster care?"

"Yeah, he knows. He's just been busy. You know that man is going to go far is life. He really has changed for the better."

Something about the way she said it set off an internal alarm, but I dismissed it. "Busy doing what?"

"Working, and being a good man." Pookie's face suddenly lit up with a big smile.

"Only if you say so. I really don't want to talk about him right now."

I changed the subject. "Look, I may need your help if I need people to write letters to the judge about what kind of person I really am. I need letters to show that many tough things happened to me after my mom died, but I've really changed. Are you down?"

"I'm not much one for writing, so I don't know if I could help. How many good characteristics would someone have to point out, except for you being a shallow and shady bitch?"

"What? Are you serious?" I looked at Pookie strangely. That internal alarm started going off again, but a bit louder this time. Had I made a mistake in confiding in Pookie?

Pookie laughed. "I'm sorry. I was just trying to lighten the mood. Mikaylo tells me I need to watch my mouth sometimes, but he's getting used to it now. You know how I can be."

I frowned. "Why are you constantly talking about him? Don't you want to know what's going on with me?"

Pookie giggled. It sounded insincere, and my internal alarm started blaring. "My bad. I heard about how things went down. I'm sorry you got in all this legal mess. My baby says maybe this will make you grow up. He probably would've come, but he's cleaning the house. He has more responsibilities of his own these days."

Now I was confused. "Your baby? Cleaning whose house?"

"Well, we started hanging out, and you know . . ."

Who was "we?" "No, I don't know," I commented.

Why did I have to go and take the bait?

"We're *involved—me and Mikaylo.*" Pookie lifted her sleeve, revealing a new, heart-shaped tattoo with her and Mikaylo's names scripted across it.

A pang of jealousy shot through my stomach right away. "What! You just want to be me so bad, don't you?" I couldn't believe what I was hearing. I could feel my heart beating in my throat. Mikaylo and I had long been over, but he was my first, my first love, and the father of my child; some feelings don't die that easily.

Pookie smirked. "No, sweetie. It's not like that. Look where you are and look where I am, Honey." She looked me up and down. "You're locked up, and I'm free. Now I look fresh, and I'm being the woman I was all along, and you can't stop my shine anymore," she gloated.

A fresh wave of betrayal washed over me. "How could you do this to me, Pookie? How?"

She shrugged. "Things happen, and love is hard. You can't predict what can happen in the future. You can't control who you fall in love with, and we bring out the best in each other. He doesn't just give me dick, he gives me a piece of his heart, and that's just real talk." She stroked her tattoo. "Besides, it's not like you and Kaylo were married. Y'all have been over for over five years now. It was time for him to move on."

I shook my head. This was un-fucking-believable. "How could you mess with my child's father? He doesn't care about you or anyone else. You're flattering yourself. He lied to me and he'll lie to you."

"How could I?" Pookie snorted. "Well, how could you get stuck behind bars? Life. Obviously, you moved on with the man whose wife you murdered. Did Mikaylo not have a right to move on with his life? Why should he waste his life away because he wasn't with you?" She rolled her eyes at me. "Don't be so quick to judge our relationship."

"First of all, I didn't kill anyone. Second of all, you know Kaylo jumped ship."

Pookie's nostrils flared. The jealousy she'd harbored all these years finally broke free. Her voice dripped venom as she spat, "Don't act like you've always been responsible. Maybe you'll realize that it ain't all about you, Honey. It never was. You thought you were the shit just because your parents had that Sugar Hill type of money. Humph, you're not better! People think just 'cause we're from the hood, we're fuckups. Just like you had a right to fuck a married man and do what you thought was right for you at the time, I had a right to do what I thought was right for me."

Pookie's presence was making me itch. "I'm through this with this conversation."

"Well, I'm not. Mikaylo is the best thing that ever happened to me. If you want to ask his opinion, I suggest you buy yourself a phone card from commissary and see what he says."

I sucked my teeth. "Whatever."

"I just came to say goodbye, and to let you know that the crew didn't forget about you, plus one more little thing: I'm pregnant, and I'm going to marry Kaylo someday. Don't think you can't keep in touch, though. Write us. Hang in there!" She stood and smiled a fake smile.

I wanted to fuck her skank ass up after she laid that whammy on me. I knew Pookie had done that just to hurt me and make me jealous; she was really enjoying what she perceived as her newfound power over me. I also knew that Mikaylo got with Pookie just because he was a man whore, and she was probably more than available for him. Both of them had me questioning what I ever saw in either one of them.

I had to be honest, though; I'd grown a lot because of living in the fast lane, but I wasn't perfect. If I needed medicine for arrogance, I got it by getting the news about her and Mikaylo. Even so, I was determined that she wouldn't get the pleasure of seeing me explode. I took a deep breath, pushed my imaginary RESET button, and focused on myself and what I was up against. I didn't give Pookie the pleasure of seeing one tear fall, but as soon as my back turned and I was led out of the cell, I cried. In fact, I cried myself a mini-river. I couldn't help but to think of the horrible things that Mikaylo put me through; yet, according to Pookie, he treated her so lovingly. Pookie was the same person who hated babies when she was younger. Pookie was the same person who said that the crew should always stick together and never let men come between us. Just like they say, actions do speak louder than words. My pity party was cut short.

❧❋❧

In dim light, with the backdrop of dark shadows, I felt as if the walls were closing in on me. I'd been sitting in a steel cage, but the spaces between the bars might as well have been sheets of solid metal. I felt trapped, numb, and drained, like all of the blood had been sucked out of my body. After lunch, I shuffled toward a seat in the conference room and sat down while I waited for Grant. I didn't feel like talking to him again; Pookie had really done a number on my nerves, and I just wanted to curl up in a ball and stay there until this was all over. My head nodded slightly and I started to slouch as I forced my eyes to stay open.

❧❋❧

"I'm tired of recalling events, and I can't take it! No more bad news," I shouted at Grant. My cheeks were hot and my heart was pounding. I went from feeling sedated to exploding in no time flat. I was tired of feeling alone, and I was tired of feeling persecuted. I rubbed my temple a few times and inhaled. By that time, I tuned into his words.

He didn't react. He just gave me that same expressionless look, cleared his throat and resumed speaking. "Detectives pulled phone records, analyzed credit card statements, and went over Sammie Lee's accounts."

"Great," I remarked sarcastically. "This can't be good for me."

"A credit card charge was made. One of those credit card charges was a plane ticket. When questioned about the purpose of it, Sammie

Lee said it was for you."

"I know. It was the ticket he charged for me." I rolled my eyes and began sniffling. I felt so used. "I can't hear this sort of thing again. I can't." I shook my head.

"The ticket wasn't to Hawaii or Georgia. It was from New York to Miami."

I shrugged. "He traveled on business. That's probably why he was down in Miami."

"The authorities also tracked down a recurring number on phone records. When asked about the number, Sammie Lee stated that it probably belonged to someone his wife knew that he wasn't aware of, but the detectives checked that out too."

"This is going nowhere fast. Can we cut this short today? I don't think you understand that I'm doing the best I can to emotionally survive through in this place. I also had another visitor, who didn't exactly bring a smile to my face."

"Ms. Davis, I'll say this once for you: I'm here to do my job. Now would you really like me to leave?" he asked.

He was right; if he left, I'd be completely up shit's creek without a paddle. If I thought things were bad now, having no attorney at all would make them worse. I needed to get it together. "I'm sorry. Please continue."

"The number that appeared in a pattern belonged to a phone account of a Marcus Stevenson. With that piece of information, the detectives analyzed the times of the calls. An outgoing call was placed from that same number to a man around the same time witnesses living near the crime scene reported they saw a speeding car with tinted windows. Also, Mr. Lee has interacted with Mr. Stevenson previously. Police investigated Mr. Stevenson and discovered that he has had brushes with the law in the past." Grant consulted the notes on his legal pad. "Someone came forward and stated that he sold this Marcus Stevenson a gun on the street a week before that strange plane ticket was purchased."

I looked at Grant in confusion. "So what does all this have to do with me?"

"Good question. Sammie Lee and his wife owned property in Miami as well. The police discovered that Mr. Lee had a savings account there. A large withdrawal of cash was made several months before the plane ticket was purchased. Shortly after that, the account was closed. And, according to the dates you submitted, this was well before you and Sammie Lee ever began a relationship." He hesitated, as if he didn't want to break the streak of good news. "I'm sorry to have to tell you this, Ms. Davis, but you weren't the only one Sammie Lee had an affair with. There were more women in Sammie's past during his marriage. Several, in fact."

I began to perk up. I didn't care who Sammie Lee had been fucking in the past. I was more concerned with him getting his just desserts now.

"Multiple women have called the tip line, explaining that they met him in bars or on the Internet. Each woman told a similar story, similar to how you said your relationship with him began and continued."

I let that marinate. *Sammie, you rat bastard*, I thought. "Who is Marcus Stevenson?"

"His limo driver."

I recalled the quiet yet built man who drove the limousine. "The few times I rode in the limo, he gave me a different name. It was some generic nickname, like Big G, I think."

Grant nodded. "Stevenson has several aliases. The police are investigating them all. Further investigation turned up a sizeable life insurance policy on Lola Lee. Mr. Lee recently made a trip to see Stevenson around the time when Mrs. Lee's body was first discovered. According to Stevenson, Mr. Lee heard that detectives had been questioning Stevenson and he reportedly told Stevenson that he better keep his mouth shut, or their future plans would be ruined."

"What future plans? Did the detective find out what Sammie Lee paid for the hit?" I bounced on my seat in excitement. I could see the light at the end of the tunnel, even though it was faint.

"Well, there's a bit of a strange twist that may really shock you." Grant actually blushed as he looked down at his notes.

I raised my eyebrow at the sight. "Yeah?"

"Mr. Lee is bisexual."

"What! That bastard!" A small sense of panic threatened to erupt. Sammie Lee and I hardly used condoms because I was on the pill. What if he gave me a disease? Yet one more problem to deal with ...

"Yes. Well, actually, Mr. Lee had been, uh, on the down low for a while. Marcus shot Mrs. Lee at the request of Mr. Lee, because he thought he would finally have Mr. Lee all to himself. They agreed that a woman should take the fall to throw off all suspicion, and you fit the bill. We found a copy of your house keys on Mr. Stevenson's premises."

I suddenly remembered when Sammie Lee instructed me to give my keys to Stevenson to get my flat tires fixed while we went to Hawaii. I thought that it was odd when I handed him my car keys he insisted that I also give him my apartment keys as well stating he'd leave my car keys inside. That explained how the gun got planted in my place.

"That large sum of money that was withdrawn was to help Marcus Stevenson with a street debt, not for the hit."

"Wow." I was stunned at the bones that had come tumbling out of Sammie's closet.

"Stevenson broke down and confessed to the shooting, in exchange for receiving a lesser charge. Mr. Lee was charged as an accessory to murder, obstruction of justice, conspiracy to murder, and a lot of other charges."

For the first time since I was put in handcuffs, Grant smiled. "You're being released, Ms. Davis. And on a personal note, I suggest you choose carefully the company you keep next time."

I was being released. I was free! I was innocent! "I will. I love you. Thank you!" I said. I would have thrown my arms around him if I could, but one of them was cuffed to the table. I sighed deeply with relief instead, and I couldn't stop smiling.

I could tell that Mr. Grant really pushed those detectives to dig deeper; he was far more confident and caring than I ever imagined. What seemed like an open-and-shut case of a mistress's hatred for the wife, turned out to be anything but that. Sammie Lee had made some classic mistakes with his complex scheme, and I was so glad that he had. Considering everything he risked and the gifts he gave me, I should've known something wasn't right from day one.

As awkward as it was to be dragged through the mud by the media, their attempts to make amends were even more so. I went from a woman scorned to a pitiful victim who hooked up with the wrong person at the wrong time. Ironically, I think that $30,000 reward Sammie offered had something to do with motivating tongues to wag and prove my innocence; or rather, Sammie's not-so-innocence.

There were such things as second chances, but I still had several loose ends to tie up. Now that my own life had been protected and spared, I knew I had to get back to addressing my past—especially that part which involved my daughter.

Chapter Eighteen

STAY WITH ME

For obvious reasons, I was no longer interested in sucking dry the pockets of every man I met. I had to get Kyashira back. After I was released from jail, Ritchie came to the rescue by giving me some money to get back to Georgia. He also gave me enough money to feed myself and get a hotel room for a short period of time, so I could get to the bottom of my daughter's situation.

"Ritchie, I don't know how I'll ever thank you for all you've done," I said. I gave him a big hug.

He hugged me right back. "Don't even go there, Honey. Thank me by handling your business with my godchild right now. Be strong, and do what you have to do to bring her home for good."

What Ritchie said made me smile, but it wasn't long before I had to roll up my sleeves and dig into the dirty work. I went through the proper channels at DFSC and got clearance from the judge for supervised visits with Kyashira through her current foster parents. I didn't want Kyashira to end up a jailbird, prostitute, or someone who looked for loved in all the wrong places for the rest of her life. I wanted to get to know my child and have doctors assess the psychological or physical damage that may have occurred at the hands of Candace. From what I noticed during supervised visits with my daughter, she had a hard time feeling loved, but at least she showed no signs of extreme behavioral problems. Kyashira was shy and withdrawn and the exact opposite of me, always been outgoing and overbearing.

When I first kissed her during a supervised visit, she cried. She had one stuffed animal—a stuffed bear Jessie and Paula had given her—and she clung to that bear for dear life. The pediatrician treated her for a yeast infection, and I feared that she'd been sexually abused at Candace's house. I couldn't prove it, of course, but I just had a feeling. When I asked her if any adult had ever touched her in private places, Kyashira would just frown and squeeze that bear.

Upon my return to New York, I came back to my apartment and found that the lock had been changed. I called Mr. Brown, the superintendent.

"This is Honey Davis, and I'm calling about my apartment. I was away, but I'm back now. I know I—"

"Oh, you were away all right." Mr. Brown laughed. "I know all about it. I don't like trouble. Stay away from here!"

Great. "I need my things! At least let me get my belongings."

"The rent wasn't paid. Someone else is renting now."

"That's unlawful eviction! You can't just handle things like that. I'll gladly make arrangements to pay you, but I know you have to take me to court and give notice."

Mr. Brown snorted. "Your shit was auctioned off so I could get my money. I don't feel bad about it, neither. I would think you've had enough of court. Do you want to go back downtown? If you do, let's go, you whore!"

"Fuck you!" I screamed. *Click.* He hung up.

Since I had no home base, and now no belongings, it was emotionally easier for me to temporarily stay in Georgia so I could see my daughter for weekly visits. Kyashira already had abandonment issues, and understandably so. She was more important than fighting with my landlord. It would be in her best interest for me to be near her, anyway. I flew back down to Georgia and got a room at one of those extended stay places. I still had the money that Sammie Lee had wired to my account, since my assets had been unfrozen, so I had enough to tide me over for a bit.

I tried to build trust with Kyashira, but that was hard to do in those short visits, considering the damage that had been done. Her new foster parents were much better; at least they had children of their own, and they seemed to really care about the children they took in. I was thankful for that, although it was a little late in the game to do what should've been done at first.

"You're not coming back," was what my daughter often said each time I saw her.

"You are not in this world alone," I said, stroking her hair. "I am not going to let you down this time, Kyashira. Momma did have to leave you with relatives once, but I never knew that you'd be put in foster homes. I am working hard to make a place for you."

"They said you hated me. Not Jessie or Miss Paula, but other people. They said you never wanted me." My heart shattered as she began to pout.

"No! I never hated you. Never."

She hugged her bear. "Where's my daddy?"

This was the hardest part to explain to her. I didn't want to blame Mikaylo for all of the problems in our lives, since I made my fair share of them too.

"Your father lives in New York. I really haven't seen him in quite a while, though."

"Why not, Mommy?"

"When Mommy was a teenager, she didn't make a smart choice. Your father didn't either. When people have sex before they are mature, they are not prepared to face the possible consequences of raising a child. For us, we weren't the best match as a couple, and we didn't have any money to take care of the responsibility we both created."

Kyashira mulled this over. "Do you mean I was a mistake, and that's why you didn't want me?"

She was a smart one! "No, baby. Never that. I wanted you from the very beginning." I sighed, remembering the fight I had with my mother when she tried to force me to have an abortion. "Sometimes young mommies who don't have any adults to help them with a baby have to let the baby live with someone who can take care of her. It's just how it goes when you try to grow up too fast. Sometimes girls do that because they want to fit in with boys."

Kyashira frowned in disgust. "I don't like boys."

"Good. You have plenty of time to grow up. Most teenager mommies regret having sex so early in life. Some boys never step up to the plate and willingly support the children that they help make."

Kyashira cocked her head and regarded me. "Daddy doesn't help you with me?"

I kissed her forehead. "One day, I will tell you more about your daddy, but right now, I just want you to know that I love you, and I want you. That's what is most important."

※※

For some reason, I missed being a casual drinker. Frequenting bars and clubs gave me somewhere to be, and I always met new people. I guess that was my previous addiction, far more than the alcohol itself. I didn't want to party and get buck wild again, I just needed some sort of release after one of those difficult supervised visits. I craved an escape.

The need to take a break from issues with my daughter led me to sit on one barstool in Atlanta. I wasn't sure what to do next, except order a drink.

"What are you having?" the bartender asked.

I sighed. "A shot of vodka."

I watched him grip the bottle. As the liquid fell into the shot glass, horrible memories of using alcohol to engage men in conversation, then to drug them so I could rob them, came back. It reminded me of the night I met Sammie. I didn't realize that I'd been traumatized by those things, but I had.

"Noooo! Nooo!" I screamed suddenly. I jumped up and broke into a run, out the door.

"What's wrong with that bitch?" a patron said.

"You owe for this drink," the bartender yelled.

I couldn't turn back. I just couldn't. I found a restaurant and hid in the bathroom.

You can do it, Honey. Leave the past in the past. You've changed. All of those things you did with men you met in bars are behind you, I told myself as I studied my labored face in the mirror.

That's when I knew I needed professional help, and quick! I soon located an Al-Anon meeting location. I knew that I wasn't technically an alcoholic, but either way, I needed to go. My mother's alcoholism was something I also needed to address and since the group catered primarily to family members of alcoholics, it was a good choice for me. I secretly feared what alcohol had done to her. Valerie was my mother, but I didn't want to risk ever being like her in that way. I also realized that if I had been drinking heavily during my pregnancy, Kyashira probably would've been born with some sort of damage. Plus, if I was trying to get my daughter back, attending Al-Anon meetings would help me prove that I was trying to clean up my messed-up existence. Joining the group gave me the support I needed to face many fears and forgive myself for mistakes I made.

I decided not to return to New York. I found a job at the cosmetics counter of an upscale store in Lenox Square in Buckhead. It was walking distance from the MARTA train station and the mall. I worked my fingers to the bone for three months to prove to the judge that I could take care of Kyashira. I also got a furnished efficiency apartment, and I soon learned why a young professional I met in the mall offered me to sublet it for $500 a month, on a month-to-month basis. Roaches were the least of my worries there. As soon as I moved in, I found out that it was one of the worst apartment buildings to live in, period. The college student next door loved to blast her music as loud as she could, and the hot water didn't work half the time. I didn't feel safe walking from work at night. The person who subleased it to me had once been robbed at gunpoint. Nevertheless, it was a place to lay my head without getting trapped into a year-long lease. It also made me even more determined to work harder and get the hell out of that place!

My hustling spirit did pay off and my supervisor promoted me quickly because of my high sales record. I became an assistant manager in record time.

Guess who stumbled across me in the mall? Candace Jones! What Kyashira's former foster mother was doing in an upscale mall, I don't know. Last I heard, she'd been stripped of her foster parent status and had to make restitution to the state for all of the money she'd scammed as a foster parent, in exchange for no jail time and five years' probation. Candace—and sometimes her crew—would stop by and taunt me, but I refused to play into their bullshit. I had bigger goals in mind, and beating up a poor excuse for a human being wouldn't help me get Kyashira back for good.

I stayed positive by teaching women how makeup could enhance their beauty. It was natural for me, and sales came to me easy. I wasn't rich, but at least I could legally pay the bills. It wasn't a quick fix; I worked for almost a year before the judge was convinced that I'd turned my life around enough to deserve custody of my daughter. I learned to cook real meals, survive on a budget, work a real job, and give up alcohol and men. On nights I didn't work late, I participated in a Twelve-Step Program, and it was the start of being responsible for myself. My greatest reward was regaining the legal right to care for my own child. I got a second chance at motherhood!

The very first night I put my daughter to bed, I cried. I broke down and cried as I clung to her with thanks. It was all like a real sweet dream, and unlike anything I'd imagined before. One day at work, one of my regular clients told me that her mother had just passed. Her mother's house was empty, and she agreed to let me rent it to help me get on my feet until we both could make concrete plans. I assured her that I would be a responsible tenant who would respect her mother's place. I was more than thankful that I could provide a safe place for Kyashira to stay with me.

For quite a while, I had to convince my daughter that I did want her.

"You don't love me," she would say while hugging her bear.

"Momma does love you. We're going to be a real family," I insisted.

"Then why did you leave me and let Miss Jones beat me?"

"Oh, Kyashira," I said with a sigh. "If Momma could take all of your pain, she would."

"If we're going to have a real family, where's your mother and father?" She liked to ask questions out of the blue.

"Grandma passed away," I said, turning around to face her again. I sat on the edge of her bed. I felt a little tear form in my eye.

When I couldn't answer about my father, it inspired a burning desire within me to address that too. I decided to call him after my daughter fell asleep that night. While I was cleaning up everything else that had gone wrong in my life, I may as well tackle the last one. I hadn't spoken to him in so long, I didn't know what to say.

"Hello, who is this?" my father asked. He obviously didn't recognize my voice after so long, or the strange number that popped up on his CallerID.

"It's me, Honey." I bit my lip, wondering what kind of response I was going to get.

❧※❧

My father showed up at my job. I mentioned to him, in passing, where I worked during our phone conversation. I didn't mention that name of the store, but I suppose he took a wild guess based on my tastes. Of course, he heard all about me being in jail, and the entire mess with Sammie Lee. I was ashamed because I was sure I'd discredited him too. He never said that, but I knew. People often forget that things we do impact everyone who is close to us in our lives; consequences often don't just come our way, they multiply.

"May I help you?" I asked.

I wasn't paying attention to who was standing at the counter before I spoke. He stood there, holding a manila-colored envelope. I couldn't believe he just popped up to see me like that.

"I just came here to give you this, Honey. I won't wear out my welcome. I just want to say something that I've been waiting to say in person for a long time now."

I asked one of my employees to cover for me while I took my lunch break.

I couldn't think of a private place to talk, but the food court was the best I could think of. We walked awhile in silence and had a bit of un-comfortable conversation. I could tell he didn't want to say much until we were able to sit down.

Jerome fidgeted with the envelope while he spoke. "She tried to bleed me dry. You were right about her; I was wrong."

I was confused. "Her who?"

"The minister that presided over your mother's funeral. Reverend Daniels."

"Oh, her." Her taunting voice came back with a snap.

Jerome sighed. "She didn't try; she did bleed me dry. Well, maybe that's not quite accurate." He chuckled nervously. "She got enough, but I managed to wake up before the worst damage was done."

"I'm sorry."

"No, *I'm* sorry. I should never have put you in the position to feel that you had to leave because she let it slip that I wasn't your biological father." He looked down at the envelope. "You told me you wanted to know who your real father was that day, and you deserve to know who he is. It's not my place to keep this information from you." He slid the envelope toward me. I took it and held it, but I wasn't ready to open it quite yet.

"Despite everything that's happened, I'm proud of you for stepping up and finally trying to do right." He covered my hand with his. "I re-ally had your best interests at heart, Honey. I know that parents usually get a bad rap, but I tried to make sure you had everything because I felt guilty about why you were born. I've always loved you, and I still do; you are the only child I've ever known. My ego just had a hard time dealing with the circumstances of your birth." He paused and stared into the distance. "I'm a doctor who is used to having, or getting, all of the answers. This time, I was stuck, and there were no answers for me." He stood and looked down at me. "Should you ever need anything, you or your child, you know where I am." He nodded at the envelope. "I know you probably hate me. Do what you will with the information. It is yours to keep."

I was speechless and stunned. My father kissed me on the top of the head, like he did when I was a little girl. Tears dripped from his eyes. All he could manage to do was mouth the word goodbye. I wanted to stop him from leaving, but spite would not let me. He'd had that information and kept it from me. I needed time, and I probably needed to see what was in that envelope.

Chapter Nineteen

NO TEARS LEFT TO CRY

Kyashira had a break from school. She was beginning to adjust being with me, although things still weren't peaches and cream. I saved enough money to fly to New York for a few days. By that time, I gathered the courage to hunt down my real father. I didn't know if he was still living or dead. I had no idea if I should shake his hand or give him a hug. It didn't matter. I just needed closure.

Kyashira squeezed my hand as we walked into a rough-and-tumble neighborhood in New York City. Even my old crew would've questioned if they could handle the kind of action that was going on there. I felt like I should've rolled with five police officers on each side of us. Ritchie would've come with us if I'd asked him to, but he still would've wanted to get in and get out. Everything and anything was going on. Prostitutes were on the stroll in broad daylight. Drug boys guarded corners, staring me down, then asking if I wanted something. I just kept walking until I found the address I'd been given. I said a quick prayer for our safety and stuck to the purpose of my business.

I was stunned that my real father may have been residing in a place like that. As bourgeois as my mother was, it just really left me puzzled.

Then again, according to the documents I was given, the man in question was a patient at the clinic where my mother once volunteered.

I knocked on the door and an elderly woman in a faded pink housecoat answered the door. "Who you?" she asked.

"Hello, my name is Honey. Is there a Stanley Allen that lives here?"

I could feel Kyashira pat me on the leg. I looked down at her, and she clung to my leg tightly.

The woman pointed to a man and another woman, who were arguing in the street. The woman was half dressed, with her floppy breasts spilling out of a torn and dirty dress. We could hear their conversation as if they were standing next to us.

"Get the fuck out of my house! Don't come back, man. You put your hands on me again, I'm going to send my peoples to fuck you up," she threatened.

"Take your ass in the house. Cut out all that shit!" the man yelled. He left her, crossed the street, and approached the building where Kyashira and I stood. The old woman was still behind the door, staring at him.

"Kiss my muthafuckin' ass!" the other woman yelled.

"Don't make me have to come over there and stick my dick in your mouth!"

"How much you got?"

They both burst out laughing. I was so sickened, I couldn't believe I'd ever been in that same place of talking foul and acting terribly. In fact, their language made me cringe. "It's okay, baby," I told Kyashira, drawing her close to me. I rubbed her back warmly.

The man walked past us and entered the house like nothing was wrong. "Hello, Momma, what's happening?"

"This lady say she looking for you. She looking for a Stanley Allen." She turned and shuffled back into the house.

He looked at us. "I'm Stanley Allen. Is there something I can help you with? Anything I can do would be my pleasure." He licked his lips and winked at me lewdly.

He reached down to grab my hand and I knew he was going to try and kiss it. I yanked it back. My own father tried to hit on me! Yuck! I made a sour face. He was a pathetic old player who still thought he could pull any woman—I saw it in him. I just stared at him for a little while, with that crazy look stuck on my face as I studied his. Attractive still, but obviously a player who never had grown up. I could envision him smacking dice against the curb and still boosting clothes. My biological father was obviously a loser. Another woman came to the door, then exited and strutted past him. Her clothes were tight as hell.

"Work the pole good for Daddy. I'm coming to check on you," he shouted.

I turned to leave. I was disgusted. Kyashira and I walked away.

"Hey, baby! Who is you? Hey, you got a fat ass. Hey you—what's your name?" he shouted. Every statement got more and more obnoxious. I sighed, knowing that I'd done the right thing by not telling him who my mother was, and why I'd really come. I didn't want to put my child in a position to have to deal with a grandfather like that, after all she'd been through. Hell, I didn't want to claim him either. It was obvious that he would've brought nothing but heartache into our lives.

"I thought you were someone else. Sorry," I shouted. I walked quickly, and Kyashira barely kept up with her little legs.

"Who was that man?" my daughter asked, slightly out of breath, as we headed to the subway.

"Nobody. He was nobody, sweetie."

"Where are we going now?"

"To see your grandfather, and he is a very good person."

※※

I returned the favor to my father by paying him an unannounced visit. I closed the door to his medical practice while sighing deeply. The place was packed. I walked up to the receptionist and asked her to call him.

"Dr. Davis is with a patient right now. Who should I say needs to speak to him?"

"Just tell him his daughter and granddaughter need to see him. It's very important. In fact, it's an emergency."

The woman working the reception desk was someone I didn't know. I assumed that Miss Betty, who had been his receptionist since I was a child, had retired. She was sweet and always made the office run like clockwork. But this new chick on the block kept eyeballing me like she expected me to boost the jar of candy on her desk. She called and repeated what I said, glancing up at me the entire time. In no time flat, my father appeared. He looked confused.

"Honey! I'm surprised to see you. Is everything okay?"

I nodded. Everything seemed okay for the first time in a long time. "This is your granddaughter," I started, then broke down crying. He came over and put his arms around me, and I hugged him. "I'm sorry, Dad. I'm so sorry. I love you! You took care of me and gave me a nice life. You are my father, and I am so sorry."

He ushered us into his office. Even though I tried to be discreet as I could, I knew I was attracting attention. As soon as he closed the door, we embraced real and strong. He bent down and looked at Kyashira in the eyes. A soft look came across his face.

"You're beautiful. You look just like your grandmother. What's your name?"

Kyashira clung to my leg. "Kyashira."

He picked her up and held her like he didn't want to ever let go. "I like that name. Do you think you'd like a lollipop?"

"Yes!"

"You have such nice manners, Kyashira."

"Thank you, Grandpa."

I was stunned. I never told Kyashira to call him that; it just came naturally for her. My father smiled wider than I'd seen in a long time. Being a grandfather came naturally for him, too.

Like magic, Kyashira smiled as he took a small lollipop from a container. She hadn't even done that with me, no matter what I gave her.

"When you truly love someone, that love lasts forever," my father said as he continued to hold his granddaughter. "I made mistakes. You made mistakes. We're only human. I think we should both pick up pieces of our lives and move on."

He nodded. "Grandpa is old. It's time to get down." He set Kyashira on her feet with a little groan, but he was beaming.

Kyashira continued to suck on her lollipop. "He's funny," she said, looking at her grandfather.

"He sure is."

⁂

My last stop was to see what was poppin' with Ritchie. He was still in his old spot in Harlem, but that crazy Tatiana was gone like yesterday's news. I was happy to hear that. I introduced Ritchie to Kyashira, and thanked him for what he'd done. Ritchie was the only one who stayed in my life because he proved himself by helping me with her. He told me that even if he had been able to accept collect calls, he could not have come to visit me anyway because of his police record for shoplifting. I never knew he had a record! Worse, that evil heifer

Pookie never told him what I said, so he just figured that I didn't want to see him when I was in jail.

"Pookie will get hers, don't worry," he said. "I never liked her non-dressing ass anyway." We laughed together, and it felt good. "I will stand by your side, no matter what. You know that, ma." He bounced Kyashira up in the air and she squealed with joy. "Thanks for bringing my god-daughter by. That was a good look. She's cute," he said.

"Good looks run in the family, Ritchie," I teased.

Ritchie and I were talking when someone knocked the door. Given the history of those knocks when I was around, I prayed to Jesus that it wasn't Tatiana. I heard a familiar voice. It wasn't Tatiana's voice; it was Pookie's!

"Shit," I said under my breath. I hoped she didn't come walking into the apartment, picking on my baby. Disrespecting me was one thing, but I wasn't about to let her start trouble with my child.

"Why you tryin' to stop me from comin' in? You ain't gonna let me sit down, Ritchie? You know my feet hurt. I'm pregnant, remember? I need to talk to you about Kaylo," I heard her say. "He moved and changed his number. I'm almost 'bout to have this baby. I ain't got no money, no diapers, no milk—nothin'! I ain't got no job either, and the doctor said I need to be on bedrest. Can you believe that shit?" Silence, then, "I thought I was in control, but I see now that he had me from the very beginning. He's not the one pregnant, so then why should he give a fuck, huh? How could I have been so stupid?"

"I'm a little busy right now," Ritchie called out. "I'll call you about this later." He made no move to open the door.

Pookie acted like she couldn't hear. She just kept running off at the mouth.

"How am I gonna take him the court if I don't know where he is? Please tell me you seen Mikalyo."

"I told you that I've got company. It's not a good time, Pookie," Ritchie told her.

"Who you got up in here that you don't want me to see, Ritchie? Don't let me find out Tati's back." The doorknob jiggled. "Open this door, Ritchie! My feet hurt and I gotta pee!"

"Slow your roll! I didn't ask you to come in."

"I don't need no invitation. Now let me in or I will scream bloody murder up in this hall!"

Ritchie sighed and shot me an apologetic look before he walked over to open his door. Pookie burst in, still flapping her gums. She waved a church fan in an attempt to cool herself off. Her huge belly threatened to burst the seams of her maternity blouse, and her nose had spread from one side of her face to the other. "Turn on the air conditioner! It's hot as a mug up in here, and I need your help with this situation. See, that's why women be using niggas or turning to the other side. Y'all is no good, treating us queens like we ain't shit."

Pookie saw me sitting there and her eyes got real wide. Her hand froze in mid-fan. She knew I'd heard everything. Karma was a bitch, oh yes it was! I paid my debt to it, and now Pookie's hour of reckoning had begun.

She plastered a fake smile on her face. "Honey! Oh girl, I'm so glad you're back home! You know what? I missed you so bad. I knew you didn't have nothing to do with that woman's death. Thank God, the truth came out. I was telling people it would. You lookin' good as always. You ain't changed a bit!"

She struggled to decide how she should react, and it was the best she could do. She reached out to hug me, like she was begging to restore our relationship, but I leaned back out of her reach. A grease-soaked scarf was tied around her head, and baby powder was caked on her chest; her huge breasts looked liked snow-topped mountains. I couldn't believe she came out of the house looking like that! Instead of cussing her out like the old Honey would've done, I wished her well by rattling of the names of some organizations that helped pregnant women, and kept it moving. I gathered my and Kyashira's things, kissed Ritchie on the cheek, and got ready to leave.

Before I left, I had some choice words for Pookie. "I told you that you had a coward on your hands in Mikaylo. You knew it yourself, too. Now you will have years of crap to deal with. Good luck with that. Ritchie, I'll holler later."

"We ought to do lunch sometimes," Pookie commented.

I chuckled. Pookie knew I pitied her. I didn't have to even speak the words.

"Not in this lifetime. I'll pass on the invite, Pookie. Write us," I said, looking down at my angel. Pookie looked like she was nearly on the verge of wetting herself. I looked at Kyashira one final time. She grabbed my hand. We walked out yet one more door. I looked back and I could see nosey-ass Pookie pushing the curtains back, watching me and Kyashira walk down the street. I held my daughter's hand as we walked away.

Epilogue

Yolanda and Carlos got married. I never saw Yolanda anymore, and only once since I'd gotten out of jail, because Carlos turned out to be a very controlling man. I guess Yolanda tended to pick the same kind of men. What could I have done? I had to let her go and live her life. I just continued to pray for her and her children (she had another one by Carlos not too long ago).

The last I heard of Pookie, she was still struggling to raise her child. Unfortunately, she was on welfare and ended up living in the projects. Pookie had the nerve to try to hit me up for money, telling me that we were best friends, and our children were brother and sister. I told her that it was just sad that a baby had someone like her for a mother, and someone like Mikaylo as a father. Mikaylo was still up to his old tricks. When Pookie tracked him down, she found out that he had gotten yet another woman pregnant, and he'd been living with her. Some people never grow up. Word had it that his new girlfriend was taking care of him, and there was talk of a wedding, until a delay was announced. That may have had something do with Pookie taking Mikaylo to court for child support. He still took no interest in Kyashira, which didn't surprise me. I've accepted it. Wasting energy on either him or Pookie was a waste of my time, so I stopped.

Ritchie gave up boosting and dealing drugs on the side after he lost one of his brothers to a drug deal gone wrong, just like he lost his father. If he could give up Tatiana, there was hope for anything. I prayed that Ritchie would become a legitimate businessman. He had it in him to be whatever he wanted to be, and Ritchie was a good person.

On a happier note, Paula was doing better. She was finally starting to accept Jessie's death. She got a new job, and she was working to repay her brother and get her and Jessie's house back.

As for me, a fresh start was in order. Kyashira, my father, and I moved to another state, away from the memory of what happened in New York and Georgia. My father sold his practice after he shared something with me.

"I'm tired of being a doctor, Honey. Don't get me wrong, I love helping people. I chose the profession because that's what my parents wanted me to do. I'd rather volunteer in a clinic on occasion."

"What would make you happy?"

"If I told you, you'd laugh."

"No I wouldn't."

"You know I always liked to cook, right?"

"Yeah." I remembered how he would sometimes make me pancakes, and once he baked a turkey for Thanksgiving.

"I know it's silly. Everyone would laugh at me, but I would love to own a restaurant."

I smiled. "Why is that silly? You shouldn't let people dictate who you want to be. Let's make it happen. Who cares what anyone else would think? I'll help."

"I'll help too," Kyashira piped up.

My father hugged her and smiled.

We named the restaurant after my mother. I know she looks down on the establishment, happy to see us all working together at Valerie's.

Business is great at the restaurant. Kyashira enjoys helping out her grandfather. They are very close. Being here has helped her to come out of her shell, little by little. She's grown like a weed and is no longer underweight. There are times when she still has flashbacks and she wakes me up, screaming at the top of her lungs. When thuggish-looking men pass her on the street, she often breaks out in tears, too. The last time it happened, she admitted to me that a man did sexually abuse her at Candace's. My heart nearly broke in two when she shared that with me. She's in therapy and it's helping her sort out the confusion and pain of her young life. I'm grateful that my Dad's been there for her, and for me. He really values their bond, and he's proud to be a grandfather.

"Grandpa, can you fix me spaghetti and meatballs?" she asked almost every day.

I'm surprised she isn't sick of it yet. I mean, she eats it like it's going out of style. It's was her favorite, so my father cooks it for her almost every day. The three of us still have some insecurities left, and we have a long way to go before abandoning them for good, but at least we are all trying hard.

Speaking of fathers, my sperm donor, Stanley Allen, turned out to be someone my mother picked up out of spite. My father explained that she said she found the worst man she could to dole out revenge; that's how she ended up with a fast-talking player from the wrong side of the tracks. When I was showing off, she was just trying to keep that dark streak in my blood away. It was ironic, to say the least.

That conversation with my father about following one's dream inspired something in me that just was sitting inside, doing nothing. I did help him at the restaurant, and still do. But I went back to school and finally earned my high school diploma. I became a volunteer for the Office of Juvenile Justice and Delinquency Prevention while I worked on my college degree. I wanted to show my daughter that her mother was doing the best she could. I went into therapy to help heal myself even more. I stayed in touch with my Al-Anon sponsor to make sure that I stayed on track, because I didn't want to make the same mistakes. It's time for our family circle of pain to be broken.

I know better than anyone that this isn't a world without rules. You get back what you put in; maybe not right away, but eventually. I told this story for the sake of Kyashira's healing, and for other people out there, so they can to understand how choices made can impact many people. I know that Lola Lee can finally rest in peace, with her murderer behind bars.

Tell your loved ones you care as much as you can, and show them that you care. I know I did. Through all of the mess, I learned how to love; I'm not talking about a man, I'm talking about myself and my family. I am finally happy with my life, knowing that I am no longer wasting my potential as a woman and as a human being. Every time I kiss my daughter, I feel that despite my mistakes, if I try hard enough, I can get a second chance and not waste it. Life is too short to take for granted.

MELODRAMA PUBLISHING ORDER FORM
WWW.MELODRAMAPUBLISHING.COM

Title	ISBN	QTY	PRICE	TOTAL
Wifey	0-971702-18-7		$15.00	$
I'm Still Wifey	0-971702-15-2		$15.00	$
Life After Wifey	1-934157-04-X		$15.00	$
Still Wifey Material	1-934157-10-4		$15.00	$
Sex, Sin & Brooklyn	0-971702-16-0		$15.00	$
Histress	1-934157-03-1		$15.00	$
Den of Sin	1-934157-08-2		$15.00	$
Eva: First Lady of Sin	1-934157-01-5		$15.00	$
Eva 2: First Lady of Sin	1-934157-11-2		$15.00	$
The Madam	1-934157-05-8		$15.00	$
Shot Glass Diva	1-934157-14-7		$15.00	$
Dirty Little Angel	1-934157-19-8		$15.00	$
Cartier Cartel	1-934157-18-X		$15.00	$
In My Hood	0-971702-19-5		$15.00	$
In My Hood 2	1-934157-06-6		$15.00	$
A Deal With Death	1-934157-12-0		$15.00	$
Tale of a Train Wreck Lifestyle	1-934157-15-5		$15.00	$
A Sticky Situation	1-934157-09-0		$15.00	$
Jealousy	1-934157-07-4		$15.00	$
Life, Love & Lonliness	0-971702-10-1		$15.00	$
The Criss Cross	0-971702-12-8		$15.00	$
Stripped	1-934157-00-7		$15.00	$
The Candy Shop	1-934157-02-3		$15.00	$
Cross Roads	0-971702-18-7		$15.00	$
A Twisted Tale of Karma	0-971702-14-4		$15.00	$

(GO TO THE NEXT PAGE)

MELODRAMA PUBLISHING ORDER FORM
(CONTINUED)

Title/Author	ISBN	QTY	PRICE	TOTAL
Up, Close & Personal	0-971702-11-X		$9.95	$
Menace II Society	0-971702-17-9		$15.00	$
			Subtotal	
			Shipping**	
			Tax*	
	Total			

Instructions:

*NY residents please add $1.79 Tax per book.

**Shipping costs: $3.00 first book, any additional books please add $1.00 per book.

Incarcerated readers receive a 25% discount. Please pay $11.25 per book and apply the same shipping terms as stated above.

Mail to:

MELODRAMA PUBLISHING

P.O. BOX 522

BELLPORT, NY 11713